OUT ON A LIMB

A.J. Truman

OUT ON A LIMB
By A.J. Truman

Cover design by James at GoOnWrite.com
Copy editing by Sarah Henning
Formatting by Caitlin Greer

Thank you to Paula, Andria, Dahlia, and Lee for getting this book into shape and to Mike for all your support! And thank you to readers for your patience and support with this book. I couldn't have done this without your enthusiasm and encouragement, Outsiders!

What's an Outsider, you say? Oh, just a cool club where you can be the first to know about my new books and receive exclusive content. Join the Outsiders today at www.ajtruman.com/outsiders.

CHAPTER ONE

Cameron

In the time that Cameron Buckley brushed his teeth, took a shower, got dressed, and watched an episode of his favorite show, Sleeping Beauty had not moved from his bed. He had actually forgotten what year the guy was, but this was nothing but a freshman move. Cameron admired Sleeping Beauty's body. The tight curls of his brown hair, the arms with burgeoning, See-I-Totally-Work-Out muscles, the perky ass under his Fruit of the Looms. Cameron didn't use a rating system for the guys he hooked up with. He wasn't a frat boy. Instead, he graded on a pass/fail system. He gave himself a mental pat on his back for his latest pass while he slipped on his shoes.

Cameron checked the time again. He clapped twice, loudly, as if he were turning on the lights. Sleeping Beauty stirred from his deep slumber.

"Morning," Cameron said. He finished tying his shoes.

The guy wiped the sleep from his eyes. Cameron saw him register where he was before slapping on a bashful smile. "Morning yourself."

"You sure were tired."

"We had an exhausting night." Sleeping Beauty raised his eyebrows at Cameron, who proceeded to check the time on his phone.

"It's eleven thirty. Don't you have class?"

"Not until noon."

"How did you swing a noon class as a freshman? My first year, all I could get were the nine a.m.'s."

"I'm a sophomore."

"That explains it."

Sleeping Beauty rubbed at his head. He definitely noticed that the guy whose bed he was lounging in was all dressed and ready to go, but he didn't seem to care. He must be new at this, Cameron thought. A total freshman at heart.

"Man, that jungle juice was strong last night, but it went down so easily."

"Jungle juice is dangerous. The sweetness is deceptive," Cameron said. He pulled a bottle of aspirin from his nightstand. "Take two of these, and you'll be fine."

"Thanks. That was an awesome party."

"It was alright. Not bad for a Tuesday night." Cameron wound up at the same parties with the same people in the same apartments, former South Campus artsy people who now lived off-campus. That tended to happen when you were a senior. He had already found his people and his groove. "I haven't seen you around there before."

"I live in McKenzie up north, but I heard about this party from my roommate's girlfriend."

The guy gazed around at Cameron's room. It was its usual mess, but the beauty of having an apartment versus sharing a dorm room was that your bedroom could be a raging disaster without anyone complaining. As long as he kept the rest of the apartment clean, his roommate didn't say a word.

"You really love movies." The guy pointed to the line of posters thumbtacked to Cameron's wall. "I never saw *Drive*. Ryan Gosling is super hot, though."

"It's a phenomenal movie."

"Cool." The guy nodded. Cameron knew he'd never watch it, and if he did, he'd probably turn it off after five minutes. Sleeping Beauty hadn't moved from the bed.

"You're a deep sleeper. You didn't hear me get up?"

"Nah. I can sleep through anything."

"Apparently."

The guy tried to look deep into Cameron's eyes. "You should get back in here." He patted the empty space next to him. His boner stretched out his underwear. "We can go for round two."

"I'm already showered and dressed."

"We can shower afterward. Together." Sleeping Beauty reached out his hand to Cameron, who gave it a light handshake.

"It's a small shower."

And now Cameron felt bad. The guy retracted his arm and sat up.

"I had a lot of fun last night," Cameron said. He made sure to always tell guys this. Always compliment them before telling them to get out. It softened the blow.

"Me, too."

"I don't mean to be an asshole. I just have to get to work," Cameron said, hoping he understood.

"You work? Like an internship?"

"Like at a coffee shop."

"Oh, that's cool." The guy finally got out of bed. He stretched his arms over his head and let out a caveman yawn. Cameron admired his chest. The sophomore was a fan of manscaping. All over, from what Cameron could remember. It was like having sex with someone who wasn't completely real.

Sleeping Beauty stumbled over to Cameron, not to his pile of clothes. Earnestness ringed his eyes as he caressed Cameron's fingers. Cameron felt the dread sink in. He braced himself for impact.

"I really did have a good time," the guy said. He had cut himself shaving, just under his chin. It was one imperfection that made him stand out in Cameron's mind. "And I think we should go out sometime." After Cameron didn't give him an immediate answer, the guy asked, "What do you think?"

"You don't have to do this," Cameron said. "We had some great sex last night. We don't need to justify it into something more."

"I'm not. I like you."

"We've known each other for twelve hours. Jungle juice was involved in half of that, and lube was involved in the other."

"You're funny." He stroked Cameron's cheek. "I don't know, I enjoyed talking to you at the party."

"But that wasn't a real conversation. We were flirting. Our talking was all sexual subtext meant to get us into bed together. And it worked. It worked very well."

Cameron thought he saw dejection cross the guy's face, but then it was gone.

"You're playing hard to get, aren't you? I get it," Sleeping Beauty said. He wrapped his arms around Cameron's waist.

Cameron put on his game face. He knew this was merely the denial part in the five stages of drunken hookups.

"There's nothing to play here. Do you really want to go down this road? I'm graduating in three months. Then I'm moving out to Los Angeles a few weeks after that. Do you think it's wise to try and hang out and possibly turn this one night stand into a relationship when it's only going to break apart three months later? We had a great time last night. You have an amazing dick, and I'm glad I got to enjoy it, but we don't have to turn something fun into something serious. Let's not sully this experience."

Sleeping Beauty nodded his head slightly. He seemed to get it. Cameron felt like the Miracle Worker breaking through to young Helen Keller.

"It's not your fault. It's the Puritans' fault." Cameron handed him his heap of clothes.

"The Puritans? Like from the 1600s?" The guy untangled his clothing and began to sort them out.

"Exactly. They were the first settlers in the United States. They were deeply conservative and religious. Like the Amish, but not as crafty. And because they were the first settlers, their conservative beliefs are embedded in our culture. No matter how much we evolve as a society, we still have those Puritanical roots."

"My ancestors emigrated to Ellis Island in 1906."

"Even so, the heart of American society is tied to Puritanism. If only the Greeks or Romans had discovered America. Then we all could've been having orgies nonstop." Cameron paced back and forth in front of his audience of one. "But no. We were settled by Puritans."

"Not Christopher Columbus?"

"He discovered America, but he didn't settle here."

Sleeping Beauty nodded.

"My point is, America is still a Puritan nation. We are all inherently conservative about sex. It's ingrained in us that sex should be tied to love. We can't just have sex with people. We have to rationalize it as falling in love or trying to have a relationship with that person when really, all we wanted was to get off." Cameron knelt down beside his latest hookup. "Now, I have to ask you, when you were talking to me last night, when you were smiling at me and putting your hand on the small of my back, when I asked you 'Hey, do you want to get out of here' and you said 'Fuck yeah,' were you really, honestly, truly thinking 'This guy could be my boyfriend?'"

Cameron was damn near out of breath. He gazed into this guy's eyes for recognition, for some sense of understanding.

"I guess...not."

"Precisely!"

"I thought you were really hot," the guy said.

"And I thought the same thing. We were physically attracted to each other. We were horny. And we were drunk. We may be Puritans at heart, but we are animals in our bones."

Sleeping Beauty buttoned up his shirt and buckled his belt. Cameron handed him his shoes, which had gotten kicked off by the door.

"Yeah, I get it." The sophomore's eyes lit up like he cracked a long word in a crossword puzzle. "I always hate the awkward texting after hooking up with a guy I'm not interested in."

"Let's not do that to each other."

He pulled out his phone. "Do I have your number?"

"No." But he still had his phone out, ready to take it down. Puritanism was a hard force to shake. "No need."

"What if you wanted to do this again?" His eyes shifted to the bed.

"I'll know where to find you."

Sleeping Beauty smiled and nodded. He tied his shoes and nodded again. "This is awesome."

"I'm glad I could enlighten you," Cameron said while walking to his bedroom door. When he opened it, the guy knew that was his cue to go.

"Seriously. I hate that everything has to mean something all the time. And so it won't be awkward if we see each other at another party?"

"Nope."

"Because we're not Puritans."

"You got it, man." Cameron led him to the back porch of his apartment, which had a staircase to the street.

Sleeping Beauty froze at the door. Awkwardness rained down on him. The goodbye. No matter what, the guys always made the goodbye part weird.

"So...I guess I'll see you around?"

"Probably," Cameron said, refusing to let the moment get the better of him.

The guy's face flushed red. He lifted a tentative hand to Cameron's cheek and gazed into his eyes. "I had a really good time, Cameron," Sleeping Beauty said softly.

Cameron eyed the errant hand and then shot the guy a look.

"Right." Sleeping Beauty snapped out of it and removed his hand. "Old habits."

Cameron shut the door once the guy left and breathed a sigh of relief. If only he could spread his message to more than one guy at a time. Sex was not love, nor was it a gateway to relationships. And relationships were just a gateway to disappointment. He thought that maybe one day, when he was working in the entertainment business, he would write a movie where the two leads were friends who had sex but had no desire to be in a relationship. Not every story had to have romance.

CHAPTER TWO

Walker

Walker Reed watched the minutes of his life drift away. He couldn't remember what day it was. They all blended together, like his closet full of dress shirts. Maybe it was Tuesday. It didn't matter much. Each day was the same. The same routine, the same motions, the same conversations. The other day, in the elevator at work, one guy turned to his female co-worker and said "Another day at the grind." She laughed and responded, "You know it." Why was she laughing, he wondered. It just made Walker depressed.

The minutes were passing even slower with the same morning traffic. Walker scratched at his beard and turned on the radio, his usual routine for dealing with traffic. A song came on that instantly transported him back to his college days, just as he drove past his alma mater Browerton University. He remembered strolling to class with his boyfriend, giving him a clandestine ass squeeze before running into his lecture hall. The biggest worry on his mind was writing a five-page paper. He had to laugh when kids got stressed out about homework. *You think that's stressful? Wait until you get a mortgage.*

Since he was stuck in gridlock, Walker pulled out his phone and looked up some of his old college friends and acquaintances on Facebook. He was grateful to have a way of knowing what's going on with people without having to ask them. A tinge of sadness crept inside him when he saw just how old some people looked. This hot straight guy with flowing, Jesus-like blond hair from his political science class was now bald. Another guy he used to see at the student gym had major love handles. But Jesus was a partner at a huge Manhattan law firm, and Love Handles was a junior senator for Indiana. And Walker was still crawling down Susquehanna Avenue.

"Another day at the grind," he said to himself.

Walker didn't have highlights in his day. He called them blips. A minor deviation from the norm. One of his favorite blips was getting his morning coffee. His office was located in the south building of four identical gray towers at the edge of the city, just off the highway. People at his work called it The Complex, which reminded Walker of a prison. Each building had a Starbucks in their lobby, but Walker preferred venturing to the west building. One of his favorite blips of the day was right before he opened the door, every part of him wondering if his favorite barista would be behind the register.

And he was! It made Walker grateful for the long line. More time to steal glances at this guy.

"Hey there! Welcome to Starbucks. How's it going?" the barista asked with a flicker of recognition.

"Just making it through the work day." Walker always hated his response. He never sounded as cool as the barista.

The barista shrugged strands of his brown hair out of his face, giving Walker a clear view of his blue eyes, the shade of the sky on a perfect spring day. He began to write on a coffee cup but stopped.

"Grande vanilla latte, right?" He asked with a smile that Walker liked to picture throughout his day.

"Good memory!"

The barista wrote the order on his cup. Here was the part where Walker tried to think of something to say. He had only a few seconds before he would pay for his purchase and had to move on. The line was waiting. This challenge to engage in conversation with the cute barista, to make himself noticed before having to move on, was a major blip for Walker. It got his blood pumping, and made his eyes clear. This was what it must feel like to be a baseball player up at bat. He had one chance every day before fading back into the crowd.

At that moment on that day, fate smiled on Walker Reed. Because the cute barista yawned.

"Late night?" Walker asked.

"Early morning," the barista cracked. "I was at a party and drank way too much. Why do I make myself drink jungle juice?" He shook his head at the memory.

"Getting drunk on a Tuesday night? You're like a college student."

"I am a college student."

"You are?" Walked asked. "At Browerton?"

The barista nodded. "Only for a few more months."

"Getting kicked out?"

"Ha!" The barista laughed. *I made him laugh!* Walker gave himself one hundred points in whatever imaginery game he was playing.

"I went to Browerton."

"Really? What year were you?"

Walker didn't want to answer. It would only bring down this moment. "Let's just say my fifteen-year reunion is this fall."

"Man, that means I have to do math. You're no fun, Walter."

"It's actually Walker."

The barista grabbed Walker's coffee cup to re-examine. "I've been writing Walter this whole time. For months."

Walker shrugged. He was too transfixed by the barista's eyes and his Starbucks smile the first time to correct him. He had just wanted to savor that moment. And then he figured it would be weird to correct his name after letting *Walter* slide a few times.

The barista crossed out *Walter* and wrote in *Walker* on the cup. "Better late than never."

Walker handed him his usual ten dollars, and the barista made the requisite change, which Walker always tossed into the tip jar. He figured the barista was flirting with him for a bigger tip, and so Walker shoved in another dollar.

"All right," the barista said. "Well, have a good morning, Walker."

"You, too." Walker moved over to the waiting area with the other impatient businessmen. But this blip would not subside. He felt like he had already had his morning caffeine for the week. He returned to the register.

"What's your name?" He asked the barista. The female customer shot him a glare. "Now that you know mine." Walker's heart pounded in his chest.

"It's Cameron."

"Like from *Ferris Bueller*?"

"You got it."

The customer cleared her throat loudly. Cameron smiled politely at Walker, a signal that meant this conversation had to end, but Walker detected something genuine in his look, something that suggested that this wasn't the horrifically awkward experience Walker was imagining.

He grabbed his coffee and burst back into the center of The Complex. He realized that the sun was shining and a cool breeze swept between the buildings. It was a beautiful day.

Φ

Over the almost fifteen years he worked at The Berkwell Agency, his workspace had shrunk from a large cubicle with a window to a smaller cubicle with no window to finally a long table he shared with ten other people. Management had embraced the open workspace, although they still got to keep their offices. Some days in the winter, Walker never saw the sun. He thought after all his time here, and his promotion to Associate Media Director, he would have earned an office. Alas, they kept making the offices more open. Or more shared. Only vice presidents and above received the luxury of a door and walls.

Walker logged into his email and groaned under his breath. Sure enough, in the span between leaving his car, getting his coffee, and walking to his desk, Patricia had sent him three emails.

He felt his blood pressure rising, beating against the inside of his chest, just by reading the subject lines. That's all he had to read with Patricia. She either started emails in the subject line and continued them in the body, or she sent them with no subject line at all. They never went more than two sentences. She didn't text or instant message. Her email was stream of consciousness.

Subject: I think we need to discuss

Radiance's fall initiative. What would it look like to shift dollars out of TV and into print? Have our competitors continued to spend as aggressively in print?

Subject: How is the

Facebook execution coming along? What's the ETA on launch? Have we received feedback on the creative from the clients?

Subject: Can you pull

Our media spend for the last five summers? Were we able to maintain share of spend throughout?

This was Walker's inbox all day every day for the past six years. By now, he was used to his boss's machinations.

Like her, he used to think they were curing cancer, until he realized that nope—they were just trying to sell shampoo. Patricia and other co-workers talked about work all the time—in the break room, in the hall, whispering to each other outside a conference room. They found this all so important.

Before he finished his cup of coffee, another one had been placed next to his keyboard like clockwork. Lucy smiled above him.

"You're the best. You know that?" He said warmly.

"If only I could get my kids and my husband to say that to me, my life would be set." Lucy was Hispanic with curly brown hair, a full face, and a bright outlook that managed to survive cubicle culture. She wasn't trying to be CEO, which made her a delight to be around. "Are you ready?"

"For what?"

"We have a meeting."

"We do?"

"Check your email."

And in the five seconds Walker wasn't focused on his computer, Patricia had managed to send another email.

Subject: Meet me in my office

"Just a subject line," Walker said. "That's not a good sign."

"We should go," Lucy said. She was able to laugh off Patricia. Work never got to her like it did for Walker, and he couldn't understand why.

They strolled over to the wall of offices that overlooked The Complex. Walker wondered if Patricia appreciated having a view, or if she saw it merely as a piece of status. She typed away feverishly on her laptop. Papers and Post-its were arranged at right angles on her desk. Walker and Lucy took their seats.

Patricia kept her blonde hair in a controlled ponytail that hung down her neck like a tie. She had a stick figure body and, in a different life, could've been a movie star. Walker wondered if she would've enjoyed jetsetting, premieres, and celebrity-filled parties as much as putting together media plans to sell shampoo.

She pressed her fingertips together and kept her back yardstick straight. "I received some news this morning." She nodded to herself, keeping Walker dying of suspense. "The client has put our account into review."

Lucy's eyes bulged, and Walker's probably did, too. Major blip. Patricia continued talking.

"They recently hired a new CMO, and he wants to see what other media agencies have to offer."

"Don't we have a contract with them?" Lucy asked.

"It's up at the end of their fiscal in June." Patricia stood up and walked over to their side of the desk. Her heels made her tower over Walker, which he suspected was not coincidental.

"So much for loyalty," Walker said. "When we won the business six years ago, they had a four percent market share. Now they have seven."

"A year ago, it was ten," Lucy said.

"That's not our fault. They have terrible creative." Walker couldn't watch a Radiance Shampoo commercial without rolling his eyes. They were as corny as a terrible '80s sitcom. Not the way to lure a younger demographic. Unfortunately, the Berkwell Agency didn't create the ads; they just decided where to place them.

"We haven't lost the business yet. They're letting us throw our hat into the ring to pitch."

He remembered being promoted to Associate Media Director when they won the business. He couldn't wait to craft a fresh media strategy and energize the brand. He forgot what it felt like to care that much about a job.

"There are plenty of agencies that have rewon their clients' business," Patricia said. "It's not easy, but it's not impossible. This new CMO wants to show off. Now, it's our time to prove to them just how valuable we are. It's going to be all hands on deck for the next few weeks."

"Are they putting their creative agency into review?" Walker asked. Patricia retreated behind her desk.

"I don't know, but it doesn't matter. We need to come up with the most innovative, dynamic media strategy they've ever seen. Walker, I'm sending you a list of reporting I need pulled ASAP. I want to see how they've spent every ad dollar over the past ten years, and how this correlates to their share of voice. We're going to dissect the strategies of all their main competitors, down to the commercial placement, to find commonalities that we can fight against. We've been doing the same thing year after year. That ends now."

Walker groaned internally. Patricia's cool façade was showing the tiniest of cracks and was bound to shatter during this process.

"What happens if we lose the review?" Lucy bravely asked.

Patricia gave Lucy a look saved for dramatic moments in action thrillers. She didn't have to say it. They all knew if they lost the account, then they lost their jobs.

"Please send me the reporting and analysis by end of day, Walker."

Lucy and Walker made a beeline back to his desk. "How's that for a Wednesday morning?" she asked.

He really needed some more coffee.

CHAPTER THREE

Cameron

Over his tenure at Browerton, Cameron had done what he needed to do to get good grades. He had made the Dean's List once or twice, mostly as a fluke, but he wasn't like many of his classmates killing themselves for a perfect GPA. You didn't need straight As to make it in Hollywood. Hell, some of the most successful people in the business didn't even go to college. Yet for his screenwriting classes, Cameron applied himself like he was gunning for magna cum laude status.

He found himself walking extra fast to get to the first day of his final screenwriting class. The Radio-TV-Film department didn't offer many screenwriting courses, and they filled up quickly. He would've rioted if he was denied entry to Advanced Screenwriting as a senior.

Cameron's apartment was a ten-minute walk from campus. A sharp pang of sadness ripped through him. He felt so disconnected from campus life, from Browerton. So far away. He walked past underclassmen galavanting around their dorms and huddling in groups on benches. That used to be him and his friends. He was in this weird limbo where he was working at Starbucks and living off campus, yet had to remind himself he was still technically a student. He pushed past it. He was onto bigger and better things on the West Coast in a few months.

Most lectures for the Radio-TV-Film department were held at Flynn Hall, smack in the center of campus. It was one of the oldest buildings at Browerton, but had recently been remodeled to keep up with the twenty-first century. It kept its sweeping staircases intact, though. Cameron trudged up two elegant, but steep flights, to room 204.

The classroom was one long conference room table. Besides his love of writing, the other main reason he took this class was sitting at the head of the table. Professor Elizabeth Mackey didn't just teach screenwriting; she lived it. She had a script produced into a successful movie in the early 2000s. She still was represented by one of the top talent agencies in Hollywood.

"Let's talk dialogue," she said from her chair. Cameron was instantly rapt. There was something about the carefree, but confident way she spoke that made him pay attention. "One of the big issues script readers see in Hollywood is that all of your characters sound the same. There should be subtle differences in how your characters talk, and those differences will define each of them. If you think about one of the talkiest movies ever, *Pulp Fiction*, one of the first scenes is John Travolta and Samuel L. Jackson talking about burgers and TV pilots. But really, you pick up on who these characters are, what makes them tick."

She played the clip from the movie. Cameron had thought *Pulp Fiction* was just a bunch of random conversations punctuated with gratuitous violence, but after Mackey's explanation, he saw how the chitchat revealed character. He was loving this class already.

"We're going to do a little exercise now. I want you to write a short scene, no more than two pages. Two characters max. One character is asking the other character to borrow five dollars."

"Are they friends or family?" Robert asked, a student who Cameron had suffered through many a class with over the years.

"You tell me. Through dialogue. You can do whatever you want, set it wherever and whenever. But I want to get a sense who these characters are through this exchange of money and what they say and don't say."

The class spent the next half hour scribbling away on notepads and on laptops. Cameron clicked away on his computer, deleting half of what he wrote, then deleting the whole thing and starting over. He pictured the scene as if he were watching it on screen. Well-lit, cuts back-and-forth between the characters. He cast that hot, bearded Walker guy from Starbucks this morning as the main character. Stern, with hints of bubbly insecurity. His mind always imagined scenes as if they were in a movie or on TV, ever since he was a little kid. That's how he knew he was destined for a career in Hollywood.

He had a creative breakthrough somewhere at the twenty-five minute mark, typing and typing until the tips of his fingers became numb.

"Pencils down...or whatever," Professor Mackey said. Robert cracked his knuckles for the whole class to hear. "Does anyone want to volunteer to get critiqued?"

"I thought this was just an exercise?" Panic creased Robert's forehead. Cameron imagined his helicopter parents waiting on the other side of the door.

"It is. I'm just asking for volunteers. Anyone brave enough to share what they wrote?" Professor Mackey raised her eyebrows, waiting for someone to pull a Katniss and volunteer as tribute.

Hands remained firmly planted in laps.

"I'll go," Cameron said. He figured what the hell. He welcomed feedback, and he didn't think his scene was completely horrible.

Professor Mackey printed out copies and distributed them amongst the class. They took a few minutes to read, and this time, nobody was shy about speaking.

"This isn't correct," Robert said, shaking his head at the pages. "You were supposed to write a scene where one character asked the other for money. In your scene, Roger is flat-out giving Eloise the money."

"And if Roger is giving it, and she obviously needs it, why isn't Eloise taking it?" A fellow classmate pursed her lips.

"He's asking her to ask for it. Eloise doesn't know how to depend on other people so—"

"Cameron, the writer isn't supposed to talk during critiques. Just listen," Professor Mackey said with a warm tone in her voice that soothed the frustration and hurt flaring inside his chest.

"I like that Eloise always calls him 'sir.' It's like she hates him and is being a bitch, but she still has respect for him."

At least someone in this class got it. Cameron would not miss discussion sections in the working world. At a real job, if you said something stupid, you would be called out on it.

"But why didn't she just ask for the money herself?"

"There's a lack of continuity between her words and her actions. It didn't ring true for me."

"You used the wrong version of their. It's their lives t-h-e-i-r, not t-h-e-r-e."

Cameron acted like a statue. No movement, just freaking listening. The discussion around Cameron's piece eventually died down, and they turned their heads to the professor, who had acted like a neutral moderator.

"Nice work, Cameron," she said. "You made these characters come alive, and the fact that it triggered so much discussion means your writing left a mark, which is always a valuable quality."

Cameron managed a polite nod. Nice work was the equivalent to a participation trophy.

A few more volunteers went, and the discussions were much more pleasant. He was packing up his laptop, when Professor Mackey put her hand on his backpack.

"I just want you to know that your writing is fantastic," she whispered to him.

Cameron's head shot up.

"I didn't want to interfere with the critiquing process, but I don't want you to get discouraged. Professor Kenmore told me about you. He said I was lucky to have you in my class."

"Thanks." Cameron blushed. That was better than any A on a paper.

"Well, you're a natural." She played with her reading glasses dangling from a string around her neck. "I'll see you in the next class."

Cameron heard the music swell in his head as he exited down the steep staircases of Flynn Hall. Now was a good place to end the scene and fade out.

CHAPTER FOUR

Walker

Walker stretched before he got in his car. His muscles cramped from sitting all day. His body felt heavier, like something left in the fridge for too long. His office had an ergonomic specialist come in to adjust everyone's chair, but it made no difference. Walker was tired and sore from answering emails and sitting in meetings and filling out Excel spreadsheets. And his cavemen ancestors thought they had it rough…

He checked the clock in his car and cursed under his breath. His job was supposed to be an eight-to-five with an hour for lunch. Five was merely a suggestion. At a stoplight, he watched a gaggle of college students cross the intersection. Probably off to some bar or party. He wondered if Cameron was doing something fun. Getting drunk on more jungle juice.

Campus was but a speck in Walker's rearview mirror when he reached Petty Marsh, a new gated development in the hills of Duncannon. He drove down streets with cute names, past lawns landscaped to within an inch of their life, each McMansion blurring into the next. He turned right on Lillypond Lane and stopped at the house with the wraparound veranda. Walker parked on the street. Two SUVs sat on the circular driveway.

"Sorry I'm late." Walker shook his head. "Work…"

Doug nodded and kept his hand on the front door. His hair was combed back meticulously, with his glasses resting on his head. He still had his boyish looks, like he never left Browerton.

"They're really working you hard down there." Doug tapped his wedding ring against the door. *Clack clack clack.*

"They are." Walker hated that he apologized to him once already. He wouldn't do it again.

"I have friends who work in advertising. None of them work as hard as you."

They're my friends, too, Walker thought. Though it was clear which side they took in the divorce.

"Doug, I'm tired. Is he ready?"

"Hey, Walker." Ron poked his head next to Doug and stuck out his hand.

"Good to see you, Ron." Walker shook it a little too hard. He enjoyed watching him wince.

"Dinner's getting cold." Ron kissed Doug on the cheek, making Walker wince. He disappeared back inside the house.

"Is he ready?" Walker asked again.

Doug glanced over his shoulder and tensed slightly. His lips drooped at the corners. Bad news was coming Walker's way. You don't spend fifteen years with a person and not pick up these infinitesimal shifts. "Can I talk to you for a second?"

He stepped outside and shut the door.

"Is Hobie okay?" Walker asked.

"He's fine. We're throwing a party for him on Sunday. You got the invite, right?"

"Yeah." The invitation had a trampoline background. *Hobie's Jumping Jivin' Sixth Birthday Party!* Doug left no stone unturned when it came to parties.

"Well, Hobie's actual birthday is Saturday—"

"I know when my son's actual birthday is."

"*Our* son." Doug shot back, a sharp blade in his diplomatic demeanor. "Anyway, he wants to stay here for the weekend, for his actual birthday and the party."

"So you'd have him for the entire weekend? This is my weekend, Doug. I'm being nice letting you have him early on Sunday."

"I understand, but he really would like to be here for the whole weekend. He wants Ron to make him a batch of birthday pancakes, and he wants to sleep in his bed."

"Ron can make him the pancakes on Monday morning, and Hobie has a bed at my place. It's an awesome racecar bed." One that cost nearly as much as his own bed and was superior to the regular humdrum bed at Doug and Ron's.

And Ron's special birthday pancakes? Bisquick.

"Monday morning isn't his actual birthday. He really wants to have all this on Saturday, the whole pomp and circumstance, if you will."

"I haven't had a full weekend with him in three weeks." Walker had to switch around his last weekend because of a work deadline. And now with the media review, he knew it was only going to get worse.

"And who's decision was that?"

Walker seethed with rising anger. He rubbed at his temples and worked overtime to keep his cool. Doug remained calm as always.

"It would mean a lot to Hobie. I know you want to make him happy, Walker."

Walker plunked down onto the rocking chair on the porch. Doug sat in the wicker chair across from him.

"I know this is a surprise, and I know it isn't easy."

"No. Don't you psychoanalyze me. I'm not one of your patients, Doug. Did you put this idea in Hobie's head? Why spend time with Walker when you can spend your birthday with your fun dads!"

He and Doug had agreed to a joint custody arrangement originally. But then work got busier, Hobie started school, and Doug could arrange his client appointments around Hobie's schedule. And he had Ron to shoulder the responsibilities. Walker's joint custody eroded little by little, a few hours here, half a day there. Now he was down to two days a week and every other weekend.

"I didn't put this idea in his head," Doug said.

Walker wished he had. That would've been easier to handle than the truth Doug was leaving unsaid. Walker felt the punch to his solar plexus.

Silence hung in the air.

"You might not have given him the idea, but you certainly aren't discouraging him."

"Can you blame him?" Doug raised his voice. He was on the edge of his chair. "Whenever you pick up Hobie, you're late, and then you're tired or in a mood or distracted. Kids are smart. They pick up on those feelings."

"Especially when their shrink fathers are pointing them out."

"What do you have planned for Saturday, for his actual birthday?"

Walker stammered for an answer. More silence in the air. Thicker than late August humidity. He caught a smug smile flit across his ex-husband's face. But that wasn't the person he hated right now. Walker didn't have pancake mix at his condo. He didn't even have Hobie's favorite cereal, which Doug had forbid him from eating since it wasn't organic.

"Fine," Walker mumbled out. "I'll have him back Friday evening."

"I can just keep him when he gets out of school. I'm picking him up anyway."

Walker scratched at his empty ring finger. "Okay."

"Thank you Walker. He's really going to appreciate it."

Φ

Walker kept looking back at Hobie through the rearview mirror. Doug let him graduate to the booster seat from the full-on harness in January. Each time he looked through the mirror, he hoped his son would be looking back at him, making a silly face like he used to.

Hobie stared out the window.

"Hey, champ! You excited for this weekend? The Trampoline Palace is going to be a good time."

"Yeah."

Hobie had wild black hair and olive skin. Genetically, he had nothing in common with his dads. That didn't stop

Walker from seeing his brown eyes and long nose in his son's face.

"I'm going to miss you this weekend, but I hear Ron is cooking up some of his famous pancakes."

"Yeah. With whipped cream, too."

"What makes them so special? Is it the whipped cream?"

"He puts butterscotch chips and blueberries in them."

"My stomach is growling! Can you hear that?" Walker roared like a lion. Not too far off from his stomach's real sound.

"Stomachs don't growl like lions, Dad."

"You got me." Walker didn't even know his son liked butterscotch. He would've gotten butterscotch topping for ice cream sundaes or butterscotch pudding. Why didn't Doug tell him? Doug's pettiness never ceased to amaze him. He made a mental note to pick up butterscotch something tomorrow.

"Hey, I got some shipments in from Amazon. There are some leftover boxes you can play with at the condo." It was getting harder to keep on a happy face. Walker was like a comedian bombing.

Walker looked in the rearview mirror, waiting for a response. Hobie shrugged his shoulders. "Thanks."

He and Walker used to take the discarded boxes of their Christmas gifts and make a Christmas monster robot that terrorized the tree and stockings. Hobie would smile so wide the top half of his head could become unhinged. The memory formed a lump in Walker's throat.

Hobie wasn't smiling now. He watched himself kick his feet out. Walker remembered when Hobie would spend car rides asking him nonstop, non-sequitor questions, screaming them at Walker. Some of them were real headscratchers, like why gas stations were only located on street corners or how did sidewalks get cracks in them. Were people really that heavy?

"So what do you want for your birthday, champ?" Walker asked him extra loudly. He wondered if almost-six-year-olds knew what desperation was. At a stoplight, Walker reached behind him to rub Hobie's leg. "A tent for the backyard? That could be tons of fun, especially in the summer."

Hobie stopped kicking. He pulled his foot back hard.

The lack of contact burned Walker's hand. "I saw a new Avengers Lego model in the store. We can put it together." Walker focused back on the road. Dead air filled the car. Comedians probably liked getting booed more than no reaction at all. "Hobie? You okay?"

Hobie looked at Walker through the rearview mirror, all serious now. "I already showed you what I wanted."

"Are you sure, champ?" Walker racked his brain, but nothing was coming up. Kids weren't the most reliable, but Hobie wouldn't lie about this. He saw in his eyes that this was the cold, hard truth.

Think, Walker. He scrambled through their last few visits. His mind drew blanks. He could remember how much Radiance spent on print last year, but not what his son wanted for his birthday.

"Want to give me a hint?"

Hobie sighed. "It's a bike."

Yes! When they were at Target grocery shopping, Hobie pointed out the bike with training wheels. Red with black stripes. Walker remembered, but not fast enough.

"I knew that. I was just testing you. What's the fun of a birthday gift if you know what you're getting? The surprise is the best part!"

Hobie returned to looking out the window. Which was a relief for Walker, since he could dab away tears in his eyes unnoticed.

CHAPTER FIVE

Cameron

"And our next category is…sports!"

The rest of the bar cheered while Cameron threw his pencil onto the table. He shrugged his shoulders for his trivia teammates. "Welp, maybe we'll win next week."

"Why is there always a sports round?" Ethan asked.

"For the bros in here," Henry responded. They took swigs of their beer.

Cameron swiveled his head to one of the corner booths of the bar where a pack of five nerdy guys and girls eagerly awaited for the next round to start.

"How does Brain Trust know so much about sports? They look like they spend all their time in a lab."

"They're either mad geniuses or cheaters," Ethan said.

"One day." Henry scowled at the booth. "One day."

"Alright, teams!" The MC said over the mic. "Send your designated member up to collect the next round of clues."

The three guys looked at each other in a "Not It" way. Finally, Ethan relented, as usual, and went up. He was the youngest, after all.

Cameron had met his roommate Henry through the Browerton network of gay parties. He didn't exactly remember how he met his good friends. They all just careened into each other's lives. Ethan had only entered their circle of friends this winter, but was a welcome, if uptight, addition.

"You guys need to start bringing your boyfriends to trivia," Cameron said. "They know sports things."

He worried that his friends purposefully left their significant others at home so as not to make him feel like a fifth wheel. Which was a sweet gesture, but totally unnecessary.

Ethan slammed the sports sheet on their table. There were pictures of sixteen sports stadiums, and they had to name each of them.

"And zero points for us," Henry said.

"Wait. That's Wrigley Field." Ethan pointed to a stadium in the top row.

"One point." Cameron wrote it in. He tapped the pencil against the table as silence overtook their team.

Ethan said his usual refrain: "We'll get 'em next week!"

They all continued drinking their beers.

"So, Cameron," Ethan said, pointing at him with his beer bottle. "I may have seen you leave Dean's party with that cute guy. Are you going to see him again?"

Cameron understood that being the lone single guy in his group of friends opened his romantic life up for scrutiny. He thought of Sleeping Beauty resting in his bed as if it were a lazy Sunday. Before he could respond, Henry laughed loudly.

"Ha!"

"What's that supposed to mean?"

"It means a big, fat Greek no," Henry said, almost defiantly.

"You don't know that," Ethan said. "You guys seemed to be hitting it off."

"That's just flirting. I'm guessing you gave him the Puritan speech." Henry looked at Cameron, waiting for an answer.

"It's a good speech," he answered.

"Ha!"

"What's the Puritan speech?" Ethan asked.

"It's what Cameron says to all of his flings. Basically, if you exchange phone numbers after having sex, then the Puritans win. Or something like that. Seriously, Cameron. I've heard you recite the damn thing enough times. It's a good thing you're in that screenwriting class because you need some new dialogue."

Cameron gave his roommate the finger. "The guy slept in my bed until almost noon. I got showered and dressed and he was still there! Plus, he shaved everything down there. I have razor burn."

"And how is that different from the guy whose fingernails were too long? Or the guy with a pimple on his forehead? Or the guy who put ketchup in his spaghetti? Or the guy whose laugh was too loud?"

"Those are all valid reasons. They demonstrate serious character flaws."

"Maybe those guys just weren't the one," Ethan said.

"Cameron's not looking for the one, just one night."

"False!" Cameron laughed off Henry's comment, though it stung somewhere deep down. "I'm not about one-night stands. I just don't see the point in tying myself into a relationship during the prime of my life. I'm graduating in a few months. You really think it's smart to get serious with someone right now?"

"Greg and Ethan are making it work."

Ethan blushed from being in the hot seat. His boyfriend Greg was applying to special-ed teaching jobs in the Northeast, and Ethan had his sights set on Harvard Law School. So yes, they were making it work. And good for them, Cameron thought. But he didn't want to be tethered to someone in that way. He had the energy and excitement of a pinball, and he wanted the freedom to bounce around.

"I'm moving to Los Angeles in T-minus five months, as soon as our lease is up. Now is not the time to find a boyfriend."

"What about your first three years at Browerton?" Henry asked.

"College is supposed to be fun! I grew up surrounded by straight jocks in Ohio. Excuse me for wanting to indulge." People at Browerton were crazed about finding a significant other. They all wanted that college sweetheart story to tell their kids. Cameron's parents were college sweethearts, and that did not go so well. "Let me guess. You think because I choose to hook up with guys, that means I'm secretly unhappy with my life. Not the case. I love my life. And let's not forget about all the people who are miserable in relationships."

Henry grit his teeth. Even Cameron's blood pressure climbed thinking about Henry's terrible ex-boyfriend.

Luckily, his current boyfriend Nolan was a great guy, and that was all in the past. But Cameron knew that Henry let himself get in that situation because he kept telling himself the same crap he's telling Cameron now.

"What happened to that actor I tried setting you up with?" Henry asked. "You hooked up with him and then didn't call."

"Because he was an actor! I refused to let myself suffer through his improv showcases."

"Another excuse. Another reason to run," Henry said.

"I do not run!" That got the attention of a neighboring team. "I don't even jog."

"Yes, you do! You are a Kenyan sprinter when it comes to guys. You hook up, they want to see you again, you get scared, you call it a fling, you cut it off at the knees. And here we are greeting you at the finish line, squirting Gatorade in your face."

"Well, that's a lovely visual," Cameron said.

"It's not the worst thing in the world to be in a relationship, Cameron."

That was easy for Henry to say, and for Ethan to agree with. They both had boyfriends. They were both madly in love. It worked for them, but Cameron had other things on his mind. Like his future. He preferred to get his happiness from his work and from himself rather than hanging it all on a guy.

"Monotony is just not for me."

"You mean, monogamy," Henry said.

"Same difference."

It was times like these Cameron wished he had less opinionated friends. Why did he let his life get picked apart in such detail? Was that his role as token single friend? It was usually fun, until they managed to hit a truthful nerve.

"We are not tanking this round," Cameron said defiantly. He glared at Brain Trust, plugging away at their answer sheet. He chugged the rest of his beer, stood up, and scanned the bar.

"What are you doing?" Ethan asked.

"I am going to find us someone who knows sports." He slammed his bottle down on the table. "It's time that we win for a change."

He looked out in the sea of anonymous faces, until he found one that rang a bell. His lips quirked into a smile. "I'll be right back."

CHAPTER SIX

Walker

Walker kept drinking beer until the aftershocks of work wore off. Patricia was true to her word when she said that they'd have to work harder than ever to win this review. He had to blink several times, even close his eyes in the car when he got out. Staring at a screen all day was making him blind, he was sure of it. Maybe it was for the best that Hobie wasn't staying with him this weekend. He needed to recuperate. But it still left a hole in his heart.

He ordered another beer. He knew the alcohol had to be working because he started seeing things. Like the cute barista, walking toward him.

"Grande vanilla latte." Cameron pointed at him. "Walker, not Walter."

"Hi." Walker tried not to stammer. It was the ultimate compliment when somebody remembered your name.

"How well do you know sports? Specifically sports stadiums?"

This was not the beer talking. It was actually him, looking just as sexy without the green apron.

"I beg your pardon?"

"My trivia team and I know nothing about le sports. I only enjoy when they interview athletes in the locker room. And I know this makes us sound like stereotypical gay guys. Trust me, there are plenty of gay men who know le sports. It's just not us. That's why we need you."

"You're so sure I know sports?"

"It's le sports, and yes. You're wearing a tie. You know things."

Walker flipped his tie around in his fingers. Nothing made you more of an adult than a tie. It was the crow's feet of clothes.

"You owe me," Cameron said, pointing at him. "I gave you an extra shot of espresso the other day."

"Fair enough."

Cameron passed him the trivia sheet. "What are you doing in a college bar?"

"I didn't realize this was college kids only." Walker felt something coming to life inside him, like an engine revving first thing in the morning. He wanted to compete at Cameron's level. His energy was infectious, and he forgot how exhausted he was.

"There are classy adult bars around here, too. The kind with a jazzy piano and work happy hours and cocktail napkins for your drink."

"I prefer McFly's." Walker surveyed the dingy surroundings. Sticky floors and dark lighting, full of charm. "You know this place used to be a McDonald's?"

"Seriously?"

"Yep. That line of booths is where the registers used to be. McDonald's was even grimier than McFly's." It came back to Walker crystal clearly, details he forgot that he had remembered. "It was a twenty-hour McDonald's. Everyone used to come here after parties. This place was dead during the day, but you couldn't get a seat at two a.m. Chances are if you couldn't find a hookup at a party, you could find one here."

"Love at a McDonald's. It doesn't get more all-American than that."

A smile flitted across Walker's face. "The week they were closing, they sold hamburgers for nineteen cents each. Like a liquidation sale. My freshman roommate and I each got ten. I woke up the next morning to the sound of him puking into a trash can." Walker could still remember the sounds, and unfortunately the smells. The edges of the memory glowed in his mind like a photograph.

"I can't believe this place used to be a McDonald's."

"And you know that yoga studio on Rogers?"

Cameron nodded.

"It used to be a tattoo parlor."

Walker wished he could listen to Cameron's laugh on repeat. The guy knew how to wield such a powerful weapon.

"Who knew Duncannon had such an edge?" Cameron brushed hair out of his eyes. "Now it's a sterilized yuppie paradise."

Walker couldn't complain. He was part of the problem, and he liked that his son got to live in a safe, clean city. Although with that came skyhigh property taxes, but he wasn't going to bore Cameron with such details.

Cameron moved right next to Walker to call over the bartender. He ordered two shots. Walker smelled his woodsy cologne, even some remnants of Starbucks, and nearly pulled Cameron into his lap.

"We need to toast to McDonald's," he said. He handed Walker a shot. "Don't worry. It's just vodka."

Just vodka. It had been too long since Walker's last shot. He eyed the glass of clear liquid with trepidation, but it turned out it was like riding a bike. The alcohol streamed down his throat and gave him a healthy burn in his chest.

"So why are you and your friends here and not at the Royale?" Walker asked.

"What's that?"

He felt a sinking feeling in his chest. "You've never heard of the Royale? Do people not go anymore?"

Cameron shrugged in complete confusion.

"It's this gay eighteen plus dance party that was held above this abandoned pizza parlor. I think at least three-quarters of the gay population at Browerton had their first gay experience on the dance floor of that place." Still no reaction. "Come on! They don't do it anymore?"

"I guess not. Sounds deliciously sketchy. Did you feel your first boner grinding into your thigh at the Royale?"

Walker nodded. "We used to look forward to it every week. We would pre-game in someone's dorm room and then stumble over, ready to dance. There would be guys there from all over. Townies, closeted husbands, high schoolers who snuck in. Once we saw a member of the Browerton football team there, but it was an unspoken rule that what happened at the Royale stayed at the Royale." Walker breathed out a lengthy sigh. "And now it's gone, apparently."

"That sounded like fun. There's this dance club in the city that has a massive gay dance party called Revolution once a quarter. It's three floors."

Walker doubted it was as good as the Royale. He felt a little bad for Cameron and his friends that they couldn't experience that. *Today, being gay is more accepted*, he thought, which was great. But there was something to be enjoyed in the secretiveness.

"How long ago was this?" Cameron asked, wiping beer off his lips.

"Fifteen thousand years ago."

"Seriously."

"It's not that far off."

"Are you really being coy about this?" Cameron raised his eyebrows, waiting for an answer. It was freaking adorable. "I'll tell you my age. I'm almost twenty-two and a half."

"You're young. You still use half years to describe your age." Walker gulped his beer.

Cameron rolled his eyes. "Why is it that as soon as someone hits thirty, they think they belong in the AARP?"

"You think I just hit thirty?" Walker sat up a little straighter and checked himself out in the mirror behind the bar. He could see the exhaustion ringing his eyes and his hairline just starting its slow death march.

"Barely. Maybe a day ago." Cameron was still close to him, still smellable. "You're still hot for a senior citizen."

Walker raised his beer and clinked it against Cameron's empty bottle. Their arms rested against each other's. They shared a silent moment that Walker felt throughout his body.

"We need to do something about that." He nodded at Cameron's empty bottle.

This time, Walker hailed the bartender.

"Teams, you have one more minute. When you're finished, bring them up," the MC barked into his microphone.

"Crap!" Cameron shouted.

"Le sports!"

Cameron slapped his hand on the answer sheet, reminding them of their mission. "Do you know any of these stadiums?"

Some looked familiar to Walker. He knew more about sports than Cameron, for sure, but not that much more.

"Do you see that basket of hipsters in the corner booth?" Cameron nodded behind him, and his description was pretty much spot on. "That's Brain Trust. They're here every week, and they always win, and they always act surprised and fake modest when they have to go up to accept their prize. And the leader of the group insists on making a speech."

"For winning pub trivia?"

"This needs to end tonight." Cameron handed him his pen. "Fight with us, Walker."

Walker was able to write in a few answers, more than he originally thought. He could hear the clock ticking down the seconds in his head. It was stupid pub trivia, but he found himself getting into it. He wanted to do a good job for Cameron. He managed to fill in answers for every single stadium. "Here you go."

As soon as he handed off the paper, Cameron ran it up to the MC. He thought the guy would go back to his friends, but to his pleasant surprise, Cameron returned to his spot, their arms touching on the bar.

"You may have won us the game," Cameron said. "I think that calls for a shot."

Walker waved a hand at the bartender. "On me. I don't want to know how much you make at Starbucks."

Cameron waved his hand over Walker's hand. "On me. You may have helped us win a thirty-five dollar tab at the bar."

Walker raised his hand higher than Cameron's. Their arms were nearly intertwined. "On me. Because I've enjoyed talking with you."

Cameron turned to him and flashed a thin-lipped smile that had mischief at the edges. "Who says we're done talking?"

CHAPTER SEVEN

Cameron

Cameron Buckley woke up in an empty bed. A very comfortable bed, with a thick, billowing comforter, smooth sheets that caressed his skin, and pillows his head sunk into like marshmallows. But an empty bed nonetheless.

And he was naked. He looked under the sheets to double check. Yep, naked.

He squinted at the sharp rays of sunlight streaming through the bedroom windows. Cameron surveyed his surroundings. He died and went to Crate & Barrel. He marveled at the details of this well-decorated room. The off-white walls and curved floor lamp in the corner. He ran his fingers across the mahogany night table. He stared at himself in the mirrored sliding closet door at the opposite end. His hair stuck up at all angles, and he was still naked.

"Good morning." Walker charged back into the bedroom wearing nothing but a towel. He had given Cameron such a hard time last night about being older, but the guy was in better shape than many of the unkempt slobs that roamed Browerton's campus.

"Did you sleep okay?" Walker asked.

"I think so?" Cameron rubbed at his temples and realized that he was hungover.

"I have Advil if you need it. My head is pounding."

"I'll be fine." Cameron had had worse hangovers. It was a good thing he worked at a coffee shop. Did they really drink that much last night?

Walker scrolled through emails on his phone. While Cameron's inbox was usually filled with Gap coupons and random newsletters, Walker's emails looked serious.

Cameron eyed the floor and the dresser, but he didn't see his clothes anywhere. He also didn't see any discarded condom wrappers.

"I have to ask you something," he said, his stomach swirling with something other than alcohol. "I can't believe I'm asking this question. I've never had to ask this question, but I really need to know the answer."

Walker put a hand on his shoulder. "Nothing happened last night."

"Oh thank goodness." Cameron fell back into the mountain of pillows. He only had two pillows on his own bed; this guy had six! "Not that I wouldn't want to, but I'd want to be able to remember it."

"I'm not in the habit of sleeping with unconscious men."

"That's a wonderful quality to have." Cameron breathed a sigh of relief, then bolted back up. "Wait. Then why am I naked?"

"Because you wanted to play Naked Twister." Walker removed a pair of boxer briefs and socks from his slick dresser, which matched both nightstands.

"What's Naked Twister?"

"You don't know? You seemed like an expert last night."

"We played Naked Twister?"

"I don't know. We were walking back to my place, and you kept saying that you wanted to play Naked Twister. You ran inside, tore off all your clothes, jumped onto my bed, and yelled 'Naked Twister!' at the top of your lungs."

Cameron clamped a hand over his mouth. He was going to melt into the floor.

"I did not do that."

"Oh, you did. I have it on video."

"What?!"

"Kidding." Walker put on his boxer briefs under his towel. *There's a naked guy in his bed and he's being modest?*

Cameron took a deep breath. "And what happened next? After I yelled..." He gulped down hard. "'Naked Twister.'"

"Then you passed out."

"And?"

"And I put you under the covers, turned off the light, and stayed on my side of the bed."

Warmth spread through Cameron. He got lucky, and not in the way he originally thought. He had fallen into bed with a total gentleman. Thanks to the gentleman's tight black boxers, he got to see what he almost had. Cameron smiled to himself.

"So why are *you* naked?" He asked Walker.

"Because I showered."

Cameron marveled at Walker's bare chest, damp from the shower. He didn't look to be a gymrat, thank goodness. He had some definition, but overall Cameron was turned on by the maturity, by the heft. It wasn't the same hairless, muscular chest that he'd seen with his other college hookups.

"Who's H.J.?" Cameron nodded at the tattoo of H.J. inside his bicep.

"Someone very close to me."

"Your boyfriend?"

"Not my boyfriend." Walker slid open his closet door. Lines of starched shirts and pressed pants greeted him. Cameron's closet was a discount rack at an outlet store by comparison.

"What do you do?" Cameron asked. "Lawyer?"

"I'm a media planner."

"Cool."

"Do you know what that is?"

"Nope."

"I help figure out how to sell shampoo." The man searched for the right clothing combination to wear. "Media is any type of advertising you pay for, as opposed to public relations which is media that is free."

"Oh, so you make the ads."

"No," Walker seemed to say with a sigh. "We don't make the ads. We just decide where to place them to best reach consumers."

"Do you have to wear a suit?"

"No, thankfully. No jeans, though."

"Well, that sucks. I'd go with the dark green." Cameron pointed to the pair of pants next to the regular khakis Walker had chosen. He took an extra beat to admire Walker's ass in those boxer briefs. "It'll match the shirt you picked out better."

"Thanks." Walker took his advice and slid the closet door shut. Cameron noticed just how much space was between them.

"Are you nervous?" Cameron asked him through the mirrored door.

Walker stopped buttoning up his shirt. "I'm not really sure how this goes. It's been a while since I..."

"Played Naked Twister?"

Walker blushed and pulled out a tie from another drawer in his dresser. There was something hot about watching Walker knot his tie. It was a few seconds of intense focus and precise moves.

"I had fun," Cameron said. "From what I can remember."

Walker sat on the edge of the bed. "I did, too."

He rubbed Cameron's back, gently but with a firm hand, melting Cameron like butter on a hot skillet. Cameron picked up the fresh scent of shaving cream, and dragged a hand across Walker's freshly shaved neck. Walker gave him a direct look in the eye that broke through his cool for a split-second. A tiny alarm went off somewhere in Cameron's head.

"I should probably get dressed." He leaned back, out of Walker's reach. He slipped out of bed, wrapping himself with Walker's comforter. "And I'm sure you have to be at work soon."

"Yeah." Walker's shoulders drooped with what Cameron thought was the sting of rejection. *Unintentional rejection*, he thought. He jogged into the hall and brought in Cameron's heap of clothes.

"Thanks."

He threw on his clothes and took the precious seconds he had left to give himself a brief tour of Walker's condo. He marveled at the real furniture. Cameron figured none of it was secondhand or bought off Craigslist. Walker went into actual stores and purchased these items. Cameron's apartment had a garage sale décor, which is how he and Henry acquired most of their furniture.

Real art hung on the walls. A real ficus sat in the living room.

"Do you want anything to eat?" Walker called out from the kitchen, which had real stainless steel appliances. Including a dishwasher!

"No, I'm fine." Cameron shrugged it off. He ranked this hangover a six on his richter scale.

"Are you working this morning?"

"Nope." Cameron became distracted by the closed door at the end of the hall.

"I can drive you back to your apartment."

"No need. I'll walk." He felt compelled to open the door. There might be a cadre of chopped up college bodies in a freezer or something.

"What are you looking for back there?" Walker's voice became fainter.

"Nothing." Cameron turned the doorknob. The door squeaked open. He was hit by bright sky blue walls. His eyes went straight to the racecar bed in the corner and a chest of toys by the window.

Hobie was spelled out in block letters on the wall.

"Are you looking for something?"

Cameron jumped and knocked his foot into a Lego building of a castle. His ankle took a chunk out of a tower. Pieces spewed across the carpet.

"Shit!"

"What are you doing?" Walker ran over to pick up the literal pieces of this mess.

"Who's room is this?"

"My son's."

Cameron's throat immediately shut down for business. He steadied himself against the doorframe. Walker, who he got drunk in a bar and naked with, had a son, a young son by the looks of this room.

"Please tell me you're divorced."

"I am," Walker said somewhat dejectedly. Cameron realized how cold the question sounded once it turned out to be true.

"I'm sorry."

Walker shrugged it off.

"About the Legos, too."

Cameron watched him corral the last of the pieces into a pile by what remained of the castle. He was thrown through the ultimate loop, but he also found himself intrigued. Walker wasn't just some guy in a bar. He was a father and divorcé. Most Browerton students usually had the same stories, the same paths. Cameron enjoyed hearing something new. It gave him something to focus on while he planned his exit.

"How long have you been divorced, if you don't mind me asking?"

"Two years."

"Still kind of fresh."

Walker shrugged. More like a humoring shrug. Cameron was well aware about the wounds from parents splitting up, though only from the child's point-of-view.

"How old's Hobby?" Cameron asked. Walker whipped his head around in surprise, until Cameron pointed to the Hobie sign hanging on the wall.

"It's pronounced Hobie, like rhymes with Toby. He's about to turn six."

"Kindergarten, right?"

"Yep." Walker fixed the pillow on Hobie's bed, which only made him seem more attractive to Cameron.

"So are you still in the closet? I mean, does your ex-wife know you hook up with guys?"

"Ex-husband." Walker gestured out of the room, and Cameron followed his lead back to the kitchen. "We had a civil union."

"That's so cool. You're living the gay American dream." Except for the divorce part, but in Cameron's mind, that was as much a part of being an American as a white picket fence.

Walker offered up a glass of water, which Cameron gladly accepted. He had an open kitchen, complete with a breakfast nook and stools, overlooking the living room with a vaulted ceiling, skylight, and fireplace. Cameron wondered if he would have an adult condo like this in the future, and a husband, and a kid. It was all too much to think about now.

"How did you meet your ex-husband? I'm sorry if I'm prying. It's interesting. I'm still in college mode, so I just assume everyone meets at parties or in discussion section."

"Well, actually we met at a party our junior year at Browerton."

"You were actual college sweethearts?"

"We were."

He refilled Cameron's glass as soon as he was done. None of Cameron's hookups ever offered him a glass of water, or vice versa. He should've been hooking up with thirtysomethings this whole time. "Walker, you are just an enigma wrapped inside of a mystery tucked into a luxurious condo."

Walker gave him a sly half-smile, and Cameron found himself blushing.

When they got outside, Cameron zipped up his sweater. It was a cool March morning, but he'd walked home in far less in far colder temperatures. Walker's SUV hung out in the driveway. There was a car seat in the back, which made everything feel all too real for Cameron.

"You live really close to campus," Cameron said. "I'm surprised I haven't seen you around there."

"I haven't been back, not since my ten-year reunion."

"Really? But it's right there."

Walker shrugged.

"No looking back," Cameron said knowingly.

"What?"

"I'm the same way. When I leave a place, I leave it for good. No use getting bogged down in old memories. When I was in high school, this really popular senior graduated, but he kept coming back to hang out with his old teachers and younger friends. And when they all left, he would sometimes just drive through the parking lot. It's sad."

"Maybe it was a really nice parking lot."

Cameron busted out laughing. Then he stopped, and there was silence. He knew what came next.

To Cameron, good-byes were like going to the dentist. They were dreaded, nervewracking, uncomfortable experiences, yet an unavoidable part of our society.

Walker looked at the pavement, then up at Cameron. Nervousness bounced off him like a satellite signal. "There's a great restaurant not too far from here."

"Look, you don't need to do this. You don't have to retroactively turn last night into a date." Cameron pushed back the dentist drill. "We got hammered and had some fun. We had a good time. Let's just leave it at that. Nobody's getting hurt here."

"That sounds great, actually."

Cameron did a double take. Walker didn't flinch. "It does?"

"Yeah. You're graduating. I have a kid." Walker nodded, perking up about the idea. "That makes sense."

"Then why did you ask me out to dinner?"

"Knee jerk response, I guess. To make things—"

"Less awkward!" This guy kept getting better and better. "I hate that we're wired this way. You asked me on a date to make me not feel cheap. I would've avoided your calls."

"The date would be even more awkward because we both knew this would go nowhere. And you'd probably order the most expensive thing on the menu and get drunk on wine."

"Why put ourselves through that?" Cameron couldn't stop smiling. He'd never been this giddy saying good-bye. But finally, someone got it. It was the high note Cameron needed to go out on.

"It was really nice meeting you, Walker. Your bed is very comfortable."

"You, too."

"And I'm really sorry about Hobie's castle."

"It's okay."

"Okay."

Usually, this was when guys acted all tough and swaggered away. But Walker opened his arms for a hug, a surprise for Cameron. He took the mature route yet again.

Cameron hugged back, but pulled away quickly. An extended whiff of Walker's aftershave would prove deadly to his decision-making abilities.

"I'll see you around Starbucks," Walker said.

"Have a good day at work!" Cameron powerwalked away. He couldn't stop thinking about how well that went, how well the whole night and following morning went. It might have just been the best hookup he'd ever had, despite no hooking up involved. As he made a right turn and headed toward his apartment, a sense of sadness swarmed over Cameron when he realized that he would never spend this much time with Walker again—exactly as he wanted.

CHAPTER EIGHT

Walker

Subject: Why were we in

The Food Network Magazine three years ago? We're a shampoo brand. We should not be advertising in food magazines.

Patricia's incessant emails had become more incessant thanks to the review. She spent her days scrutinizing every aspect of every media plan they executed for Radiance over the past six years. *Why did they run a commercial on ESPN two-and-a-half years ago? Why weren't they doing more with beauty websites?*

Walker pictured himself yelling at his computer screen. He wished that Patricia would conduct a modicum of due diligence for these questions rather than treating Walker's email like Google. But he did the mature thing, took a cleansing breath, and calmly emailed back that The *Food Network Magazine* skews heavily female, that ESPN was part of an old campaign for Radiance's male shampoo brand, and that running on popular beauty websites would have cost them money they didn't have in their media budget.

He thought that once he got promoted to Associate Media Director, he would be more in control. He would have a team he could manage. He did have associates and supervisors under him, but Patricia preferred to communicate directly with them, lest she have to trust anyone.

"Just breathe," Lucy said in the breakroom. "She's just nervous. We're all nervous."

Walker's chest tightened up, thinking about them losing the review. He should spruce up his résumé, but the thought of applying for other jobs sounded worse than eating chopped liver.

His mind would rather think about Cameron. He had tried focusing on his email and on pulling past reports, but it was no use. Naked Twister would never leave his head.

"What's his name?" Lucy asked.

"What?"

"You have a stupid grin on your face." She filled up her water bottle. It had pictures of her kids around the sides. "Nobody is ever that happy about working in Excel. Who's the guy?"

"It's no one." Walker blushed. A flash of Cameron, naked under his covers, watching him get dressed this morning flitted through his mind.

"Liar!" Lucy said too loudly. Walker gestured for her to keep it down.

"Sorry." She clapped quietly. "I'm just so happy for you, Walker. You need to get back on that saddle. It's been a while."

"It hasn't been that long of a while." He went through his mental sex calendar. "Has it?"

"It has. There was that high school teacher last June. And then you got freaky with that one guy shortly after the divorced was finalized."

"How do you remember that?"

"I've been with the same man for twenty-six years. I need to live vicariously through you. I'm old."

"Well, so am I. This guy," and here Walker leaned in close to Lucy and checked to make sure the room was empty "he's a college student."

Lucy clamped her hand over her mouth.

"He's twenty-two," Walker added, as if that made it that much better.

"Walker!" she whisper-yelled. "Walker!"

"I know." Walker shook his head. It had been a few days since he and Cameron parted ways on his driveway, and he hadn't had the nerve to see him. He started going to the Starbucks in his own building.

"I'm glad you had fun."

The statement dinged him just slightly. It was supposed to be fun, and only fun. He wasn't supposed to be thinking about a drunken night this much. He didn't wonder about the guys he had sex with after his divorce. He couldn't even remember their names.

"No wonder you look so tired." She let out a squeal of laughter. "He must've made you feel young again."

"He made me feel alive." Walker felt a pall come over their table, as if the further removed he was from his night with Cameron, the more his own light dimmed.

Five minutes later, he and Lucy went back to their workspaces, into the quiet of the office. A huge space of people saying nothing, all typing away at their computers. Walker crawled through his work for another hour. He figured that eventually he would forget about Cameron, and his life and work ethic would return to normal. There was something so profoundly sad about that, he thought.

After answering the last of Patricia's questions, for now, he took an early lunch at 11:30, and beelined to the west building of The Complex.

He snapped out of his work daze the second he spotted Cameron behind the counter. He wasn't used to seeing the Starbucks so empty. Cameron smiled at him, while wiping down the counter.

"Hey," he said, unsure where to go from here. Nerves slingshotted across his body.

"Hey, Walker. What can I get for you?"

Walker hadn't thought about getting a drink. He wasn't thirsty, and his mouth was a cottonball at the same time. "My usual, I guess."

Cameron wrote on his cup and passed it to another barista. "So what brings you down here for a midday coffee?"

"Oh, you know...caffeine addiction." *I wanted to see you.* The words were right there. Cameron treating him like a customer was not making this easier. "Has it been busy?"

"The usual amount. Everybody needs their coffee."

"Work's been...well, I needed a break."

The barista at the end called out Walker's order. He picked it up and made his way back to Cameron's register, feeling awkwardness sink in.

"Do you have a break coming up soon?" Walker realized as soon as he walked in here, he had no plan.

"I don't. I only work until noon, then I have class."

"I forgot. You're a senior. No morning classes."

"Exactly. And I don't even want to go to this one. It's this pass/fail sociology class, but since I failed the last test, I should probably attend the lecture."

"That sounds interesting." Walker never got to take a sociology class, or anything like it. He was a business major, at his parents' insistence. That meant math and econ and marketing.

"I fell asleep in the first lecture. Honestly, I'm so checked out. Major senioritis. I'm ready to start a career."

"Be careful what you wish for. I'd take a college lecture, especially one about sociology, over work any day of the week."

"Okay." Cameron nodded. "My class is at 12:30."

Walker laughed, then realized Cameron wasn't joking. "I have work."

"Did you hear what you just said?"

"I have a lot of things to do, unfortunately."

"Just say you're taking a long lunch."

"I have to get this report done and research our competitors' past campaigns. We're in review, so we have to..." And for the first time, Walker listened to himself. He heard himself clearly, heard every miserable word coming out of his mouth. "Let's do it."

Φ

Walker wanted to kick his younger self for every lecture he skipped, every time he snuck in a magazine to read. Class was one hundred times better than work. His mind reblossomed as he listened to the professor talk. It had been a long while since he learned anything. At work, he just *did* things, things he had done before. His body craved knowledge like a missing nutrient.

Walker and Cameron sat in the back of the lecture hall listening to the professor passionately talk about the evolution of American cities. He was a million rows away, but it felt like a conversation over dinner. Walker didn't remember his professors being this vivid. Most of his classes at Browerton were blurs of memories smeared together like a baby's fingerpaintings. He could recall going to class but not what was taught.

Cameron leaned over his seat and whispered into Walker's ear. "I can't believe your version of playing hooky is coming to class."

"The world works in mysterious ways."

"The world." Cameron returned to his seat. "Right."

"Just listen," Walker whispered in his ear. "Don't think about the exam. Don't think about taking notes. Just let yourself be interested."

Cameron leaned back in his seat. He closed his notebook. Walker watched him try to focus.

The professor clicked onto a slide about gentrification of cities. He discussed how the Upper West Side in Manhattan evolved from a dangerous, violent, lower class neighborhood, to a yuppiefied area with cute shops and little crime. Walker wished he could visit New York. *One day*, he told himself.

"That's interesting, right?" Walker asked.

Cameron gave a reluctant nod.

The professor next talked about the people behind gentrification: DINKs. Double Income No Kids. Walker smiled at the acronym. That's what he and Doug were.

Doug had dared them to move to a bad part of town because gays were supposed to be at the forefront of gentrification.

Walker was the most attentive person in that class, and soon it seemed that the professor was talking directly to him. He felt a shift rumbling through him. The windows of his brain were opened, letting in sunshine and brushing away the cobwebs. He found himself sitting up straight and forgetting that he had a cell phone with email.

He realized that his brain was doing what it was supposed to all along. It wasn't blindly going through the motions. It was absorbing knowledge. He turned his neck, and Cameron was looking at him with warm eyes, and a hint of admiration.

"What?" Walker asked.

"Nothing." Cameron didn't flinch. He remained fixed on Walker, which made Walker a little turned on. "I like watching you like this."

"Engrossed?"

"Impassioned."

Walker didn't know how to handle that. Was that a compliment? "We can go soon."

"I don't want to." Cameron rested his head on Walker's shoulder. He closed his eyes and looked peaceful.

Walker contemplated putting his arm around Cameron. Was that what he wanted or was he just bored? Ultimately, Walker didn't move. But he remembered why he wasn't as focused on classes when he was a student. Cute boys were just too distracting.

Walker didn't go back to work after class. He and Cameron meandered all throughout campus. Memory after memory flashed in Walker's head. The past was so close, yet out of reach. They visited parts of the campus he hadn't been to since he was a student.

"Why are we going to a library?" Cameron asked, following behind Walker. "Has one class turned you into a total bookworm?"

"Just trust me."

They entered the Browerton library, which wasn't anything to look at on the inside or outside. Walker hadn't been in here in years, but he could've found his way with his eyes closed. They walked past a computer terminal, and just after the reference desk, Walker and Cameron made a sharp left down a narrow hallway.

"Where are you taking me?" Cameron asked.

"Just trust me."

The hallway twisted around like the bottom of a pretzel, then spat them out into a cavernous hallway with exposed, faded brick and stone flooring.

"My friends and I used to call that the Time Machine Hallway."

At the end of the hall were two massive, wooden double doors that could've been the entrance to a castle. Instead, they led to Waring Library.

"Waring Library houses the university's music archives," Walker said.

Cameron slid his fingers over the dusty shelves filled with old recordings and sheet music. He marveled at the cathedral-like ceilings and low lighting. Album posters hung on the walls. A few new ones had been added in fifteen years, but the music library still had the untouched old-timey, classic feel Walker remembered.

"This is so un-library like," Cameron said, his head swung back to stare at the design etched in the ceiling. "Like, I'd actually want to hang out here."

"It used to be the main library in the early 1900s."

"Back when you were a student?" Cameron just had to throw that one in, but Walker took his sarcasm in stride. He found it endearing.

Cameron ran over to the record section, where rows of old records were pressed together in yellowed jackets. There wasn't a librarian here to instruct them to walk. "How old do you think these are?"

"What does it matter?"

Cameron thumbed through albums, blowing away dust. "What do you mean?"

"What does it matter how old a record or a library is? It's more than a number." Walker's voice echoed in the hollowed space.

"Did I strike a nerve?"

Apparently. Walker leaned against a column and just watched Cameron and all his flitting energy. He wondered at what point he stopped being excited about things. When did experiences stop being new?

Cameron sidled over to him, and his scent cut through the musty smell permeating this place, which probably explained why nobody visited here much.

"I think it's cool," Cameron said. "This place has character."

Cameron pointed at the molding above Walker's head. Fine detailing grooved in swishy lines. "The concrete monstrosity known as our regular library doesn't have that."

Walker pushed himself off the column. "I didn't bring

you here just to show you crown molding." He nodded his head in a "follow me" gesture. He led Cameron to a bookcase against the far wall that had a thick layer of dust.

"When I was in school, this was the place where guys would come to hook up."

"With other guys?"

Walker nodded. Cameron's eyes pleaded to tell him more. The memories flooded back into his mind. "The music library was always this abandoned." Walker gestured to the emptiness around them. "Perfect place for guys in the closet, and even openly gay guys to get it on at the dawn of the twentieth-first century, especially by the musical theater shelf."

"Very appropriate."

Walker thought he felt his phone buzz. Many times, he felt a phantom buzz in his pocket. He never kept his phone on silent just in case he needed to be reached about Hobie. He saw ten new emails in his work inbox and just as quickly shoved his phone back in his pocket.

"That's not all." Walker brought Cameron around to the side of the musical theater bookcase. Dozens of people had carved their initials into the wood.

Cameron's hands ran over a carving at the bottom dated F.K. + L.B 11/07/63. "It's amazing that a few weeks after these two fellas hooked up, JFK was assassinated. I don't know, like I wonder if people realized that they're a part of history."

"I think people are just trying to live their lives."

"Was it...was it bad then?" Cameron asked. "For gays?"

Walker realized that Cameron lived in a world where he could go to gay bars and hang out with his friends in public and not have to worry. Sure, there would always be assholes out there, but more people and institutions also had his back. He didn't have to live his life in such a coded way.

"It wasn't like the 1950s or anything. More guys were coming out and staying out when I was at Browerton. There was a small LGBT group, but we still felt like outsiders. It's not like it is today."

Cameron nodded with a glint of respect, and something more Walker couldn't decipher.

"Where's your carving?" Cameron rested against a brick wall. He looked like an album cover.

Walker squatted to the bottom row. W.R. + D.E. were inside a heart.

"College sweethearts," Cameron said.

Walker hurtled back in time, to when he and Doug snuck down here. Doug's hands were down Walker's pants as soon as they got inside. He took Walker in his mouth while Walker played lookout. It was another world away and a painful reminder of the present.

"Time flies," Walker said. "You better savor your last days here."

"Ugh, no. I hate protracted goodbyes. Everyone's so scared about the future, but I can't wait."

"That's right. Hollywood awaits," Walker said with a tinge of melancholy.

Cameron took a few steps closer to Walker. Every muscle in Walker's body was on high alert, ready to move closer. The warm, yellow light gave this moment a glow of instant nostalgia.

"Thanks for taking me here," Cameron said.

Walker nodded and felt something in his pants. He

pulled out his buzzing phone. "Hi, Patricia."

"Walker, where are you? We're supposed to have a meeting to discuss Radiance's social media strategy. It's 2:30."

"Yeah, I'm sorry. I'll be right over. I had a long lunch, catching up with an old friend."

"Walker, I don't need to remind you we are in review. Please be more cognizant of your schedule. I'll see you back at the office."

Walker slipped his phone back into his pocket. Cameron was browsing through old albums.

"Busted?" he asked.

"Busted." More than busted, Walker thought. Patricia threw a bucket of ice water at him.

They left Waring Library, retreated down the Time Machine hallway, and were back in the cold, modern furnishings of the main library.

Cameron went through the revolving door. Walker followed quickly after him.

"Back to the grind," Walker said with a shrug.

"Back to the homework grind for me."

"You're still doing homework? I commend you."

"I consider watching movies homework. It's research."

They shared an awkward laugh, but before Walker could launch into his goodbye, Cameron beat him to the punch.

"Maybe we should exchange numbers," Cameron said. "Just in case you feel like playing hooky again."

And so they did. And when Walker returned to the office, he met with Patricia and dutifully discussed Radiance's social media strategy, all with a dopey smile on his face.

CHAPTER NINE

Cameron

Cameron paced back and forth in his bedroom, phone glued to his ear. He took deep steps from one corner to the other, even dipping into his closet. His phone never left his ear.

"That all sounds great," he said.

"It's a pretty decent place, considering we're paying under three-thousand a month in Santa Monica," Porter said. "The building owner is this old Swedish guy, and I think my Swede cred got us the place."

"That's awesome."

"You'll have to share a bathroom with Grayson. Do you remember Grayson? He was my year."

"Yeah. The name is familiar." Cameron had no recollection of either Porter or Grayson. They were background players in his Browerton life, apparently. But they had a spare room in Los Angeles at a good price, so of course he remembered them vividly.

"So you're in?" Porter asked.

"I'm in. I can scan the owner my application and wire a security deposit."

"Cool."

Cool didn't even begin to cover it. Cameron held the phone to his chest as he danced around his room. Mostly spinning because of lack of space. He lost some gravity as the moment lifted him up.

"You still there?"

Cameron banged his ankle against his dresser, which put a light damper on things. "Yep. Still here."

"When did you say you'd move out here?"

"September first." Five months away. Five whole eternities, really. The leases on most off-campus housing ran from September to August, to align with the start of the school year. Cameron wished he could move out sooner, but he couldn't afford to pay two rents at once. Plus, he still had to save up for the move. He gulped hard when Porter told him what the cost of rent plus utilities came to monthly. More than double his current setup. He hoped it only took him a few weeks to find a job in Hollywood.

"Oh, I forgot to mention the best part," Porter said. "We're six blocks from the beach."

Cameron pulled up Google Maps on his computer to verify. He stared at the swath of blue on the map, mere inches from his future abode.

"You're gonna love Santa Monica. You can walk up and down the beach. There's bike paths, walking paths. Any time of day, it's gorgeous out there."

"I'll bet." Cameron could hear the waves crashing, the salt spraying in the air. He didn't hear Porter hang up, and he didn't care.

He ambled out to the living room. His mom had given him their old purple sofa. The thing was as old as Cameron, but still in great shape. It was the one real piece of furniture in this place. Non-Ikea, non-thrift store. He sank into the cushions like chocolate melting into a smore.

Cameron was one step closer to turning his Hollywood dream into a reality. He wanted to celebrate, but Henry was out with Nolan and Ethan was having dinner with Greg and his parents.

The silence in the apartment hit him. He heard a car drive by on the street. Cameron hated any type of silence, from empty houses to awkward pauses. To him, it was a continuity error, like watching characters in a movie veer from the script or break the fourth wall.

He turned on his TV and played *Little Miss Sunshine* in the background while he worked on his screenwriting assignment. That was that writer's first produced screenplay, and he won the Oscar. Maybe Cameron would be so lucky. He tried not to think about the thousands of aspiring screenwriters thinking the exact same thing at this exact same moment. The movie filled the apartment with noise; it made him calm.

He looked up from his computer. Two hours had evaporated into thin air. *Time flies where you're having fun.* It was seven o'clock on a Thursday night. He locked down an apartment in Los Angeles, steps from the beach. He should be out. Tonight should not be a calm night on the couch. He picked up his phone from the coffee table.

"Hey," Walker said, somewhat distracted.

"Is this a bad time?"

"No." He sounded hesitant. "No, it's good." Much better.

Cameron sat cross-legged on the couch. "What are you up to tonight?"

"Um, just hanging out and relaxing with some TV."

"Rough day at work?"

"Back-breaking," he deadpanned. Cameron heard the TV in the background and tried to figure out what he was watching. "If you wanted to come over and ogle my furnishings again, I could order a pizza."

"I have a better idea. Have you ever been to Cherry Stem?"

"Is that a bar?"

"It's a gay club. We should go dancing."

"It's Thursday."

"Thank you for the reminder, Human Day Planner. Tonight's '90s night. Have you ever danced to a remixed version of 'Ironic'?"

"I have not."

Cameron could almost hear Walker smiling through the phone. "Tonight's your chance."

"I'm sorry. I have work tomorrow."

"No, no, no." Cameron jumped off his couch and got into pacing mode as if he was in front of a jury. "That is not a valid excuse. We all have things tomorrow, but that shouldn't stop us from enjoying today." Cameron didn't know where he came up with such a good line. He would write it down for his script.

"It does sound fun. Man, I haven't been to a club in years."

"Don't you think that needs to change? There's still life in you, Walker."

Cameron heard a crash in the background. Definitely not a TV show.

"Dammit," Walker said. "I have to go."

"So is that a yes?"

"Maybe."

Cameron took that as a victory. "I'll pick you up in a little bit."

Φ

It didn't take long for Cameron to get ready. He wore a tight T-shirt, jeans, and a pair of pristine white sneakers that were sleek but also comfortable for actual dancing.

He strolled down the adorably suburban street, much different than the dirty, unkempt block of his apartment.

Cameron rang the doorbell.

"Dad's here!" He heard a kid yell from the other side.

Fuck.

The kid yanked the door open. He didn't hide his disappointment at who he found.

"Hi!" Cameron said with the energy of a tour guide. "Is your dad home?"

Walker chased up to his son with his coat. He also couldn't hide his surprise at seeing Cameron.

"Hey." Cameron shrugged his shoulder. "I'm early."

"Um, yes. You are."

"I took your maybe as a yes. I figured we could go early so you'd be home at a decent hour." His eyes drifted to the tiny, dissatisfied stranger below. "I should go."

"No." Walker stepped aside. "Come on in."

Walker rested his free hand on his son's shoulder. *What's the kid's name again?* Cameron tried imagining the block letters on the wall. *Henry? No. Hobnob?*

Be serious.

"I thought we weren't allowed to talk to strangers," the kid said.

"Hobie, he's my friend." Walker had a calm, yet firm tone with his son. Like sexy Mr. Rogers. "This is Cameron."

Cameron didn't have little nieces or nephews. Little kids didn't frequent his Starbucks. His experience with kids was limited to watching them throw temper tantrums in stores and the little girl in *Beasts of the Southern Wild*. He squatted down and pet Hobie on the head.

"It's so nice to meet you!" Cameron didn't know where this enthusiasm was coming from suddenly. He was a helium balloon, and the kid was planning to pop him.

"Hobie." Walker gave him a nudge on the shoulder.

"Nice to meet you, too."

"Gee whiz. You are so polite!" He was possessed! *Who is this person?*

They meandered over to the living room. Hobie sat on the ottoman directly across from Cameron while Walker made them coffee. His blinking stare intimidated Cameron.

"So, Hobie. I heard your birthday party was tons of fun!"

Hobie nodded.

"Did you eat cake?"

Hobie nodded again.

"What kind of cake did you have?"

"Vanilla."

"And did you get to blow out the candles?"

Hobie nodded. Cameron imagined this was worse than Chinese water torture. He thought kids were supposed to be nonstop talkers. Why wasn't this kid saying the darndest things?

"What grade are you in?"

"Kindergarten."

"Very cool." Kindergarten was a blur to Cameron. There may have been the alphabet on the wall. "Can you read?"

"A little."

"Oh. Can you recite the alphabet?"

"Yes." Hobie didn't say anything. Though he technically answered Cameron's question.

"That's great! The alphabet is wonderful! And so is reading!" He couldn't stop exclaiming every freaking thing he said. Even Hobie was finding it a bit much.

"You have a really cool racecar bed."

From the mirror above Hobie, Cameron watched Walker's head jolt up from the coffeemaker. His eyes bulged.

"You were in my room?"

"I…no…"

Hobie leaped up. "Dad! Why did you let him in my room? He's a stranger?"

Cameron was saying every curse word in the book to himself.

"He saw it from the hallway when I went to get something. He didn't go inside."

"That's an invasion of privacy!" Hobie said with a stomping of the feet.

Cameron wondered how he knew what any of those words meant.

"Hobert James Reed. Do not stomp your feet."

Hobie jumped over Cameron's feet and ran down the hall. Cameron was five seconds away from the fetal position. *Fuck. Fuck again. Never enough fucks.* He swiveled his head to Walker, who closed his eyes and listened.

"I'm so sorry!" Cameron whispered.

Walker waved it off. He held up three fingers.

Three...two...one

"Dad!"

Hobie stomped back to the living room, inches away from Cameron's face. "Did you touch my Legos?"

Cameron was on the verge of confessing. The lights were so bright. He wanted his one phone call.

"I'm sorry, Hobie. I don't know what you're talking about." His voice remained chipper. His insides crumbled away. He was lying to a kid.

Hobie pointed a finger inches from Cameron's nose and turned to his dad. "He hurt my feelings!"

"Hobie! We do not accuse people around here." Walker said *accuse* slowly so his son could comprehend. "I broke it when I was cleaning the other day."

Cameron breathed a sigh of relief. Hobie bought it, or at least knew this was a losing battle. He plopped down on the ottoman. Cameron managed a pity smile at the kid, but he wasn't in Hobie's good graces yet.

Walker brought Cameron a coffee, which Cameron gulped down. Too bad it wasn't spiked with something.

"I'm sorry, Hobie." Walker brought him a chocolate milk with the straw. "It was an accident."

Hobie looked at the carpet and nodded.

"How about this weekend, you and I work on putting it back together? I'll even get that new dragon set that you saw in the toy store. Every castle needs a dragon."

"Ron and Dad got me it for my birthday."

Quiet descended over the room. Cameron knew Hobie meant his other father. Walker held onto his brave face, though Cameron saw the hurt flicker in his eyes.

"Dragons are so cool!" Cameron said, desperate to break the silence. "They breathe fire."

"I know," Hobie said.

The doorbell rang. Hobie jumped up. Now the kid had a smile on his face. He couldn't open that front door fast enough. Walker noticed, and Cameron wanted to give the poor guy a hug.

"Hey, Doug."

"Evening, Walker."

Walker's ex wore a J-Crew ensemble that had barely creased during the day. He kissed Hobie on the cheek, and then he noticed Cameron on the couch. More awkwardness abounded. Doug's eyes narrowed at him for a second before warming to a smile.

"I see you have plans."

Cameron stood up and shook Doug's hand. "I'm Cameron, a friend of Walker's."

"A friend," Doug repeated. Cameron needed a parka to fight against his chill. "Well, I didn't mean to interrupt your evening."

"Oh, you haven't," Cameron said with a hearty *fuck you* grin slapped on his face. "The night is young."

"Very, apparently." Doug maintained a smile that Cameron wanted to scrape off his face.

"Dad, I'm ready to go." Hobie tugged on Doug's jacket.

"Hobie, it's not polite to interrupt." He knelt down and helped him put on his jacket. "Did you have fun today?"

Hobie shrugged. "Dad broke my Lego castle."

Doug stood right back up and eyed Walker. It was a good thing he didn't have a blunt instrument in his hand.

"It was an accident," Walker said. Cameron avoided eye contact with Doug or else he'd totally be found out as the Lego destroyer.

"Don't worry, Hobie. You'll put it back together again. I have complete faith in you!" Doug captured his son in a tickle fest. Hobie screamed with laughter. "Okay, why don't you get in the car?"

"Hobie!" Walker yelled while trying to sound pleasant. He couldn't hide the edge in his voice. He knelt down and held his arms open. "Why don't you give me a hug and kiss goodbye first."

"Right," Doug said. "Go on, Hobie."

Hobie did as directed, but it wasn't with the same amount of enthusiasm that he had for his other, bitchy father.

"And say good night to Cameron," Walker instructed.

"Good night, Cameron." Hobie was halfway out the door already. Cameron waved back.

"I'll meet you in the car, Hobie!" Doug said, before turning back to the adults. "Walker, try to be a little bit more careful when you're cleaning. You know how much care and effort he puts into building his Lego structures."

Walker nodded like a scolded child, which infuriated Cameron. He was probably one of those parents who expected the world to bow down to the demands of his son. Now he knew where Hobie learned *invasion of privacy* from.

"So Cameron, what do you do?"

"I'm in college. And I work at Starbucks part-time."

Doug raised an eyebrow at Walker. Walker looked down at the carpet. Like father, like son.

"Oh, what's your major?" Doug stifled a laugh. "It's been a long time since I asked anyone that question."

"It sure looks like it's been a long time," Cameron shot back with a passive-aggressive laugh of his own. Doug narrowed his eyes at him.

"Well, have a good night." Doug shut the door hard.

CHAPTER
TEN

Walker

Walker was engaged in a fierce battle with his mouth. He had already yawned three times in the past ten minutes, and he would. Not. Do. It. Again. He pressed his lips together like an airlock seal.

He and Cameron waited on line outside Cherry Stem, while a bouncer stood guard at the door. The sweeping wind sent shivers through Walker's too-thin jacket. He forgot how cold it could get at night, especially this late. Behind them, a guy wore a tank top and short shorts and didn't have a goosebump on his skin.

Across the street, a billboard advertising Dollop, the new cupcakery in town, shined atop an apartment building. Dollop's owner, a woman perky enough to try her hand at the cupcake game, smiled from high above. She didn't have a Mona Lisa smile, more like Mona Lisa axe murderer. It was transfixing, to say the least.

"How are you holding up?" Cameron asked him. He wore a pair of those earmuffs that go behind your head and didn't mess up his mussed hair.

"I'm great." Walker gulped back a yawn.

"Here. Have the rest of my coffee."

"I'm fiiiiiiinnnnnnnne." Escaped yawn. *Damn.* "I'm fine."

Cameron smiled at him and leaned against a poster advertising '90s night. "It's not even that late. It's only 9:30."

"What time do you usually go to bed?"

"Two or so," Cameron said with a nonchalant shrug, as if he thought that was actually normal. The admission made Walker groggy. "I'm a night owl. And you are most obviously a morning person."

"I don't really have a choice." Walker poked his head above the crowd. They still weren't moving. He knew they were only outside to make the club seem crowded and thus cooler. He hated that they were playing this game, but Cameron's bouncy energy was cute, and a little infectious.

"What are you going to do when you get a job in Hollywood? Once you're working forty hours a week and have kids, you'll see. You'll come to the other side."

"Screenwriters don't work nine-to-five, only when inspiration strikes. And I'll pass on the kids. I don't have the right birthing hips."

"Even when I was in school, I couldn't sleep in. I was just…up. It drove Doug crazy."

Cameron's expression changed to one of disgust. Walker didn't blame him.

"I can't believe you were married to that guy, or whatever."

"Doug's not a bad guy. It was just an awkward moment." Too awkward. He worried what Hobie thought. Or rather, what Doug would tell him to think.

"Thanks again for covering with your son. I've basically ruined his life."

"He's six. He's already forgotten it."

"You're good with him," Cameron said. "You're firm, but fair. And it may be hard to see, but he loves you, too."

"Thanks." He knew Cameron was just being nice, but it was still good to hear.

"I'm serious. I've seen some shitty fathers. When I was little, my friend and I were yelling in the backseat about something, and his dad pulled the car over, slapped my friend hard across the face, then continued driving like it was nothing."

Walker's blood boiled at the thought of parents hitting their kids. He'd never do that to Hobie, no matter how much he could get on his nerves sometimes. Hobie was a good kid at heart.

"Hopefully your dad wasn't that bad," Walker said.

Cameron laughed a little too hard, like a live studio audience during a bad sitcom. "I'll spare you that sordid little story. That woman is eyefucking the shit out of me."

Walker glanced behind him, and sure enough, the Dollop lady was staring them down from her billboard perch. With a bright smile, naturally.

"That billboard makes me want a restraining order, not a cupcake," Cameron said.

Each time Walker looked up, the billboard just seemed more terrible. "The cupcakes should be front and center. Nobody cares about her."

"Maybe she's trying to cultivate a Martha Stewart image."

"That billboard isn't helping." Walker shoved down another yawn. This one inflated his chest like a balloon. "And it's the wrong tact. If she wants to be the next Martha Stewart, she needs to build up a loyal customer base first. She can do that through cupcakes. If they like her cupcakes, they'll like her." Walker felt a yawn rumbling in his lungs. He covered his mouth and gulped it down. "Cupcakes can be an impulse buy. You see a billboard of cupcakes, you're gonna want a cupcake."

The yawn unleashed itself. He pressed his forearm into his mouth. Cameron watched in amusement.

"You really care about cupcakes."

"It's not that. A lot of small businesses don't know how to advertise. My work-study job at Browerton was getting advertisers for the football and theater programs they hand out. These ads were awful. No creativity. Stupid taglines. Just plain ugly. Dollop takes the cake."

"You mean cupcake."

"You can't imagine how frustrating it was to have to bite my lip and run these ads. And then the businesses would complain that they weren't seeing results."

"Well, what would you do for Miss Cupcake?"

"I don't know." But Walker did. His brain got instantly decluttered. He was in some type of trance. His tiredness seemed a thing of the past, as his mind spun like it was drenched in caffeine. He pulled out an old receipt and pen from his pocket. "Turn around and bend over."

"I thought we were just friends!" Cameron said, making Walker blush momentarily, then he was back to trance mode.

"I want to show you something."

Cameron complied. Walker began sketching out his design, using Cameron's back as a desk. His hand could barely keep up with his mind.

"Can I sit up now?" Cameron asked.

"One more minute." Walker put the finishing touches on his sketch. He stretched out his cramping hand. It was a series of wayward lines, but they all came together to resemble...something.

Cameron's eyes bulged open when he got a look.

"See, I'd put the cupcakes on most of the billboard. Beautiful, buoyant cupcakes. And then her picture would go on the right with the address. People read ads left to right, so you hook them with cupcakes, and then you bring it home with the personal touch."

"Homemade. Homegrown. Welcome Home," Cameron read off the paper. "You just came up with this?"

"It's a very, very rough idea. Just for fun." Walker already hated the tagline and wanted to change it.

"Those cupcakes look good enough to eat. I had no idea you could draw." Cameron's eyes shifted from the sketch to Walker back to the sketch. "Holy shit."

Walker shrugged off the comment. "It's really rough."

"There's no way I could draw something as good as this. Is this what you do at your job now?"

Walker let out a sigh only he could hear. "No, I work on the media end."

"What does that mean?"

"A company hires a creative agency to come up with a marketing campaign, create the ads, write the taglines. Then they come to a media agency like mine to decide how and where to advertise this cool new campaign to reach their target consumers. Do we run magazine ads or TV ads? Which networks should we advertise on? What time of year? How much will it cost?"

"Well, that sounds interesting."

"It's not," Walker said, without filtering. Usually, he put a happy spin on his job. Didn't everyone? "We're the hub between the client, the creative agency, the networks and publishers. They all get to create something or make decisions. We're just the middle men. My co-worker Lucy calls us professional handholders."

It felt nice to say these thoughts aloud. Walker turned red as he realized how uncool it was to complain about your job, yet Cameron only had a supportive smile for him.

"The real world sucks," Cameron said. "Let's dance!"

At that moment, the line moved again, as if the world bent to Cameron's will. Maybe it did when you were twenty-two.

Φ

Not much had changed from the last time Walker visited a dance club. Loud music and oppressive bass made his ears throb, though they never bothered him in his twenties. Red lights flashed across a packed dance floor going crazy for "MMMBop." The only difference was the pack of wallflowers on their phones off to the side, and even on the dance floor. Walker remembered having to stand around awkwardly when he didn't dance without a cool device as a prop.

"To the bar!" Cameron shouted. His body moved and bobbed to the music as he walked.

The bar was packed two guys deep, but Cameron used his charm and tight T-shirt to squeeze in while Walker waited at the periphery. Sleepy tears beaded at his eyes. He stifled a yawn that threatened to roar out of him. He couldn't help checking Cameron out. He knew they were friends, or something, but his eyes kept noticing the fabric pull against his biceps and the curve of his ass.

Soon, Walker's ears and eyes adjusted to the sensory overload of the club. He found the consistency of the beat soothing, like it was rocking him to sleep...

"Hey."

Walker's head snapped up. Cameron handed him a drink.

"Are you falling asleep on me?"

"No," Walker said through a hoarse throat. His back strained to keep him upright.

"That'll do the trick." Cameron pointed at his drink. "Red Bull and vodka."

That was basically the espresso of club drinks. The guy wasn't messing around. Walker eyed his cocktail.

"It's good! I promise!"

Walker took a sip and managed to keep it down, even though it was like chugging expired cough syrup.

"Let's dance!" Cameron yelled and led the way to the floor.

Walker's body struggled to perk up. He really hoped his drink kicked in soon. An image of his warm bed popped in his head. He shoved it aside and focused on the music and Cameron's biceps.

Cameron parked them smack in the center of the floor. Walker tried to mimic Cameron's dance moves, but it wouldn't be easy. Cameron writhed around like his bones were JELL-O, squatting to the floor and bouncing back up, hips matching the beat. Walker bobbed his head and tapped his foot. He was a boat and a two-day car trip away from rusty.

"Are you having fun?"

"Yes!" He said, defensively.

Cameron seemed to have a spotlight permanently on him, and Walker wanted to be worthy of his orbit. He tried dancing behind Cameron for a few songs, pulling him close, but Cameron kept spinning around to face him. He didn't seem like a guy who could be claimed. He just wanted to dance.

Walker did, too. Kind of.

After a few songs, what little energy Walker had had dissipated. He was just shuffling his feet back and forth.

"You doing okay?"

"Yep!" He said.

Luckily for Walker, the opening bars of the next song were a vital shot of adrenaline.

"What song is this?" Cameron asked. His dancing wound down while Walker was just getting started.

"'Gangsta's Paradise'!" Walker yelled. "This was my jam in high school!"

He counted down the final beats until Coolio started rapping. His mind went to autopilot as he recited the song word for word. He hit every inflection and every pause. Walker even had his pimp swagger still down. He spun around and pointed at Cameron when the chorus came on.

Cameron shrugged, completely clueless.

So Walker lip-synced that, too. Then he thought *screw it* and just began singing out loud. The club was so noisy he doubted anybody heard him, and if they did and didn't sing along, they weren't worth his time. He gasped for air as every lyric came through a 1995 portal straight out of his mouth. Cameron and the boys around him were still doing their crotch-out mating dances. They were trying to be cool, and he pitied them.

"You're a dancing machine!" Cameron said, full of snark.

"You can be, too!"

Cameron looked around at the other guys, all scoping each other out. They gave Walker ample side-eye.

"Fuck them!" Walker said. "I guarantee your soulmate is not on this dance floor. You're allowed to have fun."

Cameron pretended to be amused, but Walker felt himself breaking through his ubercool façade.

"I'm pointing to you at the chorus again, so get ready!" He built it up, built it up, his swagger getting more exaggerated. He dipped down to the ground, sprung up, and pointed to Cameron as the chorus came on again.

This time, Cameron remembered the words.

They sang their hearts out. Cameron's smile was irony free. Walker and his friends had never enjoyed clubbing like this. They were always on a mission: drinks, hookups, finding people, ditching people.

They brought it home for the final chorus refrain. Walker used his fist as a microphone. He needed to catch his breath once the song ended. He needed hydration.

"That was kind of amazing." Cameron leaned in, and Walker caught a whiff of the musky sweat in his hair, as well as the Red Bull and vodka.

Walker cupped his friend's waist. "Kind of?"

Cameron didn't push him off, not right away. He shook his glass of ice. "Refill?"

"Water."

They returned to the bar, now three people deep.

"You hang out over there." Cameron nodded his head at an empty VIP booth. He stroked Walker's hand. "I'll Lewis and Clark my way to the bar."

Walker sauntered over to the black leather booth, which curved around a table in the corner of the bar. A reserved card stood next to an empty bottle of champagne, yet there was no sign of people. As soon as he sat down, he knew this was a bad idea.

His exhaustion came whooshing back. The sore throat, the heavy eyes, the tired muscles—they were planning their attack. He focused on the moment he and Cameron shared earlier. He held Cameron's waist. Cameron stroked his hand. It could lead to more. But was that what he wanted? He enjoyed spending time with Cameron, and trying to make a move might muck that up, especially since it couldn't lead anywhere. He flashed back to waking up in bed and watching Cameron sleeping peacefully beside him. The comforter billowed around their bodies. Pillows cradled their heads. He was on his bed now. Cameron laid beside him. They had his bed in the club. Cameron patted the empty space next to him. Walker spooned him and pulled his warm body close. The bed had wings and flew high above the throngs of guys, over the dance floor. Dancers tried to grab at it, but they couldn't reach it. Some began throwing their glasses. Walker shielded Cameron from the orbs of propelled glass. He ordered the bed to take them higher, and the bed complied. The roof of the club burst off the walls like opening a gift box. They sailed into the quiet, black sky, nestled against each other, fingers interlaced, the houses beneath them tiny specks of civilization…

"Walker."

His eyes fluttered open. He sat up, which meant that he had been laying across the booth.

"Was I sleeping?"

Cameron passed him a bottle of water. "You were snoring."

CHAPTER ELEVEN

Cameron

Cameron was grateful he didn't have work or class on Fridays. He was a master scheduler. He shuffled out of his bedroom sometime after ten. In the kitchen, Henry was making himself an English muffin. He stood by the fridge, arms crossed, watching Cameron suspiciously as he made a pot of coffee.

"You were at Cherry Stem last night." Henry raised both eyebrows. "With a guy."

"Why the NSA hasn't snatched you up by now is beyond me." The coffee dripped into the pot agonizingly slow. "How'd you know?"

"Jordan was there."

"What's Nolan's roommate doing at a gay bar?"

"He says it's a great place to pick up girls." His English muffin popped up, and Henry moved it with a knife onto his plate. Cameron's coffee was still dripping along. "So who was the guy?"

"Remember that guy at the bar who helped us with the sports section in trivia?" Cameron couldn't believe this was the only way Henry knew him. Walker had gone from random guy in a bar to someone he considered a friend so fast that he hadn't briefed Henry yet.

"The yuppie?"

"I believe they prefer the term young urban professional."

"He's like a full-on adult," Henry said. "Wasn't he wearing a tie?"

Cameron thought about Walker's dad wardrobe full of khakis and button down shirts. "He's a nice guy."

"You're blushing."

Cameron poured himself a cup of coffee and ignored Henry on his way into the living room. He turned on the TV. Henry scrunched into the corner of the sofa beside him.

"Did you guys hook up?"

"No. He fell asleep."

"In the club?"

Cameron nodded. He laughed to himself at the memory of finding Walker sprawled across the VIP booth, sleeping like a baby. He found it cute. Walker was the one person at Cherry Stem who had zero fucks to give last night. He danced how he wanted to. He took a nap where he wanted to. When Cameron got home, he watched the music video for "Gangsta's Paradise" on YouTube before falling asleep himself.

"It was a fun night. It made me realize just how monotonous and cliché college guys are."

"You're a college guy."

"Not for much longer. Oh, I didn't tell you! I got an apartment in Los Angeles. Mere blocks from the beach."

"Already?"

"Better to be prepared, especially since I definitely know when I'll be out there."

"You can't break the lease."

"I'm not." Cameron rolled his eyes. "I got a place in LA! My plan is clicking into place. A little congratulations, perhaps?"

"Congrats," Henry said without much fanfare. Cameron thought his friend would be happier for him. Henry was well aware of Cameron's Hollywood dreams.

"Let the countdown begin!"

Henry shut off the television. Even after being roommates since August, Cameron still had not turned Henry into an avid TV watcher. "So, when are you seeing your young urban professional again?"

Cameron wondered if Walker had custody of his son this weekend, which immediately freaked him out. "I don't know. Probably at work. He frequents my Starbucks."

"He really is a professional! So, are you guys dating?"

"You and your labels." Cameron shook his head. "That's the best part! We'll never be boyfriends. He's divorced-ish with a kid."

Henry nearly spat out his breakfast. "Are you serious?"

"Yes! I met his son. He hates me. It's wonderful." Cameron did feel a slight twinge of pain over Hobie's mean stare, but he looked on the bright side. "Walker and I can hang out, but it's never going to go anywhere, and we're both totally fine about it. I'm graduating and moving, and he has a family and roots in Duncannon. There's no pressure. Nobody gets hurt."

"Wow, Cameron. This is the perfect scenario for you. Why did you never think of this before?"

Cameron thought he detected some sarcasm in Henry's voice. He was probably pissed off that his Cameron Needs a Boyfriend campaign was just thwarted.

Φ

"So Jake Gittes was getting too nosy, so what did Robert Towne write next?" Professor Mackey asked the class while queuing up the DVD.

"He gets beat up?" Robert asked.

"Not quite." She pressed play. Jack Nicholson is held against a gate while his nose gets cut. "He's too nosey. His nose gets cut."

"Isn't that a little…on the nose?" Robert snickered at his own lame joke. Cameron rolled his eyes. It seemed that Robert's main goal in life was to try and prove his professors wrong. That didn't make him smarter, just more annoying.

"Is it? How many times have you seen this type of punishment?" Professor Mackey asked. "It may seem a little obvious, but it's fresh, unexpected, reveals some character, and flows naturally within the story. It isn't just Jake getting beat up or punched in the face."

"I suppose," Robert said.

Cameron gave him the eyeroll of the century.

Professor Mackey shut off the TV. "*Chinatown* is considered one of the best screenplays ever written, if not the best. It's revered, yet it would shock you how few Hollywood execs have seen the movie. I remember going on pitch meetings, mentioning *Chinatown*, and getting blank stares."

"What were pitch meetings like?" Cameron asked, inching closer in his seat.

Mackey laughed to herself. "It's ten minutes of smalltalk and schmoozing. Then you launch into a beat-by-beat breakdown of your script. You basically have to talk someone through the trailer of your movie."

Cameron envisioned himself giving a pitch of his script to some stylish exec in his stylish office which overlooked palm trees and the Hollywood sign. He wondered if any offices actually overlooked the sign, or if that was mere movie magic.

Mackey handed back everyone's latest writing assignments. Cameron's paper had an A on it, which wasn't surprising anymore, and a note, which was.

See me after class.

Once people dispersed, Cameron held up his assignment to Mackey.

"My office is around the corner." She gestured out the door, and he followed.

While most professors' shelves were filled with dusty books that Cameron figured were solely there for ambience, Mackey's shelves were lined with old screenplays. Their names were written in black Sharpee on the binding. *Ordinary People, Shakespeare in Love, Fargo, Eternal Sunshine of the Spotless Mind.*

"You have quite a collection," he said.

"Thanks. You can borrow one whenever you want. Have a seat, Cameron."

He plopped into a hard wooden chair. Instead of sitting across the desk, Mackey sat in the other wooden chair, making them feel like equals. She had a coolness that he admired, that was lacking from many Browerton professors. She wasn't stuck in the world of academia.

"You're a great writer, Cameron."

He immediately blushed.

She smacked his knee with a copy of his latest assignment. "Why am I just finding out about you now? Right as you're graduating!"

"This is a hard class to get into." He kept on blushing. He wasn't good at accepting compliments not based on his looks.

"What are your plans?"

"I'm moving to LA in September."

"That's fantastic!" A wistful smile slipped on her lips, carrying her away. "Do you know where you want to live?"

"I have a place lined up in Santa Monica."

"I love Santa Monica! They have this farmer's market every Sunday with the best omelet you will ever have in your entire life."

Cameron pictured himself in Santa Monica, passing a palm tree, on his way to this brunch. These details made LA feel more and more like a real place. A real future.

"LA was a blast. It's like a new Ellis Island. Everyone's new. Everyone's fresh. All they have is a dream. Some people are going to soar, some will crash. There's so much ambition and energy coursing through that town. It's a roller coaster ride." She laughed to herself. "And now it's your turn."

"I can't wait."

"Of course you can't." Mackey came alive. She rubbed her hands together. "I had never driven before I moved to LA. I had a license, but only so I could drink. You will become a pro at making lefts at yellow lights."

Cameron had a twinge of pity for her. She obviously missed Hollywood. The woman had a screenplay produced! That was the definition of making it. Out of all the people who arrived at the glitzy Ellis Island, she was one of the few who soared. And now she was in the middle of Pennsylvania, stuck reading crappy writing all day and having to put a positive spin on it. No ocean, just the Susquehanna River. Cameron appreciated having her as a professor, but didn't understand why she gave it all up.

"I think this script you're working on for class, if you polish it up, can be a viable sample for agents."

Cameron's stomach somersaulted. "How do screenwriters find agents? It's all so nebulous. I can't send my script directly to an agency."

"Of course not. No agent in Hollywood reads anything that's unsolicited. Or anything period. Kidding." She flipped her hair off her shoulders. "It's all about creating a link to an agent, knowing someone who can pass your script along."

"So what do writers do until then? Starve?" Cameron asked with a laugh. There was always a gap in a successful person's Hollywood story. In the articles and interviews he'd read of screenwriters, they all loved talking about a vague "struggle" before making it, but rarely gave specifics. The screenwriter of *Little Miss Sunshine* was Matthew Broderick's assistant in the '90s, but never said what he did or how he survived for the years between then and selling his script.

"A lot of writers take office jobs or wait tables. But you should try to get a job as an assistant somewhere.

You'll be able to see how the movie development process works, and you'll make some great connections. I was an assistant to a producer for a few years until I sold my script."

Cameron sparked to the idea immediately. "What do assistants do exactly?"

"It's not just getting coffee, although that is a part of it. You read all the scripts that come across your boss's desk. You'll find out what projects are being set up around town. Screenwriting isn't just about writing. It's a business, and being an assistant is like film graduate school. And working in development means you see things from the buyer's side. They have the power."

Cameron tapped his fingers together Mr. Burns style.

"One of my old students works in development at Mobius Pictures. Arthur Brandt." She went behind her desk, put on her glasses, and logged onto her email. Cameron's ears perked up. He'd read that name in a few articles in the trades. He could never remember geography or historical facts, but Hollywood names stuck to his brain like magnets.

Mackey ripped a Post-it from her stack and wrote down Arthur's email address. Cameron's heart may have stopped for a second. He was about to receive the email of a guy who made movies.

"Arthur was in my screenwriting class. Not the best writer, but he always had great comments for everyone else. Whether they wanted to hear them or not."

The Post-it slid into Cameron's hand like Willy Wonka's golden ticket.

"Feel free to shoot him an email, say you're in my class. Maybe he can give you some advice or meet you for coffee once you move."

"That would be…" a million adjectives screamed for attention in his mind. "great."

"Arthur may seem like one of those Hollywood assholes. He kind of is, but he's a good guy at heart. He'll write back."

"Thank you so much, Professor Mackey. I'm really happy I took this class." She made him believe that his crazy LA dream could be a reality. Hope was the best gift you could give someone. He wanted to give her a hug, but didn't know professor/student protocol. He held out his hand, and she swallowed him in her arms.

She pulled away and looked him in the eyes. "And whatever you do, just keep writing. Don't fall into the assistant trap like I saw happen to other people. Promise you'll keep writing, Cameron. Even if only for fun. Don't let that creative muscle go to waste."

"I promise."

CHAPTER TWELVE

Walker

"Walker, where are we with briefing the client on the summer digital campaign?"

Walker's head shot up. The world came back into focus. He blinked sleep out of his eyes and found Patricia staring at him from across her desk.

"We're good."

"Good. What does good entail?" Patricia returned to typing an email on her laptop, yet still waited an answer.

"I put time on their calendar for next week to go over the digital recommendation."

"What day next week?"

"Tuesday."

"Good."

He didn't want to know what *that* good entailed. Patricia swiveled around to the neat stacks of paper behind her desk. Not a single sheet was out of place, and they all had Post-its affixed to the top page. She picked up the center stack, swiveled back, and dropped it on her desk with a *thunk*. Walker and Lucy traded looks. They never knew what would come next with Patricia.

"We just got back the media modeling research study from last year. This analyzed every campaign, down to the placement, that Radiance ran. It's a deep dive into what worked and what didn't. Which segments had the best ROI and how we can build on that. This will be crucial for planning our presentation for the review."

Neither he nor Lucy picked it up. He had never been so intimidated by a stack of papers.

"Anyway, I wanted to use this meeting to plan out a timeline for preparing the review presentation. We all need to be on the same page to make sure we stay focused." Patricia pressed her hands together. Knowing her, Walker thought, she probably was praying every night for them to win the review. He should, too, since his job was on the line. "I think we should have daily check-ins in the morning to gauge progress."

Walker hoped this was a nightmare. His head pounded from his sleep hangover.

"I think we can do a weekly check-in," Lucy said. Walker would hug her in the breakroom. "We'd be able to provide you with better updates."

"Twice a week," Patricia countered.

"Tuesdays and Thursdays?"

"Mondays and Thursdays. I love Monday meetings. It's a great way to set the tone for the week, don't you agree?" Patricia waited for their answers. Walker's head shot up again from the sleep canyon, and he nodded. "Excellent. I'll send out the meeting invites. Thanks, guys."

Walker and Lucy stood up to leave.

"Walker?"

He turned around. Patricia nodded her head at the research study.

"I want you to read through this and fully digest it. You're going to be the point person for all research questions. You'll need to make sure everything in our presentation aligns with the media modeling study."

"Got it."

Walker beelined to the breakroom with the study weighing down his arms. He poured himself another cup of coffee, and then he hugged Lucy as promised.

"I tried, honey." She laughed into his chest.

"We just had a meeting about a meeting."

"A series of meetings."

Walker paced around the small confines of the breakroom. It wasn't much exercise, but it was necessary movement. All this sitting. All this staring. Whatever was in Patricia's office, she should bottle it and sell it to insomniacs.

"Is the boy keeping you up?" She asked with a giggle. She wanted the goods.

"Yes, but not the way you're thinking. And he's not a boy. He's twenty-two. He can drink, vote, buy cigarettes, and serve in the armed forces."

"I have a twenty-year-old son. I know all about that age."

"Luis is twenty?" Walker remembered the boy who tagged along with his mom to work. "Don't tell me that."

Walker returned to his computer. His desk shook when he plopped down the study. A lineup of email subjects were striped across his screen.

RE: RE: ASSETS NEEDED: Radiance Fall Initiative

Meeting Invite: Monday

Meeting Invite: Thursday

Subject: Here's my proposed agenda for Thursday's meeting

Subject: Where are we with-

APPROVAL NEEDED: Banner Ad Copy

There was one email Walker wanted to send himself:
PLEASE RESPOND: How the fuck is this my life?

Φ

Walker left work early to attend Hobie's gymnastics class. Doug had scheduled their son to within an inch of his life. Gymnastics and soccer and piano lessons. Doug wanted Hobie to start learning French for fear that he was falling behind. Falling behind whom? Walker wondered. Doug didn't have any answer either, but he still worried.

The class was showing off their tumbling skills today. Walker found Doug and Ron in the stands. He couldn't not sit next to them and risk being talked about by the other parents.

"You made it," Doug said.

"I'm only ten minutes late."

"You almost missed Hobie tumble."

The instructors were still scrambling to get the kids in an orderly line. He didn't miss anything, just more smugness from Doug. Walker yawned into his arm. Doug elbowed him in the side to stop while maintaining a pristine expression for those around them. Walker was still sore from dancing last night, but it was a good sore. His body had been used for something more than sitting and typing.

Doug had friends in the stands, other parents he'd gotten to know while Walker was busy at work. Really, Walker didn't have the energy to compete with them, which was all these parents seemed to do with each other. None of it spoken, of course. That's how Hobie wound up with a trampoline extravaganza birthday party complete with artisan birthday cake.

Melinda, one of the unofficial head moms of their age group, turned around and tapped Doug on the shoulder. She always reminded Walker of a cat staring down an unworthy human.

"How is that piano tutor working out for Hobie?"

"Fabulous!" Doug knew how to play the sassy, fun gay when needed. "Now, if Hobie could just sit still enough to practice."

"Sophie was the same way. Always squirming." She leaned in and whispered. "We had her tested for ADHD, just to make sure. All clear," she said, back at normal volume.

"We also had Hobie tested."

"He's fine," Walker said abruptly. Melinda and Doug traded looks.

"Hobie just likes doing his own thing. He types at the piano keys." Doug chuckled.

"Don't worry. Sophie got the hang of it very quickly. I'm astounded at how well she plays now."

Doug slapped his lap. "When are we setting up another playdate with Hobie and the lovely Sophie? We keep talking about it every time we see each other!"

"Sophie is starting ballet on Thursdays, and she has Mandarin on Mondays. Maybe on Friday?"

"We'll check our calendars. Where did you find your Mandarin tutor? We're on the hunt for a good French tutor."

Walker tuned out. He could only take so much of this. He didn't know how Doug wasn't dropping dead from exhaustion.

In college, Walker gained about a million friends when they started dating. Doug treated each of them as they had a special relationship, but Walker knew Doug was his at the end of the day. Doug's compact size and charm reminded people of Truman Capote. Precious was his nickname on campus. He liked being the strong, silent type to Doug's social butterfly.

Walker thought they were going to make it. They didn't want to do long distance after graduation. Doug began his master's at Browerton, and Walker stayed. He turned down a job in New York City. Because he loved him. Because Doug made him into the man he always wanted to be. He thought they were forever.

And maybe they were, until Ron came along.

Doug elbowed him in the ribs. Walker was mid-yawn. He covered his mouth.

"What's the matter, Walker? Your pretty young thing wearing you out?" Doug asked, louder than he needed to. Melinda and the other moms turned their heads.

"I just had a busy day, that's all."

"Pretty young thing?" Melinda asked.

"Walker's new *friend* is graduating Browerton this June." He placed extra emphasis on friend, even though that was technically the truth.

Walker's face flushed a whole new color of red. "He's a friend."

"I met him. He seems like a great friend."

The moms traded looks that Walker tried to ignore.

Walker wanted to tell the other father of his child to shut the fuck up, but he would take the high road. The high road ate at his insides, but it was the right thing to do.

"Go Hobie!" Walker threw his hands up and clapped for his son tumbling at the moment. Doug followed suit not to be outdone.

Hobie took a bow for the parents, which cracked up Walker. Only Walker, apparently. Rather than join his class in a nearby circle, Hobie ran to the corner of the room and proceeded to jump on a pile of gym mats.

"Not again," Doug whispered to Walker.

"It's not that big of a deal."

Hobie rolled himself into one of mats like he was sushi. Walker nodded at him to rejoin his classmates.

"His instructors spoke to me about this the other day," Doug said. "He's been doing this every class. Running off to do his own thing."

"Why didn't you tell me?"

Doug didn't bother to answer that. He was the default A parent, and Walker was B, though Walker didn't know when those roles were decided.

"He's a little quirky," Walker said. "He's still tumbling. It's really not that big of a deal."

"Or it could be a sign of something else," Doug said in one of those tones that doctors used to describe spreading cancer cells. Walker rolled his eyes at his ex-husband's dramatics.

"He's fine. He's just too cool for his class."

Doug shot Walker a withering stare. He shook his head with a toxic mix of disgust and disappointment. *Yeah, well I'm bound to you, too, Doug,* Walker's eyes said back.

All of those college memories with Doug seemed far away, not just timewise. Walker didn't know how he got here, and he didn't know whom he got here with.

CHAPTER THIRTEEN

Cameron

"You should know this Cameron. How come you don't know this?"

"If it happened before the year 2006, it doesn't count!" Cameron chewed at the end of the tiny pencil. He stared at the blank answer sheet willing the right director to pop into his mind. There was an empty space in his head for this piece of trivia.

"You have until the end of this song to hand in your answer sheets," the MC said through the microphone. He turned up "Sexy Back" by Justin Timberlake. Justin was about to take it to the bridge once more, and then time would be up.

"Anything?" Ethan looked at Cameron with hope and fear.

Henry pointed his beer bottle at Cameron. "You are supposed to know all movie questions. That's your role on the team."

"Don't remind me." Cameron squeezed the pencil

tight in his fist.

There were never old movie questions in pub trivia. The furthest back a question went was a decade, maybe. Then all of a sudden, out of the blue, they were supposed to know which person received two Best Director Oscar nominations in the same year in the year 2000.

"I think it's Steven Spielberg," Ethan said. "He's been nominated a million times."

"But twice in the same year?" Henry asked. He peeled off the label of his beer.

"I don't think it's Spielberg," Cameron said. "Too obvious. *Schindler's List* and *Jurassic Park* came out in the same year, but that was ages ago."

"Quentin Tarantino?" Ethan asked. Nay, pleaded.

"He never won a directing Oscar, only screenplay."

"Come on, Cameron. We've never gotten this close. We're in second place." Ethan got right in his face. "We could win this. For the first time, we could be champions and beat Brain Trust."

"You sure it's not Spielberg?" Henry asked.

"Seventy percent sure," Cameron shot back.

They glared at the corner booth containing Brain Trust. They seemed like the group who only went to the bar solely for the purpose of competing in trivia, not to talk to anyone. They probably went home to play chess to celebrate, Cameron thought.

Not tonight.

He racked his brain of movie knowledge. He used to soak this stuff up. Did his brain run out of space?

"Justin has officially brought sexy back. We are out of time," Ethan said as the last bars of the song played.

"Did Walker sex the knowledge right out of your

head?" Henry asked.

"We haven't had sex, only talked." A light bulb flickered above his head. "It's not Spielberg. Wrong Steven."

Cameron scribbled down an answer.

"Are you sure about that?" Ethan asked, looking over his shoulder. "Not like I know any better."

"Yes," Cameron said with hesitation. He brought his sheet up to the MC.

"I'm rooting for you guys," the MC said.

Cameron glanced at the corner booth on his way back to his seat. One of the Brain Trust members gave him a Queen Elizabeth wave with rueful smile to match.

Those bastards.

"We haven't had sex," Cameron said again once he returned to his table. "Walker and I."

"Good to know." Ethan laughed to himself as he drank.

Cameron thought back to the wide-eyed wonder with which Walker watched the sociology lecture. He was glad he could give him that. Walker seemed to have this dark cloud of adulthood over him, which Cameron was eager to lift.

"I think you like him," Ethan said.

"I like him as a friend."

"'Friend,'" Henry said back with air quotes.

"I enjoy his company. What's so wrong with that? It's not going anywhere." Cameron was the one going somewhere. "You guys are just in comfortable, boring relationships and thus want to live vicariously through my life. Too bad my life can't be all drama and sex all the time."

"That means you're doing it wrong," Henry said.

"Okay, who's ready for some answers?" The MC called out to wild cheers and a light round of opera applause from Brain Trust.

He read through the list of answers. Cameron and his friends reverted to their nervous anticipation poses. Ethan rubbed his temples and looked down at the table. Henry pretended to pray. Cameron looked at his teammates with a touch of pre-nostalgia kicking in.

His team remained calm as they managed to get the first five questions correct. They knew they were right.

"And now the final question. Number six," The MC said. "And this one was apparently a doozy. Only one team got it right."

Cameron side-eyed Brain Trust. They smiled and patted each other on the back.

"And the person who was nominated for directing two films in the year 2000 is...not Steven Spielberg."

Brain Trust leapt up then shot back down just as quickly. From victory to defeat in zero-to-sixty. Such was life.

"Sorry Brain Trust," The MC said with a knowing smile. "The correct answer is...Steven Soderbergh. *Traffic* and *Erin Brockovich*. That means our winner is Taints Misbehaving!"

Cameron and his table jumped up and screamed so loud they could've shattered windows. Taints Misbehaving ascended to the stage while "We Are the Champions" played to accept their trophy and thirty-five dollar bar tab. This was as good as life got, Cameron thought.

They didn't waste a moment using that bar tab, which bought them each two more beers. Cameron actually felt a small lump expanding in his throat, and the emotion was written all over his friends' faces.

"You guys, this is one of our last pub trivias," Ethan said. "It's bittersweet."

"We'll still be friends," Cameron said.

"Yeah, but we won't all be together like this. We won't all be able to just hang out and drink on a weekday night at the drop of a hat."

"You still have two more years."

"But you don't."

"It doesn't mean life is ending. Just time for the next chapter."

"Excuse the sentimentality, Cameron." Henry glared at his shredded beer labels on the table. "Not all of us are ready to turn the page."

Silence descended over Taints Misbehaving. Cameron wouldn't let their night end on this note. Endings didn't have to be these depressing events. They were new beginnings.

"We still have a few more months. It's too soon to get mushy." Cameron raised his glass. "Let's live it up!"

He downed the rest of his beer. "Who wants shots?"

Φ

Three rounds of shots later, Taints Misbehaving was ready to call it a night. The alcohol had washed away the awkwardness from before. Sometimes, Cameron didn't understand his friends. Henry and Ethan slipped on their jackets, which proved more challenging after exhausting their tab.

"I'm going to go to Nolan's," Henry said.

"And you're going to Greg's?" Cameron asked. Ethan

nodded.

"Good idea. You guys don't want to waste your drunkenness."

"You want us to walk you home?" Ethan asked.

"Nah. I can take care of myself," Cameron replied, his voice extra loud thanks to the extra drinks. He was drunk, but used to being drunk, so it was no big deal really.

"Okay. Get home safe." They hugged each other goodbye.

"Taints Misbehaving!" Cameron screamed when they reached the door.His friends went one way. Cameron stood outside the bar. A stray car zoomed by, but otherwise Duncannon was fast asleep. He couldn't stand living in a town that had an unofficial bedtime.

Instead of walking, Cameron pulled out his phone, ready to call a cab. His finger hovered over the keypad.

Nope.

He was still in the mood to celebrate.

Φ

"Cameron?" Walker did a double-take when he opened the door. He wore a ratty Browerton shirt that hugged his chest and plaid pajama bottoms that didn't do much for the imagination.

"What's up?" Cameron hung on the door. His feet had carried him here on autopilot. "We won!"

Walker got a whiff of his breath and winced. "Who won?"

"Taints Misbehaving! We did it!"

"I'll get you a glass of water." Walker let him inside.

"Do you remember when you helped us with the

sports round? Because you know sports. I mean, le sports. Le spoooooortzzzzzz. It's a fun word to say."

Cameron strutted around the condo, taking in all the decorating flourishes he had missed on previous occasions. Walker had framed artwork on the walls. And not the same faux-arty black-and-white photo that everyone bought from Target. Real, one-of-a-kind shit.

"You know what sucks about being a senior?" Cameron said from the hallway.

Walker met him with the water and a *keep it down* hand motion.

"Everyone gets all mushy all the time." Cameron gulped a sip. Water dribbled onto his shirt. "This is the weakest vodka ever."

"Why don't you come to the living room?"

"We're not dying here. We're graduating! Why do people have to get sad? I can't wait to firmly enter my twenties. I'll take another."

He stuck the empty glass out.

"Coming right up." Walker grabbed the glass.

"Thank you, kind sir."

Walker gave him another *keep it down* signal. He made himself passive-aggressively clear, even to a drunk guy.

"Just chill out in the living room."

"Okay, okay. I'll go there in a second."

Walker returned to the kitchen. Cameron continued staring at the painting in front of him. So many dots and shapes in muted colors. Maybe it was a puzzle? Or a treasure map?

The door creaked behind him. Cameron pivoted around to find little Hobie staring at him from his bedroom.

The kid was the picture of cuteness in pajamas holding onto a teddy bear.

"Hi, Hobie!" Cameron whispered. He squatted down and waved.

"Are you here for a playdate with my dad?"

"No." Cameron giggled to himself. "Yes. I just came over to say hi and tell him that Taints Misbehaving won."

"What's a taint?"

"Hobie, get back to sleep." Walker shoved the refilled glass into Cameron's hands and rushed over to his son.

"Isn't it late for a playdate?"

"It's not a playdate."

"That's not what Cameron said."

"You remembered my name! High five!" Cameron's hand hung in the air. Hobie couldn't resist slapping him five.

"Back to bed." Walker remained firm.

"But I'm not tired anymore."

"Yes you are." Walker yawned, complete with lion's roar at the end. "See, we're all tired."

"That was a fake yawn," Cameron said. He looked to Hobie who nodded in agreement.

Walker tried to hold onto control, but his parental power couldn't match a cute kid and a drunk college student. He sighed. "Fine. Hobie, you can play with your Legos for twenty minutes. And then it's back to bed. No exceptions."

"Deal." Hobie held out his hand, and father and son shook on it.

Cameron loved that no matter how firm Walker was (or tried to be), he cared deeply for his son. A flicker of sadness burned inside him like a lighter searching for a cigarette.

"I'm sorry for breaking your Lego castle," Cameron said with actual remorse.

Hobie nodded like he wasn't that surprised. Were all six-year-olds this smart? "It's okay. When I rebuilt, I turned half the castle into a space station."

"Cool! Can I see?"

Walker raised his eyebrows. Cameron shrugged. It was Lego time. You were either in or out. Walker followed behind and sat on Hobie's bed.

Cameron knelt right beside Hobie, who showed off the castle/space station. A rocket ship sat on the drawbridge, attended to by knights and a purple squid-like alien.

"This is Monte." Hobie pointed at the knight. "He's King Dandelion's most trusted knight, and he's in charge of protecting the rocket ship along with Smort." He pointed to the alien.

"Protecting it from whom?" Cameron asked.

"Uh, everyone! It's a rocket ship in Medieval Times. All the other kings and kingdoms want it."

"Right. Duh. So do Monte and Smort get along? Like are they friends?"

Monte and Smort were on opposite sides of the rocket ship. Cameron could make out some friction in their body language.

"I don't know," Hobie said. "Monte wants to protect King Dandelion, and Smort likes to eat insects and grass."

"Okay. Got it, got it. So Monte is uptight and by-the-book. He follows orders, and I'm sure there were tons of rules in Medieval Times. But Smort comes from the future and a planet with no rules. So they're like an odd couple."

"What's an odd couple?"

"It's when two people seem totally opposite, yet still can be friends. Like peanut butter and jelly. They have nothing in common, but they work great together on a sandwich."

"I can't eat peanut butter. I have a peanut allergy."

"Oh. Sorry."

Hobie picked up Smort and eyed him suspiciously. "I don't really trust Smort."

"Because he eats insects?"

"No. Because he eats grass. I ate it once. It doesn't taste good." Hobie lifted Smort up in the air. Cameron watched the wheels turn in his head.

"What if Smort wants to be the new King Dandelion? He's pretending to play nice when really he has this whole agenda."

"Yes!" Hobie said back, though he seemed confused by half those words. "You're really good at this."

"I hope to do it for a living one day." Cameron shrugged modestly. He believed he had a gift for story. Hobie should come to his screenwriting class. He was already head and shoulders above most of the other students.

"Time's up," Walker called out from behind. He patted the bed, which Cameron soon realized was for Hobie, not himself.

"Okay. A deal's a deal," Hobie said with a real yawn. Cameron wondered if he really understood that. Doug probably put those words into his mouth a long time ago.

"Thanks for letting me play with you," Cameron said.

"Thank you for helping, Cameron." Hobie smiled wide and showed off all his baby teeth. Cameron buzzed with something more powerful than beers and shots. "Dad, can Cameron tuck me into bed?"

Cameron whipped his head around at Walker. He had no idea what that entailed, but he let Walker know he could handle it.

"Why don't Cameron and I do it together? Since he's a first-timer."

Hobie nodded and climbed under the covers, pulling them right up to his chin.

"Hey Cameron, I'm playing soccer this spring!"

"That's awesome!"

"Will you come to my first game?"

Cameron looked to Walker, who didn't have an answer. It was his call. "Sure! I'd love to."

Walker showed Cameron the steps delicately, like he was teaching him how to operate an airplane.

"You don't want to tuck too hard and turn him into a mummy!"

Hobie rocked back and forth to show Cameron what mummies do. "I won't be able to get out of bed."

"I think I get it," Cameron said, though actually nervous. He was finally on Hobie's good side and didn't want to blow it.

"We'll each take a side," Walker said. He took the far side, and Cameron took the other. "Ready?"

"Ready as I'll ever be," Cameron said. He and Walker jammed the covers under Hobie's legs. He giggled and squirmed the whole time, but by the end, he was a comfortable sardine.

"Sweet dreams, Hobie." Walker brushed back his son's hair and gave him a kiss. Cameron hated that he was getting all mushy.

CHAPTER FOURTEEN

Walker

Hobie was down for the count. He took an extra moment to watch his son sleep, his compact chest rising and falling. He wished he could bottle moments like these up for a shitty day.

Walker found his friend in the living room, staring at pictures on the fireplace mantle, nursing his glass of water. When Cameron turned around, he saw flecks of sleep weighing in his eyes.

"I can call you a cab home. My treat."

"You're good with him," Cameron said quietly. That wasn't sleep in his eyes. Something much heavier.

"So are you."

"I played Legos with him for five minutes. You're...you're a really good dad." Walker wasn't used to such a serious Cameron. But then Cameron began laughing, more like nervous exhalation. He waved everything off, mocking his self from a few seconds ago.

"Did you draw this?" He picked up a framed picture of a newspaper cartoon sitting on the edge of the mantle. In the cartoon, two old ladies—one named Bush, the other Gore—were at a bingo hall. The state of Florida was calling the number, and both old ladies shouted bingo at the same time.

"Do you remember the 2000 presidential election and the recount drama? The hanging chads?"

"Of course I do." Cameron studied the picture. "I learned about it in history class."

Walker groaned to himself. "I was one of the cartoonists for *The Browerton Bugle* my junior and senior year. That one got syndicated in a few other college newspapers." Walker had forgotten that cartoon was there. He passed by it so often that it became a decoration more than an accomplishment.

"I remember the sketch you drew at the club…" Cameron brought the picture over to the couch. "You are amazingly talented."

"Thank you." Walker didn't need to look at the cartoon. Doug had gotten it framed as a Christmas gift. A wince of pain shot through Walker's chest when he held the frame up close, and he was back in his apartment, knocking this out in a two a.m. burst of inspiration.

"How many cartoons did you draw for the paper?"

Walker shrugged his shoulders. "Maybe fifty or so."

"Fifty? Wow!" He held up the frame in triumph, and knocked it against a lamp. Walker took it from him and placed it on the coffee table.

"That was a long time ago." *A long time ago.* Not just measured in years, but in life stages.

"You still got it." He took a sip of water, and Walker dipped the glass back.

"Finish that one up, then you'll have another."

"I'm not that drunk. Am I?"

"Whatever will keep you from throwing up on my area rug." He filled Cameron's glass to the brim with water. His guest sipped at the edges.

"Sorry," he said. "I'm just now realizing that drinking thirty-five dollars worth of alcohol in a half-hour was not my smartest move."

"Do you need to lie down?"

Cameron glanced over Walker's shoulder, to his bedroom. Home of the world's most comfortable bed, according to Cameron.

"Can I lay down on it for one minute? Just until I'm sober enough to go home."

"You'll be sober in one minute?" Walker knew this was a losing battle. He stepped aside.

Cameron waltzed past him and belly flopped onto the bed. The comforter whooshed out around him.

"And don't worry. This isn't a cheap ploy for sex. I'm really here for the bed."

Walker hung by the door. "That's quite the confidence booster."

Cameron made a snow angel with his blanket. Walker almost forgot that Cameron seemed on the verge of tears mere minutes ago. Almost.

"Why didn't you try to pursue it?" Cameron asked.

"Being a political cartoonist? It's extremely competitive. You can probably count the number of people who make a living off it on one hand."

"That means it's possible."

"Not anymore. My time has passed." Walker shrugged his shoulders. He'd told himself that so many times that he never flinched at its ugly truth anymore.

"Why don't you get comfortable?" Cameron gestured to the empty half of the bed.

Walker didn't have to ask if this was another cheap ploy for sex. Sadly, he knew the answer. He worried if he could control himself. But Cameron could. Cameron set the boundaries, and he followed.

He kicked off his shoes and stretched along the right side of the bed. He stuffed the remaining pillows under his side, mirroring Cameron. He could pick out touches of gray in his blue eyes.

"Everything is always possible," Cameron said. "I mean, the film industry is insanely competitive. There are only so many movies made each year. But I'm going out there, and I'm not going to give up until I succeed. It's all about perseverance."

"It's easy to say that now, before your journey has begun. We'll talk again in a year when you're really in the trenches."

"And I'll still have the same attitude." Cameron yawned, and Walker followed in one continuous burst of air.

"I think you should have a back-up plan."

"Walker…"

He held his hand up. He was determined to impart what little wisdom he had. "You don't want to be chasing a dream so long that you're stuck. I know guys who tried to make it in advertising, and now they're years behind the rest of the working world."

"Is that what you wanted to do?" Cameron asked pointedly.

Walker pictured himself flipping through old issues of *Adweek*, reading up on the big agencies in New York. It was a lifetime ago.

"You would've been good at it."

"Maybe." Walker smiled to himself. "I know it doesn't sound sexy and cool, but there's nothing wrong with a steady job that you like."

"But don't love."

"You'll love having money in your back account and insurance when you go to the doctor."

"You really seem to love it."

The words jabbed at Walker, stronger than they let on. He picked at a stray fabric on his pillowcase, an expensive pillowcase that working at Berkwell allowed him to afford. But it was just a pillowcase.

"Sometimes, when I'm at my desk at work, or I'm in a meeting, I'll ask myself, 'How did I let myself get here?' I have friends who kept pursuing their dreams, through down times and unemployment and moving to new cities, but they stuck at it. And they're succeeding. Why couldn't that be me?" Emotion clogged his throat. He knew the answer to his question, but he didn't want to say it aloud. "You reach a certain point in your life when you realize you can't hit the reset button again."

Cameron placed his hand over Walker's. "You still have one more reset in you. I know I'm probably too young and bright-eyed to say this, but the cement hasn't dried yet."

"You're right. You are too young to say that."

Walker didn't mean to sound so harsh. Cameron would learn the bitter truth about life eventually. "What do your parents think about your film dreams?"

"My mom says I should give it a shot, but I know deep down, she wants me to go to law school or something with a higher success rate. I'm an only child, so all of her eggs are in my basket."

"No pressure there," Walker said.

Cameron cocked his head, which Walker had to resist finding irresistible. "She understands this is what I want to do, and she wants me to try. She never got to pursue her dreams. Life got in the way." The dim light of the lamp glowed around Cameron's face. Walker noticed that look on his face from before.

"What's wrong?"

"Do you want to watch some TV?" Cameron looked ahead. "You don't have a TV in your bedroom?"

Walker shook his head no. TV was the last thing he cared about right now.

"Is it okay if I shut my eyes for a few minutes?" Cameron asked. "I have a headache."

"Sure," Walker said, stumbling over the word. "I have Advil."

"That's okay." Cameron turned away from Walker.

Walker remained on the bed, an ocean of tension between them. Seconds crawled past. He didn't want to leave the bed. He hoped that just being here, next to Cameron, was enough to make the guy feel better. Walker soon felt himself dozing off, only to be pulled back by the sound of Cameron's meek whisper.

"My dad left when I was five." Cameron spoke to the wall. He had no intention of moving. "When he would come home from work, he would carry me on his shoulders and walk around the neighborhood singing Bob Dylan songs. And then he'd tuck me in at night and check for monsters under my bed. One day, he never came home. He left us a note on the kitchen counter. He didn't want to be a husband and a father. I slept by the door night after night, just hoping he'd come back, until I realized that I was being a fucking idiot. People don't come back."

Cameron didn't turn, didn't move. His body was a tense knot folded into itself.

Walker turned to him and became his big spoon. He wrapped his arm over Cameron, and gave him his warmth. They lay there in silence, neither of them thinking this was a cheap ploy for sex.

CHAPTER FIFTEEN

Cameron

Cameron woke up in a familiar bed with familiar arms spooned around him. His mind scrambled for a second before remembering the details of last night. Trivia, Legos, talking about TV. Talking about his dad. Cameron turned red at the memory. Damn Walker for being such a great listener, and a flawless big spoon.

Daylight poured in through the windows and reflected off the mirrored closet doors. Walker's peaceful breath brushed against his neck.

Their positions hadn't changed from last night. They lay on top of the covers in their clothes. Cameron wanted to know what time it was, but he didn't want to move.

"Dad?" Hobie called out from the other side of the door.

Walker woke up. He took in their surroundings and dressed state. "Did you say something?"

Cameron pointed at the door.

"Dad? Is there school today?"

Walker rolled out of bed, literally, smack onto the floor. He checked the alarm clock, which he had never set. "Shit."

The time was 7:45. Early for Cameron, not for everyone else.

"Hobie, give me a second. Okay, bud?" Walker shouted to his son.

He paced around the room, nodding at different items. His mental to-do, Cameron figured.

Walker took off his ratty Browerton shirt. Cameron enjoyed the view. "I'm going to hop in the shower." Then he stopped. "No. I should get Hobie ready first. Hobie," he called out. "Did you brush your teeth?"

"Do I have to?"

Walker continued talking to himself, the stress of the morning piling up exponentially. "I'll get him dressed and ready. But that means he'll have to wait while I get ready. I can give him cereal, but we don't have time to let him pour. He'll hate that. Shit, and I have to let Patricia know I'm going to be late."

He paused mid-pace. Cameron was sitting on the bed, watching this whole exercise. He held up a hand. "Don't worry about me."

Thank you, Walker's face seemed to scream at him.

"You can head out," Walker said. "You don't have to stay for the circus."

"There's a circus?" Hobie yelled through the door.

"It's a metaphor!"

Cameron should've left to let them get ready on their own, but he didn't want to leave the guy hanging. Walker didn't get to enjoy more than three seconds of waking up in bed.

"New plan. You shower. I'll watch Hobie."

"Really?"

"Yes."

"Do you know what you just agreed to?"

"I want to help." Cameron found himself eager to spend more time with Hobie. The kid was a game, and last night, Cameron made it to the next level. Cameron got off the bed and pushed Walker toward his bathroom. "Besides, I've taken care of drunk friends having emotional breakdowns in a Denny's parking lot during a hailstorm. This should be a cake walk."

Walker stopped at the bathroom door and looked at Cameron with genuine appreciation. "Thanks."

"Shower. Now."

One door closed and another was about to be opened. Hobie stood in the hallway in his pajamas. Cameron affixed his hands on his hips and stared down the scrawny, pint-sized ragamuffin. How could somebody so small cause so much whirlwind? It was the butterfly effect in full force.

"Why are you wearing your normal clothes?" Hobie asked.

"I, um, forgot to pack pajamas."

"You had a sleepover? On a school night?"

Cameron avoided going down that rabbit hole. "Hobie, I am here to help you get ready. What first?"

Hobie blinked at him blankly. Walker was obviously the leader of the morning routine.

"Have you brushed your teeth yet?"

"Do I have to? They're baby teeth! They're going to fall out anyway!"

"I'll take that as a no." Cameron straightened his posture to mimic Superman. He was Morningman to the rescue! He stretched his arm. "To the bathroom!"

He pretended to fly down the hall to the bathroom next to Hobie's room. Hobie flew right alongside him, his stubby legs scurrying to keep up.

Cameron needed sunglasses to handle the bright yellow paint of the bathroom walls. One Spongebob toothbrush lay at the base of the sink with a tube of kids toothpaste rolled up from the bottom.

"My dad says we don't need that much," Hobie said to the glob of toothpaste Cameron squeezed onto the brush. He didn't have to specify which dad. The unfun one, obviously.

"Fair enough." Cameron wiped off half and placed the ball on the edge of the sink. He handed the brush to Hobie. "Here you go."

Hobie didn't take it. "I don't want to."

"You have to."

"Brushing is stupid."

"There are a lot of stupid things we have to do."

"But why do I have to brush if my teeth are just going to fall out anyway?"

"Because the tooth fairy doesn't accept dirty teeth."

"My dad said the tooth fairy isn't real."

Cameron made a note not to bring up Santa to the kid. He held out the brush with a smile this time. "Come on, Hobie. You need to brush."

"You can't make me. You're not my dad."

He had a point there. Kids could be smart at the worst times. What was he doing? Cameron had zero experience with small children. Now he was supposed to get this one ready for school. He was the very definition of in over his head.

Hobie went back to his room to play with Legos. Walker was so good at the firm dad thing, but Cameron couldn't play that card. He searched the medicine cabinet and found an extra, unopened toothbrush. He globbed on the toothpaste.

"All right. If you have to brush, then I have to brush, too," he said. Hobie looked up from his castle/rocket ship, unimpressed. "Hobie, brushing can be fun. You get to do the foaming beast thing."

"What's the phony bee sting?"

Cameron smiled with a plan. "You've never let yourself foam at the mouth?"

Hobie gave him an odd look. Cameron may have hooked him. "Follow me."

Back in the bathroom they went. Cameron put the unused half-ball of toothpaste back on Hobie's brush. Poor kid with his pea-sized, recommendation amount of toothpaste. No wonder brushing was a bore.

"Brush each side of your mouth for thirty seconds. Let's see who can get foamier beast mouth. I'll time us. And...go!"

They scrubbed feverishly at their mouths. Hobie watched Cameron through the mirror and copied his circular brushing style. Toothpaste foam bubbled up from their mouths and dribbled down their chins. Cameron used to do this with his mom, and it wasn't lost on him that he was passing it down.

"Switch sides!"

Cameron made zombie moaning sounds. He bulged his eyes and stuck out his arms, going full-tilt monster. "Roooooaaaarrrrr." The foam dripped from his mouth.

Hobie had a matching beard of foam and roared his kid heart out.

"Let's see who can get more foam!" Cameron said. He and Hobie brushed harder. He spat a puddle of excess foam into the sink. Hobie made a noise like static on the TV. Cameron copied him but let Hobie be louder.

"Foooooooooammmmmmm Monsteeeeeerrrrrr."

Hobie tried to say something but the foam was too much. He laughed and drops of foam splashed onto the mirror.

Cameron bared his teeth, coated and dripping with you-guessed-it. Globs of foam piled up in the sink. He forgot how much fun could be had before eight a.m.

"And time!"

They spat their remaining toothpaste foam into the sink. He didn't know how it happened, but most of Hobie's face was foamed out. He obviously won. Cameron poured him a cup of water to rinse with. They flashed their clean teeth at each other.

"See, that wasn't so bad."

By the time Walker left his bedroom, Cameron and Hobie were seated at the breakfast bar. Walker was ready for work in a solid blue tie, a button-down shirt that displayed the curve of his pecs and khakis that showed the curve of his butt. Just something Cameron happened to notice.

He stared at them dumbfounded. "You're dressed, Hobie."

"Cameron helped me pick out an outfit!" Hobie showed off his long sleeve shirt with a sailboat smack in the middle. Unlike Cameron's friends, he wore it unironically.

"It felt like a day for sailboats," Cameron said, off Walker's surprised look.

"You didn't have...I could've gotten him dressed."

"I know."

"Thank you." Walker's eyes bore into him with such intensity that Cameron felt himself sweat like after a great workout.

Cameron spotted Hobie while he poured milk for both of their cereals. Walker flitted around the kitchen looking for something to do. He wiped off the clean counters and glanced down at Hobie's feet, which had a pair of tied sneakers. Cameron grinned when the guy realized he could take a breath.

Walker opened the pantry and grabbed a breakfast bar.

"You have time for a real breakfast," Cameron said. "I already took out a bowl for you." He nudged said bowl over to Walker, who filled it with cereal.

"Hobie, can you pour some milk into my cereal?"

And then there they were. All eating breakfast together.

Like a happy family?

Cameron looked down at his breakfast, his appetite vanishing with each second. The sound of munching and crunching filled the vaulted ceilings.

Post-breakfast, Walker slipped Hobie into his yellow raincoat. A light drizzle misted over the gray sky.

"I'll drive you back to your apartment."

Cameron was already outside. "That's okay. I'll walk."

"But it's raining."

"I don't melt."

Walker soon got the message that this was non-negotiable. "Is everything okay?"

"Yeah." Raindrops sprinkled on Cameron's hair and shoulders, but he ignored it. He didn't care about getting wet. He just wanted to get home.

"Thanks for your help this morning." Walker leaned in for a hug, which Cameron reluctantly accepted. He felt like an intruder, and he wanted to leave before he was busted.

"Say good-bye, Hobie."

Hobie motioned for Cameron to squat down.

"Bye, Hobie!"

He didn't respond. His tiny, number-two pencil arms pulled Cameron into a hug. Cameron smelled the fresh scent of toothpaste lingering around his mouth.

Φ

Cameron laid on his bed for a good part of the morning staring out the window. He listened to birds chirp, one of the telltale signs that winter might actually be gone for good. Up here, winter was like a horror movie villain. Never dying for real.

He woke up some time later to more birds chirping, a yellower tint of sun, and a buzzing phone.

A buzzing phone.

Cameron ran his hand around his nightstand like a metal detector on the beach. *Beep beep beepbeepbeepbeepbeep*

"Hello?" He didn't recognize the number.

"Is this Cameron Buckley?" A man with a dudebro accent asked.

"Speaking." He wiped his hand over his face and stifled a yawn.

"This is Arthur Brandt. I received your resume from Professor Mackey."

Cameron popped straight up. Grogginess? What was that?

"Hi, Mr. Brandt. I'm sorry. I didn't recognize the number." It was a 310 area code. LA proper. Cameron swooned.

"It's Arthur, and that's to be expected. Is this a bad time?"

Cameron got off his bed and paced around the room. "No. Not at all."

"I figured a college student would be around in the afternoon."

"You figured right." Cameron pictured him sitting at his desk, feet up, stylish blazer, palm trees in the background.

"Professor Mackey told me that you're one of her most promising students, and I had to talk to you."

This wasn't just talking, Cameron knew. This was his chance to impress.

"Film is my passion, and I can't wait to start working in the industry."

"What have you seen recently?"

Cameron rattled off the list of movies and TV shows from memory. "And I'm really excited about the lineup of movies that Mobius has coming out."

"It's been a helluva ride. I've been here five years. I've been developing this script called *Makeshift*

Coriander by this hot, young writer, and I'm hoping to get it into production by the fall."

"*Makeshift Coriander*? That script was on the Black List last year!" The Black List was an unofficial survery of Hollywood readers of the best unproduced screenplays around town. He didn't need to consult the Internet for this. Cameron Buckley knew his shit.

"Right. It's an unbelievable script. A female assassin impersonates a world renown chef in order to cook a poisonous meal for the President of the United States. What a hook."

"I love that the main character is female and that she didn't have a romantic interest. I feel like Hollywood doesn't write roles for women like this anymore."

"Yeah. Every actress over thirty-five is chasing this project down. Wait, how did you know about the no romance part? Did you read the script?"

Cameron cringed. "Yes. It was floating around online, like most of the Black List scripts."

"Don't worry, man. I get how the Internet works. Good on you for taking the initiative to read those screenplays."

Cameron spun like a ballet dancer. "How do you decide to put a movie into production?"

"You need to have a star and director attached. Then you need to make sure the financials work out. Both sound simple but can take years to happen," Arthur said with a laugh.

"Or they get thrown into turnaround," Cameron said. He inhaled a breath. This was like a date minus the sexual tension. He never got a chance to talk this kind of inside baseball stuff with his friends. He had just met another person in an exclusive club, and he knew the language. It made him feel better about all those hours watching movies and reading the online trades and breathlessly waiting for the weekend box office to show up online. He wasn't alone.

"I am seriously impressed, dude. You definitely know more than I did at twenty-two. So you want to be a screenwriter?"

The way Arthur asked the question made Cameron pause. It sounded almost like a trap of some sort. Cameron was familiar with looks he received from family and family friends when he told them he wanted to be a writer. This call had been going like gangbusters, and Cameron didn't want to ruin the momentum with his strongest link to a career in Hollywood.

"I'm keeping my options open. I definitely want to know more about development and seeing how scripts get shaped for production."

"Cool. You don't want to limit yourself too soon. Les Moonves wanted to be an actor before he became President of CBS," Arthur said. (Cameron knew that.) Cameron breathed a sigh of relief that he wasn't sure was necessary. "I'd be happy to pass your resume along to HR. When are you moving out here?"

"September." Cameron hoped he sounded somewhat calm and collected because inside, he was freaking out.

"Just in time to escape the cold. Shoot me an email if you have any questions in the meantime. We'll grab a drink once you're in town."

"Sounds good. Thank you so much." And Cameron was up again. Floating around the room. High-fiving the ceiling. But his high came to quick halt when Walker flashed in his mind.

"Cameron?"

And then he was sitting.

"Still here." Cameron knew he sounded calmer now.

"You remind me a lot of myself. I think you'll do great."

CHAPTER SIXTEEN

Walker

Walker entered familiar territory. He and Cameron strolled
down a block of three-flats not far from campus. In
Walker's day, this was where fratty North Campus folk
lived as upperclassmen. But now, Cameron's friend's
boyfriend lived here with his friends. Gentrification had
done it again.

"Are you nervous?"

"No."

But of course he was. He couldn't deny the ultimate
truth that he was a thirty-six-year-old father who was
attending an off-campus college party. He prayed not to
run into anyone he knew. Not like that would happen. The
adults he knew had adult friends and did adult things.
Walker did, too, but he couldn't refuse Cameron.

Cameron couldn't have run fast enough from his
apartment the other morning. They hadn't spoken since.
Walker worried he and Hobie had finally scared him away.
Walker felt his whole body light up when Cameron texted

him this afternoon about going to a party. He said yes before realizing he'd be the one non-student here.

"It's just a small gathering. A few drinks with friends," Cameron assured him as they continued up the block. Walker heard music blaring from two apartments they passed. When he was a freshman and had little social pulse, Walker and his friends would roam this block and crash any parties they heard. Later in the night, when everyone was drunk and coming and going, the notion of "invites" disappeared.

I'm going to a party with a friend. He told himself that story over and over, even though his heart did a somersault whenever Cameron smiled at him. Walker clutched the bottle of wine he brought as a gift. Because that's what adults did when they were invited over someone's house. They brought a bottle of wine.

Cameron examined the offering. "You didn't have to get anything. They're having a keg, and Nolan's roommate Jordan has a bunch of top shelf liquor. He's kind of a snob about it, but at least he shares."

"Some people might like wine."

"This isn't a book club."

They reached the last apartment complex, a U-shaped, three-story building with bay windows on both ends. It was a layout familiar in these buildings. Walker could picture the exact layout of Nolan's place.

The labels on the buzzers were scratched off or peeling, new names affixed over old, like a billboard. Maybe if Walker peeled long enough, he'd find a familiar name. Cameron buzzed the middle one.

"It's Cameron and Walker," Cameron said into the speaker.

Nothing, then a long buzz. They entered the black-and-white tiled lobby. Flashback after flashback of parties past filled Walker's head. Cameron held open the inner door for his friend, and they trudged up to the third floor.

A lithe, energetic guy opened the door. His eyes immediately lit up at Cameron, then examined Walker like a science experiment.

"Henry, this is Walker."

"It's great to meet you!" Henry said. "Thanks for your help with trivia."

Walker shook his hand, which caught Henry offguard for a moment. He showed him the wine, which caught him offguard for a longer moment.

"It's one of my favorite bottles," Walker said.

"I think my mom loves this one, too."

Two strikes before he even got in the door.

Cameron and Walker squeezed inside, where the temperature spiked a good ten degrees. So much for a small gathering.

People clustered in groups throughout the long, narrow apartment. Yes, he knew it well. On the right, they would pass the living room and dining room complete with bay window before making a sharp left down the main, narrow hallway. Bedrooms one and two were on the right, with the lone bathroom on the left. Predictably, there was already a line. And then onto the final piece, the light at the end of the tunnel. The kitchen, with a small line of scratched-up counter space and fridge at the end. Then through the back door to the porch, which housed the smokers.

The kitchen seemed much smaller thanks to the bevy of people circling the keg and the bar. Cameron hugged the rest of his friends, stationed around some form of alcohol. He pointed his arm at Walker.

"Walker, this is Ethan, Greg, and Nolan."

The three guys waved. The one in the middle—Greg, maybe—clapped a hand on his shoulder. "Let's get you a drink."

"I brought this." Walker flushed red as he held up the bottle of wine.

"Thanks. I'll take that." Nolan plucked it from his hands and slid it onto the kitchen table where it rested next to a roll of paper towels.

"We've heard a lot about you," Ethan said. He seemed eager to please and would probably be a helpful ally tonight.

"Should I be afraid?"

Nolan handed him a beer in a red Solo cup. Last month, Walker attended a craft beer festival. He doubted this was one of the selections.

"Your son sounds so adorable," Ethan said. "I loved Legos as a kid."

"Thanks." Walker nodded. They didn't have kids to ask about. Nor did they have jobs. That ruled out ninety-eight percent of his normal conversation topics. "So, what year are all of you?"

A sophomore, junior, and senior. He thought maybe he could have better luck connecting with the latter.

"Do you know what you're doing next year?" He yelled to Greg over the crowd.

"I'm hoping to get into Teach for America."

"I had a friend who did that. She hated it." Walker bit his lip. Greg looked down at his beer. "I mean, that was years ago."

"I hope so."

"And it was a little bit her, too. She liked to complain about everything." Walker couldn't remember this girl's name, just that she hated Teach for America.

The guys looked down at their drinks. Even Walker relented and took a sip. The beer tasted like used bathwater.

"What's it like being a dad?" Henry asked him. He meant it like any other smalltalk question. What's it like studying abroad? What's it like majoring in chemical engineering? Only it wasn't.

"It's...it's great."

"Cool." Henry looked down at his phone. But so did most people in here. "Good Lord." He shoved his phone in Ethan's face, who burst out laughing. "I know, right?"

"Laura K. Niles needs to get off social media."

"What do you think of her?" Cameron asked Walker, like he was supposed to know who that was.

"She's okay."

"Her music's glorious, but she's a trainwreck of a person," Ethan said. "Did you listen to her new album?"

"It's out?" Cameron asked.

"She put it on Spotify this morning."

Cameron whipped out his phone and in a split second was on Spotify, which Walker had just heard about a few months ago.

"Oh!" Ethan screamed, slapping Henry's arm. "I didn't tell you!"

"Ow and what?" Henry asked.

"I found Brain Trust's Instagram feed."

"I love that band!" Walker shouted out. He received blank stares in return.

More people jostled their way into the kitchen. Walker was practically on the kitchen table. Sweat beaded on his forehead. There was a whole living and dining room. *The alcohol isn't going anywhere!*

"Apparently, Brain Trust has been talking smack about us ever since our victory. Are you on Instagram?" Henry asked him. "I'll follow you."

Walker shook his head no. "I'm on Facebook."

He could hear a record scratch to a stop.

"My mom loves Facebook," Ethan said.

Φ

Walker breathed in the fresh air of the smoker's porch. The breeze felt extra cool against his sweaty skin. He got some odd looks from the smokers across the way. He did the polite head nod, but that didn't seem to help. He hoped to hide out here for the rest of the party.

"Catching a breather?" Cameron jumped onto the porch from the kitchen.

"What am I doing here?"

"You're hanging out with some friends on a Saturday night."

Those guys were not his friends. They were nice, and they tried, but Walker stuck out. He couldn't help it. Age wasn't just a number.

"Thanks for coming. They really were excited to meet you."

"They seem like good guys. I hope you all stay friends."

Cameron took a drink from Walker's beer. He'd only had three sips, and that was just to blend in with the crowd. "Are you still friends with people from Browerton?"

"Friendly. People drift, people fade in and out of your life." Doug still had a strong group of friends from college. Even though it was amicable for the most part, the divorce forced people to take a side. They were always on Doug's side, though. The friends Walker gained when he and Doug began dating left just as easily.

"You know what's cool, though? Really cool." Walker leaned closer and caught hints of Cameron's familiar cologne. "No matter how long it's been, how many years, when I see people from college, it's like we're twenty again. All the memories and the jokes, and even the drama, come back like they just happened."

"Big problem." Henry joined them outside. Walker didn't know how he wasn't gasping for air in his fitted v-neck sweater. "The keg is kicked, and Jordan is hoarding the rest of his alcohol. He did this whole monologue about us being freeloaders."

"Can we get some more?" Cameron asked.

"The stores are closed."

"You know, there is the wine," Walker said.

Cameron and Henry traded looks.

"It's actually really good. Trust me on this." Walker was determined to prove his worth. Wine's worth.

He moved between them back into the kitchen, which was empty now that there was no more alcohol to be had. He found his bottle of wine on its side tucked in a napkin holder.

Henry passed him a fresh Solo cup. Walker searched Nolan's drawers and came up with a thin steak knife. He twisted the knife into the cork, Macgyvering it into a corkscrew. *Would they even know what Macgyvering means?*

"You see, wine gets better with age. Hard alcohol is all well and good now, but once you're meeting friends after work for a drink or going to dinner parties or regular parties, where it isn't about who can get wasted the fastest, you will realize," he uncorked the wine and took in the sharp aroma. "That wine is your friend."

Walker poured himself and the others a cup. "It's the classy, and surprisingly economical way to get buzzed. You can pick up a decent bottle for five bucks."

"I do love being classy, y'all," Cameron said.

"And when you come home from a long day of teaching kids or shuffling papers in a cubicle, a glass of wine can take the edge off." He handed over the cups to Cameron and Henry. They hung on his every word. *Behold the power of wine.*

"It smells like my parents," Henry said.

"That's natural. That feeling will go away, I promise you." Walker raised his cup. The others followed. He glanced at Cameron, who flashed him a knowing smile. "To you, gentlemen. To the future. To getting wasted like an adult."

They cheers'd. Wine soothed Walker's throat and coated his stomach like the old pal would.

"That's some good shit," Henry said.

Cameron nudged Walker's shoulder. "Way to go, Wine Guy."

Henry held up his cup again. "To the Wine Guy."

That became Walker's name for the rest of the night. Wherever he went, "Hey Wine Guy!" It was like he had introduced these kids to texting. Their lives would never be the same.

He relaxed on a ratty couch with Cameron and other students talking about old professors. Many of them hadn't changed; a few had gotten worse. This didn't feel so weird anymore. He was talking to people at a party. Age was irrelevant. He was the Wine Guy.

"Hey Wine Guy, what are your thoughts on Two Buck Chuck?"

"I think it's okay. Great when you're twenty-three and broke, but as you get older, you realize the value in paying slightly more for something slightly better."

Walker thought back to all the college parties he attended as a student. Not much had changed. Even with people looking at their smartphones every two seconds and pulling up clips, it was still about people talking and connecting.

"Oh shit!" Nolan yelled. Blue and red lights from outside lit up his face. "It's the cops!"

People ran over each other to escape or find refuge. It hit Walker that he was at a party with underage people, many of whom had drank wine he brought.

"Fuck on a stick." Cameron jumped up. He pulled Walker down the hall. People crowded into the kitchen.

"The back porch?" Walker asked.

"They always station one cop there. It's a trap."

As they passed bedroom number one, where Jordan was fighting back people trying to hide, Walker remembered the closet next to the bathroom. It would be big enough for the both of them.

"Follow me." Walker took Cameron's warm hand and led them into the hallway closet. They shoved in behind the row of coats. It was tighter than he remembered. Jordan and Nolan also had a shit-ton of crap. Cameron and Walker had to squeeze flush up against each other. Walker fanned the coats out to better conceal them.

"We're fine," Cameron said. "We're adults, and this isn't our place."

"I gave alcohol to minors."

"But it was wine."

The deep clomping of cop shoes reverbated on the floor. Walker signaled for Cameron to stay quiet.

"Evening, officer," he heard Nolan say.

"We having a party tonight?" The officer asked, and Walker's throat seized up. That voice belonged to Ed: husband of Melinda, father of Hobie's gymnastics classmate Sophie, friend of Doug and Ron. Walker shoved him and Cameron further into the closet, behind the heavy winter coats.

"I don't think there are any underclassmen here," Cameron said.

But it didn't matter. Melinda's husband couldn't find him here, not drinking with college kids and his new pretty-young-thing boyfriend who wasn't his boyfriend. He would never hear the end of it from Doug.

The clomping got deeper. Louder. Closer.

The closet was pitch black. Walker couldn't see Cameron, but he felt his body close to him.

"Do I need to go around asking everyone for ID? Because all it takes is one freshman or sophomore sneaking in here." Ed must like the macho thrill of being a cop since at home, Melinda wore the pants.

"It's your call, officer."

"Okay then. IDs out everyone!"

Walker's heart rattled like a wild animal stuck in a cage. When he was a senior, he and Doug threw a small party and still had the cops called on them. It was a testament to the safety of the town the police had nothing better to do. Walker and Doug charmed the pair of cops who had visited, inviting them to sing a round of karaoke with them. It turned them into legends for a while.

"Think positive thoughts," Cameron whispered.

The faint crackle of the police radio echoed. Ed and his partner were in the hallway. Every one of Walker's nerves stood on edge. But then he felt Cameron's arms around him, like they were protecting him. And even though that wouldn't have helped if they were caught, it made Walker calm down.

The doorknob jangled, followed by the creaking open of the closet door. Officer Ed shined his flashlight around the closet. Walker prayed that the winter coats were heavy enough. Cameron seemed to sense his legitimate fear and tightened his grip.

The beam of light inched across the hanger pole, getting closer and closer to their heads. Walker's throat shut down. He couldn't even prepare an excuse for when Ed caught him. *Hi Ed, I seem to have gotten lost on my way home.*

The flashlight clicked off just before it reached Cameron's hair. The door shut.

Walker's lungs filled back up with air.

"Success," he whispered.

No witty reply from Cameron.

Walker reached his fingers out into the blackness and felt Cameron's forehead, the smoothness of his skin, then traveled down to his stubbly cheek.

He couldn't see a thing, but he could feel Cameron's eyes on him. He could feel the heat between them. They locked into an intense gaze. Walker's thumb smoothed over Cameron's bottom lip.

He leaned forward and kissed Cameron. The energy Walker had from cheating imprisonment and gymnastics class embarrassment made him want to devour Cameron. Walker pulled him closer. Cameron opened his mouth and let his tongue enter. Walker pulled Cameron right up against him. Ed and his partner clomped past one more time en route to the door.

And then they were apart again.

"Walker," Cameron said through heaving breaths. His hands were on Walker's chest, pushing him away. "Friends."

The word punched him in the face.

The front door closed. Cheers exploded in the apartment. Music was turned on. It was a time to celebrate.

Except in this tiny closet. Walker wished he could see Cameron's reaction.

Cameron broke apart completely from Walker's grasp. The cold air slammed his exposed body.

"I'm trying everything I can not to fall for you," Walker said.

"I'm moving across the country, and you have a kid." Cameron opened the door and rejoined the party. In the light, Walker saw how red his cheeks were. "So try harder."

CHAPTER SEVENTEEN

Cameron

It was one of those early April afternoons that actually acted like spring. The sun shined across campus and nobody dared wear a jacket. It was a great day for great news.

"To Greg Sanderson." Cameron lifted his mimosa. "Who's off to teach all of America!"

"Funny," Greg deadpanned before breaking into a smile. Ethan hugged him tight, smiling enough for both of them.

Greg was accepted into the Teach for America program. He'd tried explaining it to Cameron over the first round of mimosas. Cameron knew it was highly coveted, that thousands of college kids across the country applied to work in inner city schools for two years. Like being an assistant in Hollywood, it sounded like two years of hell that would pay dividends for your résumé. Oh, and helping kids, too.

"I've always wanted to visit Philly," Ethan said.

"Big *Rocky* fan?" Greg asked.

"Big *Rocky* fan?" Ethan said mockingly. "No, big *Baby Mama* fan."

Cameron watched the cute couple be even cuter. He wondered if Greg really wanted to be assigned to Philly, or if he was only doing it to stay close to Ethan. He knew of plenty of couples where one person took a job in a certain city to stay close to the other. He couldn't tell if that was love, or obligation, or guilt. Maybe they were all the same. That's what Walker did for Doug, although Doug had him so whipped he didn't even leave Duncannon. Cameron downed his mimosa.

"And just like that, our graduates have their next steps," Henry said, a touch of sorrow in his voice. He pointed his glass at Greg, then Cameron.

"Well, mine isn't set yet. I just sent in a résumé," Cameron said.

"Yeah, but that Arthur guy is pretty high up. I'm sure he'll pass your résumé right to the top. And you'll kick ass at your interview," Ethan said.

"Or suck dick," Henry said. "Whatever gets you the job."

Cameron shook his head. He had the weirdest friends, and in that moment, he realized how fleeting this time was. It struck him like lightening. In a few months, they'll never be able to sit around on a Friday morning and drink.

Cameron stood up. The mimosas kicked in. "It's a gorgeous day, guys. The celebrating shouldn't stop."

Another round of mimosas turned into drinking beer at the riverfront turned into a *Real Housewives* marathon drinking game at Henry and Cameron's apartment. A small pile of beer bottles and cardboard amassed in the corner of the living room.

"Oh! Someone just did a z-finger snap!" Greg yelled.

They all drank.

"Which one?" Cameron asked.

Greg shrugged. Who could tell them apart anyway? Cameron liked having Greg as a friend. He wished he got to know him better. How well did anyone know anyone in college? These four years went by so fast.

After the third hour, they ordered pizza. Nolan came over after being a good student and attending class. More cardboard boxes added to the pile. Ethan continued to audibly gasp at the shenanigans onscreen, while Henry sided with the show's "villain." The day went on around them. Time ceased to exist at this party.

That was, until 5:02 p.m.

Cameron noticed the time on his phone when he answered a call from Walker. They had spent the rest of Nolan's party pretending that kiss in the closet never happened. Cameron had said it was the adrenaline of almost being caught that pressed Walker's lips into his, and Walker didn't object to the rationalization.

"Hey, Walker," Cameron said cheerfully. Henry mimed a blow job, so Cameron gave him the finger.

"Hey. How's it going?" Walker asked. He was not having as much fun as Cameron, that was easy to tell.

"Geez, Walker. Don't be so pedestrian." Cameron chuckled at his joke. It'd been in his head for a while. He was glad he got to use it, finally.

"Cameron, I need to ask you for a favor."

"A sexual favor?"

"A real one. It's serious."

Cameron got up and stood in the kitchen. He put on his serious face. "What's wrong?"

"I'm supposed to pick up Hobie from gymnastics practice in a half-hour, but I have to work late. We're having an emergency meeting, and I can't get out of it. Are you able to pick Hobie up and watch him at your apartment until I'm done?"

"Um…" Cameron was not expecting that. Not at all. Was sexual favor still an option? "I don't have a car."

"You can take a cab. I'll pay you back."

"There's nothing to do at my apartment for kids." Not unless Hobie wanted to play a live-action game of 99 bottles of beer on the wall.

"You have a TV. You can order a pizza. Add it to my tab."

I'm already ahead of you, he thought. He leaned against the counter and spun his bottle opener. Cameron felt a headache coming on. He was being forced to sober up too fast. "Can't another parent in his class watch him?"

"I don't have their phone numbers."

"Doug probably does."

"I'd rather not go that route if I don't have to."

A tense silence coated the line. Walker probably did have their numbers, and those parents definitely had Doug's number. Cameron didn't know parenting could be so political.

"Cameron, please. I know how absurd this sounds, that I'm even asking you at all. But Hobie feels comfortable with you, which doesn't happen with most adults. And I trust you."

Cameron wasn't sure if he trusted himself.

"I've never baby-sat before."

"I've seen you with him. You're a natural."

"You're just trying to butter me up."

Walker didn't come back with a retort. Cameron heard a woman calling his name in the background.

"Walker, I don't know if I can. I'm..." *kinda wasted.* But he stopped himself before saying that. Walker needed him, which stirred something in his chest that overrode his buzz.

"Cameron, please."

"Okay," he said. *I can do this*, Cameron told himself.

Walker exhaled a relieved breath. "Thanks. You saved me, Cameron."

"I'm getting my wings next week."

"I..." Walker stopped himself. Cameron had an inkling what he was going to say.

"You owe me one."

"Right. Thanks, Cameron."

Cameron hung up and put on a pot of coffee. He poured himself a glass of water, chugged it, then another, chugged it. He double-fisted water and coffee. He dropped and did pushups on the kitchen floor.

"How wasted are you?" Greg asked from the living room.

Being drunk was all a state of mind, he told himself. He gave himself a nice one-two slap on the cheeks.

I'm good.

"I'm good," Cameron said.

He thought of those parents who could lift cars to save their children. If he could harness just a fraction of that, sobriety would be his.

Cameron stumbled back to the living room. Not stumbled, walked. Walked like a sober, confident, responsible adult.

"Guys, I have to pick up something. I'll be back in a little bit. Can you clean up the beer bottles and trash?"

"What are you picking up?" Henry asked.

Cameron held onto the wall for balance. "A party guest."

Φ

Cameron took deep breaths in the cab. Deep, sobering breaths. He stared out the window, but that made him dizzy. *You are* not *picking up a child drunk. You will sober up for Walker and Hobie.*

"How's your afternoon going?" Cameron asked the cab driver, hoping conversation would help burn off the booze.

"It's okay." He pulled out his earbuds, and Cameron heard talking on the other end. "I had to make a few trips to the airport. There was lots of traffic on the highway."

"Oh, really? What kind of traffic?"

"Construction. They closed one of the lanes."

Nope. Not helping. The alcohol sloshed in his stomach like choppy seas. A child's life was going to be in his hands. He had to take drastic measures.

"Could you please pull over?"

"We're not there yet."

"I know. Please pull over."

The cabbie did as instructed, giving Cameron major side-eye in the rearview mirror.

"I'll just be one second." Cameron got out of the cab, shoved his finger down his throat, and puked in the trash can at the corner of the street. He used whisper hands around his mouth to be polite to passersby. He did it again, emptying his stomach like a girl in a Very Special Episode.

"Better," he said. Cameron did a set of pushups on the sidewalk to be safe.

He slid back into the cab.

The driver's mouth hung open. He got back on the road. "I have gum."

A few minutes later, they pulled up to the gymnastics center. Cameron looked himself over in the rearview mirror. He looked passable. He wasn't 100 percent sober, but close enough. His hair was in place, and he didn't get barf on his clothes. Nobody would be able to tell he was three sheets to the wind. Half a sheet, really. *All I have to do is pick the kid up and get him back to the apartment. That barely requires full functionality of my motor skills.*

"Keep the meter running!" Cameron said.

"Okay."

He opened the door. "I don't seem drunk to you, do I?"

The cab driver made eye contact through the mirror. "Not at all." He didn't sound too enthusiastic about it.

Cameron chewed on his gum, held his head high, and entered the facility. Posters of super-thin gymnasts lined the walls in the waiting room. Mothers shoved their children into jackets too heavy for this weather. In the corner of the waiting room, Hobie sat with an instructor. He stared up at the ceiling. The poor kid was bored out of his fucking mind.

"Hobie!"

"Cameron!"

The kid's eyes lit up like Christmas morning, and a warm feeling zipped directly to Cameron's heart. It's always nice when somebody was that excited to see him. Hobie and his stubby legs ran up to Cameron. His backpack jiggled on his shoulders.

"Are you ready to go?"

"Hi," the instructor said warily. "Are you a parent or guardian?"

"I, I guess I'm a guardian. Walker Reed called ahead about me." Words fell out of Cameron's mouth, and he hoped they made sense. "And I do believe he emailed in a permission slip requesting I receive temporary custody of the boy in that which I can escort him home this afternoon."

The instructor nodded slowly and clocked Cameron's please-don't-be-bloodshot eyes. "Can I see your driver's license? I'll go check."

Cameron handed it over. "Thank you."

Hobie tugged at his sleeve. "I did a somersault today! Wanna see?"

"Super cool! I'd love to!"

Hobie squatted on the floor, getting into position when—

"Hobie," a mother yelled behind Cameron. "You shouldn't tumble on a tiled floor. Only when there's a mat underneath."

The mother, a beacon of WASP perfection motioned for Hobie to stand up. She shot Cameron a look that turned him into an ice sculpture.

"Are you picking up Hobie?"

Cameron nodded.

"What's your name?" Her words were caked in judgement and disdain. His lips wouldn't move. Maybe if he kept silent, she would go away.

"It's Cameron!" Hobie said.

"Thank you, Hobie," the mother said in a sunshiney tone that was a complete 180 from how she just spoke to Cameron. She continued staring at Cameron, observing him. He kept grinning, like nothing was up, like nobody could smell any alcohol on him because he sprayed himself with cologne and chewed gum.

"Are you Walker's boyfriend?" She finally asked.

"A family friend."

Cameron was two seconds away from jumping through the front window and running down the street when the instructor came back with his ID.

"Thank you, Mr. Buckley."

Cameron smiled with victory at the mother.

"Take care, Hobie." The mother patted his head, which Hobie barely tolerated. "Please have either father call me when you get home, okay?"

She gave Cameron one more onceover and exited with her mini-me daughter.

"Sir, can I talk to you for a second, if you don't mind?" The instructor pulled Cameron over to a row of seats facing the cab outside. Her frown was just as dramatic as her smile. "Can you let Walker know that we had another situation today?"

"Situation? I thought Hobie was potty trained."

"Not that. Walker will know what we mean."

Cameron hated her tone. She wanted to sound soothing, but Cameron was a pro at picking up passive-aggressive bitchiness. It was the only way to survive gay life at Browerton.

"Well, I don't know what you mean, and I'm the one who has to relay this information, so please explain."

She glanced at Hobie, and he could've sworn she glared at the little ragamuffin.

"When the rest of class was waiting in line to do tumbling exercises, Hobie wandered off and started stacking gym mats like a fort."

Cameron laughed. Hobie, always building something. "Is that so bad?"

"It's being disruptive to the class."

"How so? He's not stopping kids from tumbling."

"Yes, but he should be following instructions to stay in line, like my other kids." The instructor seemed to be taking it personally.

"Perhaps you don't have enough staff working the class. Is it just you?"

"I've never had a problem conducting a class on my own. Hobie is my first student to be this disruptive."

Cameron doubted any kid being talked to in this uptight, condescending would want to pay attention. "Is he not tumbling at all?"

"He does, eventually."

"Then I don't really see the problem."

The woman's jaw clenched as she became even more flustered by Cameron's questions. "He needs to follow the rules."

"But if he's doing the tumbling and shit, then isn't he? I don't think this is that big of a deal."

"I doubt you would understand. You're the baby-sitter, not the parent." The woman stepped closer and drew to a whisper. "Hobie is the only child with same-sex parents, and, well maybe there might be a correlation. This might be him acting out, in a way."

"I didn't know gymnastics instructors all came with PhDs in psychology. 'The kid has two dads. He must be messed up.' Real fucking insightful." Cameron's chest constricted, and his pulse pounded in his temples. "Just because a kid gets bored waiting in line and decides to do something fun and creative doesn't mean there's anything wrong with him. Maybe it means there's something right with him. Maybe it means you need a better lesson plan so kids aren't left sitting around bored. Or maybe you need to get off your fucking pedastal and hire some more staff. For what these parents are paying to be here, their kids don't deserve to wait their turn for most of class. Or maybe the 'situation' here is that he can smell your homophobia and granny perfume a mile away. I'm sure certain organizations would be very interested in hearing what you and your establishment think about same-sex parents."

"Sir, I didn't mean to...I don't think I phrased my point well."

"No, your point just sucks." Cameron turned on his heel. "Let's go, Hobie!"

Φ

The *Real Housewives* marathon had no end in sight. Nolan and Henry were sprawled out on the couch, while Ethan and Greg sat on the floor.

"The prodigal son returns," Henry said with extra dramatic flair. "And who is this new houseguest you brought us?"

Hobie peeked out from behind Cameron's legs.

"This is Hobie." Cameron didn't try to move him. "I'm baby-sitting until his dad picks him up."

The interaction at the gymnastics facilities had shoved Cameron from drunk to stone-cold sober. Seeing a little kid in their midst did the same for the guys.

"We're going to have lots of fun!" Cameron craned his neck at the TV. Two women were fighting in a mess of weaves and bleeped expletives. "Is there something you want to watch, Hobie?"

Hobie remained glued to the backs of his legs.

"Hi, Hobie." Greg shuffled over and held out his hand. He had that elementary school teacher voice down. "I'm Greg. That's a cool backpack, buddy. Is that *Cars*?"

Hobie nodded.

"I love *Cars*!" Greg had the ability to sound enthusiastic but relatable, like he legit liked *Cars* and backpacks and didn't find this whole situation awkward.

"Do you want some pizza?" Cameron asked.

Hobie nodded.

"We have pepperoni and one with green pepper and onion," Henry said.

"Do you have plain cheese?" Hobie asked.

Over Hobie's head, Nolan shook his head no to Cameron.

"Sure we do, pal!" Cameron said. "We're having a cheese pizza delivered just for you!"

"I can share it," Hobie said.

"You're so generous, Hobie!" Greg said, and the guys chimed in with agreement. Hobie smiled and shied at the attention.

Hobie motioned for Cameron to squat down. "Do you have any toys?" He whispered.

Cameron scanned his apartment and found furniture and books, two things no kid wanted to play with. Hobie watched a middle-aged woman having an emotional breakdown outside of a waxing salon. His eyes bulged at the sight.

"You don't have any toys?" He asked. The fact that he was stuck here was sinking in fast. Cameron remembered going to his grandparents' house and being bored out of his mind. This apartment had to be more fun than a senior citizen's house.

"Hobie…" Cameron started, hoping an idea would come to him. "We're going to play a game." More furniture, more books. A pile of pizza and beer boxes. "It's going to be so much fun."

His head whipped back to the boxes. He smiled. "A lot of fun."

CHAPTER
EIGHTEEN

Walker

Fucking Radiance. He muttered that to himself on his drive to Cameron's apartment. He would never use their shampoo again. He finally finished going through all of the research data on their advertising. All it showed was that their creative sucked. His team was getting the commercials and ads shown in the right places, but people weren't connecting with the creative. How could any of that change for their review?

Walker wanted to leave work to pick up Hobie, but his whole team was slaving away. They could afford to. Most of them were single or didn't have kids. Lucy's kids were in afterschool activities and could take care of each other. When he went into Patricia's office, she said it was okay for him to leave, but her eyes told a different story. If he cared about his career, he would choose wisely.

The golden handcuffs. *That's how they get you*, he thought. With each new promotion, with each raise, he bought more stuff. He felt he had to compete with Doug, whose practice was successful almost immediately. Especialy after the divorce, he didn't want Hobie to think that only one parent could provide a good life for him. If Doug insisted on sticking him into a million different groups, then Walker would gladly pay for half.

He parked at the curb and raced up to the front door where he buzzed Cameron's apartment. He had known a girl who lived in this complex. She tried to get him and Doug to have a threesome with her. That was a weird night.

"It's Walker," he shouted into the speaker, and was buzzed in a second later.

He took the stairs two at a time. Walker heaved for breath by the time he reached Cameron's apartment.

Cameron opened the door, himself heaving for breath.

"Thank you so much," Walker said. "How was it?"

Before Cameron could answer, Hobie ran up to the door with a huge smile stamped on his face. A tsumani of relief rolled through Walker.

"Dad! You gotta see my robot!" Hobie pulled him by the hand into the apartment. He waved to Cameron's friends sitting on the couch, all of them looking wiped out. The dining table was pushed to the side, and empty bottles were arranged as a bowling alley. A ball of foil rested beside them.

But the main attraction lurked in the living room. A robot made of cardboard stretched six feet in the air. A stepladder rested next to it, presumably so Hobie could reach the top.

The robot had legs made of folded pizza boxes. A few pizza boxes taped together created its wide, square stomach and chest. Then the head and hands were crafted from six pack containers with the dividers as fingers.

"His name is Beerza!" Hobie exclaimed. "He's like the box people we used to make on Christmas!"

Bigger than anything they ever made. Walker marveled at the size and scope—and that this was the last thing he thought he'd find in here.

"I didn't have any toys in the apartment." Cameron said with a modest shrug.

"Do you want a slice of pizza, Dad?" Hobie ran to the dining table and pulled a slice of cheese pizza. Grease dripped onto the floor, but Cameron didn't seem to care. Walker's stomach growled at the aroma.

He ate that piece in three bites.

"We also played bowling. I got a strike! Do you know what they call three strikes in a row?" Hobie asked.

Walker played along. "You're out?"

"No! That's baseball. They call it turkey!"

"Who came up with that?" Cameron asked. "Was bowling invented over Thanksgiving? Le sports people are so weird."

"What do you think of Beerza?" Hobie asked. "Cameron and his friends helped with folding and cutting the pieces, but I told them where to put it."

Walker got eye level with his son. "It was still a team effort, Hobie."

"I know."

"Now does Beerza cook or clean?"

"No!" Hobie roared back with laughter. It was music to Walker's ears. Sometimes at night, before he went to sleep, he worried that Hobie would never laugh like that around him again.

Walker squeezed him tight. "This is so cool!"

"Can we take it home?"

"You bet!"

"Can Beerza sit in the front seat?"

"Of course not!" Walker said with the same chipper tone. *Beerza. Cute name.*

Beerza?

His attention whipped back to the bowling alley. They were all beer bottles. The robot's arms were lined with Corona, Goose Island, and Miller labels.

"We weren't drinking with Hobie," Cameron said, reading his expression. "I had some friends over when you called. This was their mess, but not one sip of alcohol was consumed in his presence. I promise."

He didn't have words. Hobie's baby-sitters never did anything like this. Hell, not even his teachers. And he doubted Doug and Ron let Hobie get this artistic and make a mess.

"Thank you," Walker said. His voice quaked with emotion.

"You already said that," Cameron said with a soft smile, one that said he understood but wasn't going to make a scene.

"How much do I owe you?"

"Don't worry about it."

Walker shot him a look.

"Okay fine. For the cab and pizza, let's say fifty bucks."

Walker handed him three twenties. Cameron didn't try to make change. He forgot all about the shitty day and shitty night he had. That all evaporated once he stepped inside the apartment. Happiness expanded inside him like a helium balloon.

"You're good with kids," Walker said.

Cameron shrugged. "Maybe I'm not terrible."

Walker grabbed another piece of pizza. "How was it picking up Hobie? Did you have any trouble?"

"No, not really."

Walker didn't quite believe him. "Did something happen?"

"No, nothing."

"Cameron said the F-word to my instructor!" Hobie slapped his hand over his mouth and giggled. Even Henry and Nolan laughed to themselves.

"I can explain." Cameron mouthed "later."

Walker trusted him. He'd deal with the fallout then.

"Well, thanks," Walker said awkwardly. He knew how much Cameron hated good-byes, and this one was especially strange. They hadn't seen each other since Nolan's party.

"No problem." Cameron pretended like none of that ever happened, or that he would never acknowledge any of that ever happened.

"Alright, Hobie," Walker said. "Help me carry Beerza to the car."

"Wait. We have to say good-bye!"

"Yeah, Walker. Don't be rude." Cameron planted his hands on his hips and cocked his eyebrows. He didn't realize how much that made Walker want to scoop him into his arms.

Hobie went to the couch and ran down the line, high-fiving Henry, Nolan, Ethan, and Greg. Then he ran back over to hug Cameron. He squeezed extra hard.

Walker just waved at the guys, and then came Cameron.

"Thank you again," Walker said, then gave him a polite hug, too. More of a bro hug than anything else.

"Aren't you going to kiss him, too?" Hobie asked.

That left all adults in the room speechless.

"Kiss him?" Walker asked.

"Yeah, like you used to do with daddy."

Cameron's face dropped.

The words hit Walker in the gut. He laughed nervously, and Cameron joined in. His cheeks got hot, and he wondered if they were as red as they felt.

"Hobie, he's not…"

"We can do a kiss on the cheek," Cameron said.

Before Walker could second guess, Cameron pulled him into a warm hug, like wrapping yourself in a fresh towel after a shower. Walker felt both their hearts beating against both their chests. Cameron pecked him on the cheek. His lips caused his cheek to sizzle. Walker breathed in his scent.

He didn't know how long they hugged. Seconds? Hours? Months? It all felt the same to him. Walker was already missing this hug, and it wasn't even over yet. Cameron dropped his hands and stepped away, his pupils wide and dark. The lights came back on. The music started up.

"Good night, Cameron."

CHAPTER NINETEEN

Cameron

It was only five o'clock, but Henry was already dancing. He shimmied next to the microwave while heating up some leftover pizza.

"I see you're all ready for tonight." Cameron pulled the pizza box out of the fridge. One slice remained. He'd heard somewhere that you could reheat pizza in the oven. He googled the exact instructions on his phone.

"It's going to be ree-dic. Can we just not spend all our time on the '80s floor?"

"But in the Top 40 last time, they kept playing Laura K. Niles. I'm kinda burned out on her songs. They all sound the same," Cameron said.

They were talking about Revolution. It was a once-a-quarter gay dance party thrown in an abandoned warehouse in a shady part of Harrisburg. Three floors of dancing, with a different theme on each level.

The microwave beeped with Henry's dinner. "We're going to Nolan's to pregame at eight-thirty. Jordan's going to drive."

"Jordan's going? Let me guess—"

"Gay bars are a great place to pick up girls," they both said.

"This is perfect. I'll have to time for an extended disco nap and some TV." Cameron wrapped the pizza in used aluminum foil, shoved it in the oven, and prayed for the best.

Henry held his plate of pizza and remained in the kitchen. His face got cloudy with emotion.

"Is the middle of your pizza still frozen?" Cameron asked.

"No. It's just...I remember you taking me to Revolution when I was a freshman. You helped me get my fake ID."

"I remember. You made out with a different guy in each level."

"And you brought home that guy who barely spoke English. The cab ride was so awkward."

They laughed over the memory. That night seemed forever ago, but it'd only been two years.

"I can't believe this is our last Revolution," Henry said.

Cameron waved off the sentimentality. He refused to let the treacly music swell on this moment. Revolution was just a sketchy dance party, after all.

He opened the oven. A plume of smoke puffed out.

"Well, looks like I'm not eating pizza tonight. Stupid Internet." He yanked out the charred remains of his dashed dinner and threw them in the trash. He took out a can of ravioli from the back of a cabinet and dumped it into a saucepan. Henry opened up all the windows.

"So what was that all about last night?" Henry asked. "You and Walker."

"Walker picked up his son and said thank you. In other news, the earth is round." Cameron knew what Henry meant, and Henry wasn't putting up with his lack of an answer.

"That hug...it looked like a pretty intense hug."

"Everything's relative." Cameron watched his food cook.

"Deflecting."

Cameron stirred the ravioli. "We kissed in the closet during Nolan and Jordan's party." Before Henry's eyebrows could judge him, Cameron continued: "But I ended it."

"Why?"

Cameron's head shot up. Henry leaned against the sink, eating.

"You know why."

"You like him." Henry pointed an accusatory pizza crust at him. "You are in serious likeitude, Cameron Buckley."

"We were just in a tight, confined space avoiding the cops. Didn't Anne Frank develop a crush on the guy she was in the attic with?"

Henry rolled his eyes. Apparently, he didn't appreciate a Holocaust reference. "And what's your grand excuse for last night?"

Cameron didn't have a quick retort for that one. Henry was right. That hug was more than a hug. It was an earthquake. Cameron was still reeling from its aftershocks.

"It's okay to like him," Henry said.

"It's inconvenient."

"That's how you know it's real."

Henry chuckled and turned down the stove. Bubbling ravioli sauce splattered out of the saucepan. "You are making the Puritans proud."

Heat burned Cameron's cheeks. There was this voice in his head reminding him of the all the reasons why he couldn't like Walker. Relationships didn't work. The rug was always waiting to be pulled out from under. Just like it was with him and his mom.

"This can't work," Cameron said quietly, not even a whisper.

Henry put his arm around his friend. "You've been saying that to yourself about every guy for years. Not every relationship will end up like your parents. You're happy with Walker. Let yourself be happy."

The voice in Cameron's head was sounding more and more like a vocal minority, a squeaky wheel hogging all the grease. He closed his eyes and pictured himself letting go.

"We should eat up," Cameron said. "Give ourselves time to digest. We don't want to dance the night away on a full stomach."

CHAPTER
TWENTY

Walker

Walker blinked his eyes and they were still there. Rows upon rows of an empty spreadsheet waiting to be filled with spend projections. The fluorescent lights beamed above his desk.

He had to plug away on these figures and email them out tonight. This task required pulling up past creative briefs from their partners, finding where they listed their price, and entering it onto one consolidated spreadsheet. In other words, data entry.

One Browerton Bachelor's Degree hard at work.

Walker's wrists numbed from typing. Piercing pain shot down the tips of his fingers straight to his elbows. Each tap of a key was morse code spelling out the important messages of *OWWW* and *Carpal Tunnel Syndrome: here we come.*

Walker worked on this sheet through lunch. His half-eaten burrito bowl sat beside him, and he was about to take a bite when his office phone rang. Nobody called him at the office ever. He didn't think he ever set his voicemail. Email was the name of the game.

"Hello?"

"I'm downstairs." The caller hung up, but he didn't need to identify himself. Walker shriveled up inside. He took a final bite of lunch, then rode the elevator down to the lobby.

The doors opened on Doug, waiting there with crossed arms. There was a time when Walker liked getting a rise out of him, because they both knew how to relieve tension.

Eons ago.

"I can't believe you," Doug said in a hushed tone. Walker led him to a deserted couch that overlooked well-landscaped lawns.

"What happened?"

"I received a call from Melinda last night. She told me about the 'baby-sitter' who picked up Hobie from gymnastics."

"What?"

"I knew she could only be referring to your rent boy. She thought he was on something."

"Cameron wasn't on something. He was probably just nervous." Walker hated how quickly Doug could get under his skin. He and Melinda ruled over the other parents, but Walker refused to follow suit.

"Nervous?"

"I'm sure Melinda was not welcoming. She probably gave him that cocked-eyebrow-megabitch-staredown that she does so well."

"Great term. I'm glad your rent boy is expanding your vocabulary."

"He's not my rent boy." Walker grit his teeth. Doug maintained a serene smile for people passing by. "Cameron did a great job looking after Hobie. They built a robot."

"Oh, I know all about the robot. Hobie wouldn't stop talking about it. Beerza, I believe is its name." Doug's eyebrows were daggers for his ex-husband. "Beer plus pizza."

Doug was probably pissed off about Hobie having a good time with Cameron more than anything else. He hated not being the superior father at all times.

"So he had some bottle cases around his apartment."

"Was he drinking around my child?"

"No!" Walker punched the couch cushion, which didn't have the effect he wanted. Cameron told him he didn't drink around Hobie, and he believed him.

"Melinda said he had bloodshot eyes."

"Let's call the police then! Open-and-shut case. Maybe next she can figure out what happened to her old nose."

"I called the facility to get some more information on the incident, and I had a lovely chat with Hobie's instructor. Apparently, your *friend* threatened and verbally abused her."

Walker was prepared for this. Cameron had told him what happened, that he went all Erin Brockovich on this woman. Walker was only jealous that he couldn't witness the scene and put in his two cents.

"I'm glad this is so fun for you," Doug said off Walker's expression. "I nearly had to beg to let Hobie stay in that class."

"He had a good point, Doug. There's nothing wrong with Hobie because he isn't some mindless drone who will just sit there."

Like me, he thought.

"And do you think it's right for them to say it's because he has two dads?"

"Your friend misheard them. Drugged-out college students don't have the best memory."

"Cameron!" Walker yelled. He didn't care who heard. "He has a name. It's Cameron. I don't call Ron 'That Guy You Fucked Behind My Back'."

Doug glanced around and remembered he didn't know anyone here. Precious was safe, for now. "I'm not even going to go there."

Walker looked out the window, across the way to the west building.

"Why didn't you call me? I could've picked him up."

That was more hours away from Hobie, more hours for him to strengthen his attachment. Walker had already lost his son for his birthday weekend. He wasn't going to let that happen again. He *was* a good father.

"Hobie had a great time with Cameron. You should've seen him, Doug. When I came to pick him up, I've never seen him so happy. Like exploding with joy."

Doug bristled at the comment, then rolled his eyes. "Why weren't you there? I've cancelled appointments with patients when things came up with Hobie. Remember when he had that virus in the winter? I was there for him. And you worked. Because we all know Berkwell and Radiance shampoo would fall apart without your guidance. I didn't ask some piece of ass to parent my child."

"Our child." Walker had murder in his eyes. Doug knew his pressure points, and he knew just when to squeeze. He tried maintaining decorum with his ex-husband. He didn't want Hobie seeing his parents fighting. But Doug decided to rip the gloves off.

"And let's get something straight," Walker said with an eerie calm. "Cameron is not a rent boy, and he's not a piece of ass."

"What is he then? Your boyfriend?"

Walker nodded. He wasn't sure if that was true, but he wouldn't give Doug the satisfaction. He and Cameron were in some type of relationship.

Doug stifled a weasely laugh. "You're serious."

"Yeah."

"He's fifteen years younger than you."

"I know."

"He's graduating in June."

"I know."

"He's not going to stick around." Doug had pity in his eyes. It was a look Walker knew well and usually shrugged off. But this time, Walker could feel heat racing up his neck.

I stuck around, he thought. *I stuck around for us, and you left.*

"I need to get back to work." Walker stood up and returned to the elevators. The heat now flushed his cheeks. He jammed his finger against the up button.

"Doug, I don't criticize your life choices. Don't criticize mine."

He got into the elevator.

"Good luck with this one, Walker. Who knows? Maybe everything will work out."

The doors closed on Doug's smirk.

Φ

He hated having Doug's voice in his head, hated that he let Doug be the voice of reason for him. Walker tried to visit Cameron at Starbucks, but his shift was already over. Cameron was the closest thing he'd had to a boyfriend since Doug. Pretty pathetic.

Walker drove to his apartment after work and jogged up the two flights of stairs to his front door.

"We need to talk," he said as soon as Cameron opened the door. Cameron didn't say anything back. Walker had the floor.

"I think...I think we should end this, whatever this is. Each time I say that we're just friends, it rings more hollow. I have feelings for you, Cameron, feelings that friends do not have for each other. But I have a son to think about, and you have a future in Los Angeles that's waiting for you, and I don't know where this is going. I don't know where it can go. Whatever is going on between us, it has to stop. We need to stop it now. Rip that Band-Aid off clean. Just cut it off before it gets worse, because it's going to get worse. We'll go our separate ways. I think that's best. We had fun, but it's for the best."

Cameron nodded and absorbed the speech.

"What do you think?" Walker asked.

Cameron took a step closer, his eyes never leaving Walker.

"I know this is abrupt. We can talk about it."

And another step. Walker caught a whiff of his deoderant, but remained focused. Kinda focused.

"Cameron?"

And his lips were on Walker's. Everything Walker had just said was chucked out the window. He slammed the front door shut behind them, and pulled Cameron against him.

Walker kissed him hard, tasting his lips and tongue, breathing in Cameron. Walker held him with a strength he didn't know he had. His need, his want for Cameron avalanched onto this moment.

He walked them backward and pushed Cameron up against his bedroom door. Cameron moaned, and he moaned back, turned on by both sounds. His hands couldn't stop exploring the nooks and crannies of Cameron's lithe body. He had stared at it for so long, nearly studied it. He wanted to feel the heat coming off Cameron's skin and the flex of his muscles. His erection mashed against Cameron's.

Walker pulled away and locked into the hazy blue eyes in front of him. He gasped for air. His heart pounded in his ears.

"Walker, are you okay?"

He nodded. *Better than fucking okay.* He could feel it inside him. This dormant version of himself waking up, coming back to life.

He pushed the two of them into the bedroom. He shoved Cameron against his dinky Ikea dresser. His hands and his tongue were magnets to Cameron's body, unable to free themselves.

Shirts flew off. Walker's took longer because of the damn buttons. Warm chest against warm chest. He ran his fingers down the slight curves of Cameron's back, smelling his smooth skin, the scent going to his head. The cock strained against his pants in an epic battle. His fingers traveled farther, past Cameron's waistband, and grabbed his firm ass. Cameron shivered and dug his fingers into Walker's back, driving him wild.

Cameron stripped to his boxer briefs, barely concealing the thick cock hidden underneath. Walker wanted to take a moment to remember this image, Cameron's body all for him. He wrapped his legs around Walker's waist. His opening was positioned over Walker's cock. He grinded against the concave part of Cameron, the hollowness that seemed to beg him for entry.

"You're right," Cameron whispered through gasping breaths. "This is a bad idea."

He had Cameron dismount. Walker got on his knees and took in the sight of that hard cock outlined against those tight boxer briefs. He massaged his hand over it, getting a gutteral reaction from the guy above. He pulled down the underwear and shoved into his mouth what was waiting for him.

"Fuck," Cameron whisper-moaned out.

Walker had never been so turned on having a guy's dick in his mouth. His own dick got harder the more he felt Cameron wobble underneath him. He was better than any random college hookup Cameron had, he knew it. He sucked that dick with joy, with sloppy abandon, letting the sweaty taste of Cameron fill him up. His lips slid from base to tip and let Cameron's cock take up his whole mouth.

He spun him around, bent him over the dresser, and slapped his pale ass. It vibrated like a tuning fork.

Again.

Harder.

Cameron gasped in pleasure.

Walker opened him up and tongued that tight ring of muscle. The musky smell traveled straight to his brain and his cock. He spat on his hole and slid two fingers inside him. Cameron was jelly under his fingers. He slammed his hand on the dresser, and the thing sounded like it was going to break. Walker went to town on that ass, slapping it again, watching his handprint disappear from the fresh skin.

"I want you, Walker."

Fuck. There was no joke, no sarcasm, nothing underneath those words except truth. Walker's cock raged against his pants. He could shoot right now.

"It's all in the nightstand drawer," Cameron said.

Walker found five boxes of condoms and two bottles of lube. At that moment, he was a little jealous of Cameron's sex life.

"It was a Christmas gag gift," Cameron said behind him. "A practical Christmas gag gift. I've only gone through a few boxes this year."

Walker lifted his head up, and Cameron smiled at him reassuringly. Walker stopped caring. He wanted Cameron. He was going to have Cameron. And the rest was history.

"Sit on the bed," Cameron ordered. He kissed Walker and unzipped his pants. Walker was ready to burst through the fabric. He hadn't had a blowjob in so long, he wasn't exactly sure what to expect.

Cameron dropped to his knees and licked his lips.

Walker moaned as he entered the warm mouth. His mind went dizzy with desire, and he reared his head back. He was not expecting this. The guy knew what he was doing and did it with more passion and energy than any of

Doug's marriage blowjobs. His tongue maneuvered around his length with precision. Walker threaded his fingers into his hair and pushed his cock deeper into Cameron's mouth. Walker was going to blow, but he couldn't. Not yet. He wanted more.

He had Cameron sit on his lap. His cock felt the curve of Cameron's opening. Walker took a moment between rolling on the condom and lubing himself up to marvel at the beautiful creature in front of him. Nothing felt more right.

He got Cameron slicked up accordingly. His pupils expanded in anticipation. He pulled Walker into a kiss, full of passion and hunger. Their lips went from airlock tight to barely touching, as he sat back down on Walker's cock. Cameron dipped his forehead against Walker and heaved out a breath. He moved slowly, getting both of them used to the sensation of Walker being inside Cameron. He breathed against Walker's neck, the air chilling Walker's sweaty skin.

"Yes." Cameron was barely audible. Goosebumps covered his flesh, and Walker held him tighter.

Walker pumped into his tight hole with greater force. His need for Cameron took over. The bed creaked under their weight. Sweat funneled down Walker's beard, dripping onto his chest. Nothing could hold him back.

Cameron cradled Walker's head in his shaking hands. Intensity and lust beamed from his blue eyes. Walker was on the edge. The orgasm built, and he pounded into Cameron, who moaned in pleasure at the force.

"I don't want this to end," Cameron whispered into his ear, his breath hitting that sensitive spot at the base of Walker's neck.

Walker grunted with orgasm, emptying himself inside Cameron. A few seconds later, he felt Cameron's hot release on his stomach. They breathed heavily into each other's necks, hugging each other tight.

So much for going our separate ways.

CHAPTER TWENTY-ONE

Cameron

The only thing covering Cameron when he woke up was Walker. His arms spooned over him, giving Cameron a peek at the H.J. tattoo, which he now knew was for Hobie.

Cameron's eyes popped open. He wanted to be fully alert for this moment. It was meant to be savored and perfectly lodged in his memory. Everything felt right. The world was as it should be to Cameron. Walker's grasp wasn't unfamiliar. There were no questions that had to be asked, no steps that had to be retraced. It was the first time when Cameron awoke in bed with someone else and knew this was where he should be.

Walker stirred behind him. His head moved off the pillow.

This was new for Cameron. Not the waking up with a guy in his bed, but the instant comfort level of being here. Was this intimacy?

As if by clockwork, a little voice of doubt nagged in his head, saying all the right words. *Arthur Brandt. Hollywood. Graduation.*

Cameron realized just how exposed he was. He pulled the blanket over himself.

"Are you sore from last night?" Walker asked.

"No." Cameron laughed at the odd question. "Are you?"

He rubbed his lower back.

"Out of practice?"

Walker arched a sleepy eyebrow. "No comment."

He curled his arms back around Cameron and kissed his neck. His chest hair brushed against Cameron's skin. Even his morning breath found a way to be sexy.

"I'll remember to stretch next time," Walker said. He read his expression, which apparently wasn't good. "What is it?"

"Before I attacked you last night, you said that we should stop. Do you still mean it?"

Walker pulled Cameron into a deep kiss, but that wasn't answer enough.

"I'm graduating soon. I'm moving to Los Angeles."

"I know. But that isn't for a few months. We have time."

"Not a lot of time."

"But still plenty." Walker kissed him, but Cameron wasn't convinced. "Do you want us to stop?"

Here is the part where Cameron got the guy out of his bed. Cameron had been in this scenario before. He knew he had a future waiting for him. Yet looking into Walker's dark eyes, Cameron's heart overrode every other part of his body. The walls he usually had in place had come tumbling down. For once, Cameron didn't have a compelling desire to run.

"I really like you, Walker." It felt nice to say what he was actually thinking.

"I like you, too." He pushed Cameron's hair out of his eyes, giving Cameron a hard-on in the process. "I don't want this to end. But I know it might. And I'm not going to worry about it."

"Let's not sully this with labels or expectations," Cameron said.

Walker held up a hand. He flashed him a sleepy grin. "Consider it unsullied."

Cameron felt relief crest inside his stomach. This must have been that living in the present thing that people championed. "I really like you, Walker."

"I like you, too."

And that was all they needed that morning.

Cameron's chest was filled with happiness at whatever this was. He rubbed his hand over Walker's chest. His skin had a natural tan that made Cameron feel translucent lying next to him. Walker's dick was branding his leg, and Cameron was in the same position.

He reached between them and stroked his hard cock. Walker moaned in his ear, which only fueled Cameron's hand to pump harder.

He turned around for better leverage. His fist moved up and down Walker's thick length. Cameron grabbed both of their dicks in his hand.

"Cameron," Walker murmured. His name had never sounded so sexy.

"Keep it down. I have a roommate," Cameron whispered. His arm flexed as he caused more friction. He rolled the cocks against each other.

"Don't stop," Walker whispered.

He didn't want to stop. He didn't want this to end.

"Fuck!" Cameron yelped out as he came. Walker wasn't far behind him. So much for keeping quiet. So much for anything he planned.

Φ

Cameron called into work sick, but Walker said he couldn't. Something about a meeting and a report. He didn't sound too thrilled about it. Walker snuck into the bathroom for a quick shower, and Cameron moseyed into the kitchen for some much needed coffee. Henry already had the pot going.

"Morning," Henry said, still sounding asleep.

"Morning. What time did you get home last night?"

"Late. Nolan and I binge-watched the new season of *Shooting Blanks*. Once you get past episode three, you realize you can't stop until you're done with the whole season." Henry peered behind Cameron at the bathroom. "I missed your escapades."

Cameron breathed a quick sigh of relief. He and Henry respected each other's boundaries as roommates and friends. He tried not to disrupt Henry's life or sleep patterns too much with his sluttery.

"So I checked, and there's one last Revolution in August, right before you move," Henry said. "We'll go out with a bang."

"Awesome." Cameron sipped his coffee.

"Get excited."

"For something in August?" Revolution was fun, but it wasn't earth-shattering. Nothing was earth-shattering in the middle of Pennsylvania.

"Be honest. You're going to miss going to Revolution."

"Maybe. There'll be other dance parties in LA. Perhaps I'll get myself invited to one of those parties at the mansion of some high-powered Holllywood bigshot and join his harem of gay ingénues."

Cameron broke through Henry's stern look. "Good. You're laughing again. There is nothing to be taken seriously about Revolution."

"Well, I still want us to go one last time."

Cameron never realized how sentimental Henry was. It was kind of annoying.

Henry peered over his shoulder to the closed bathroom door. "Is your flavor of the week almost done? I need to use the bathroom."

"Another minute or so." Cameron blushed.

"So who's in there this time? A bewildered freshman? Drunk sophomore? Senior who's been watching you from afar all these years and didn't want to graduate without letting you know how he feels?"

"All good guesses. All completely wrong." Cameron poured himself a cup of fresh coffee and smiled at the smell.

"A junior who just came back from study abroad? A transfer student still learning the Browerton ropes, one rope in particular?"

"None of the above," Walker said. He walked into the kitchen in his button-down shirt and boxer-briefs. "Mind if I have a cup of coffee?"

Henry's mouth hung open. Cameron relished his reaction. He pulled a mug from a cabinet.

"Thank you." Walker poured himself coffee and kissed Cameron on the lips.

"How was the shower? We don't have a fancy head like yours," Cameron said.

"It was fine. Do you mind that I used your pomegranate shampoo?"

"That's actually Henry's."

They looked over at Cameron's roommate. His mouth remained open, but he managed a nod of approval for the shampoo.

"I'm going to put my pants on and head to work. Good seeing you, Henry!"

Φ

The washer and dryer in Cameron's apartment complex was tucked in the deepest, darkest, dankest corner of the building's basement, behind columns of boxes and assorted junk that people kept stored away but probably forgot existed. Were Cameron a little kid, he'd be terrified to ever come down here.

He crammed as many clothes as he could into the washer, colors and whites. The larger the load, the less he had to pay for. He smiled to himself as he slid his quarters into the slots. Cameron remembered Walker at his door, and how the second he saw him, he knew he was going to jump his bones. Last night was more intense than any sex he'd had in the past. He savored each moment, like eating dinner at a fancy restaurant. Sex with feelings. Who knew?

The problem with the scary basement, aside from the obvious, was the lack of cell phone reception. When Cameron returned above-ground to his apartment, he had a voicemail waiting from his mom.

"Cam, it's Mom. Call me back please. Thanks."

Her stern tone gave him pause. He redialed immediately and leaned against his living room wall. "Mom? Are you okay?"

"Hey, Cam. Yeah, I'm fine." Her voice said otherwise. Cameron always worried about his mother as much as she worried about him. They were the only immediate family they had. They were a duo. "I saw some pictures on your Instagram. Are you dating someone?"

Cameron's mom was the only one of his friends' parents on a current social network. She was always in an in-between spot because she was usually the youngest mom, and in a way, that bonded them. She had him straight out of college. Now that he thought about it, she was less than a decade older than Walker. He didn't want to think about that again.

"Some pictures on my Instagram? That's why you left one of those nervous mom voicemails?" Cameron huffed out a breath of relief. "You know, I don't have to keep you in the loop on every aspect of my life."

"But you do, my son. I gave birth to you."

"You can't use that line everytime."

"Yes, I can. If you ever experience the pain of childbirth, you will understand. Who is that man and his son?"

That man and his son. That didn't sound like Walker and Hobie. They weren't strangers or neighborhood weirdos.

"His name is Walker, the son is Hobie. They're good people."

"Are you dating that man?" She asked. Usually, their phone calls were full of inside jokes and gossip. He overshared with his mom about boys and college life. Cameron hadn't told her a thing about Walker, but there technically wasn't much to tell up until twenty-four hours ago.

"It's complicated."

He could hear the disappointment through the phone.

"He seems a lot older than you."

"He isn't," Cameron said, and ended it at that. "We're not dating. We're just friends. I mean, we had sex, but we know that this is just a friendship thing." He wasn't sure what he was saying. None of it sounded correct. "Like I said, complicated. For now."

"It shouldn't be," she said. "Cam, you don't want to be getting involved with a family. Not now."

"I know that."

"Do you? Becase the pictures I'm seeing say otherwise. They tell me you've been spending a lot of time with this guy and his young son. Do they know you're leaving?"

"Yes!" Cameron banged his head back against the wall.

"You're a college senior. You're supposed to be having fun, screwing around. And yes, I'm probably the only mother telling her son to do that, but I settled down with your father when I was your age. I didn't get to experience this freedom, and I realize how precious it is. You only get this time in your life once. Don't squander it trying to play stepfather."

"But what if I like him?" Cameron blurted out. That must be one of those speaking from the heart moments.

"You're young, Cam. He's sweeping you off your feet."

"He is not. He's a horrible dancer." They hadn't gone on any real dates. All this just...happened. Like losing weight. One day, the jeans weren't as snug.

"I can hear you smiling through the phone," she said. Cameron checked out his reflection in the TV. Yep, he was. Like a fool. "Are you still moving to LA after graduation?"

"Of course!"

"Good. I don't want him to talk you out of going. This has been your dream. There have been countless men and women before you who've given up their dream at the last minute to chase something foolish." The weight of her words hit Cameron.

"I know," he said softly. "Just trust me, Mom."

CHAPTER
TWENTY-TWO

Walker

Despite running on minimal sleep, Walker bopped along at work. He scanned those spreadsheets and worked on those reports with glee. Not like anyone could notice. Not like people around here looked up from their own computers ever. He enjoyed the personal moment.

"Tell me everything," Lucy said the second he came into the breakroom for coffee, almost like she was waiting to pounce.

"About the Radiance consumer reporting?"

"No, about the sweet, sweet loving you got."

Walker's coffee nearly dropped out of his hands. Lucy was a mother of four. She went to church regularly.

"Yeah, that's right," she said with a rueful smile. "I can tell."

"Are my cheeks still flush?"

"Worse. You were smiling while reading an email from Patricia."

Walker told Lucy the whole story of his night. He didn't dish every detail. He doubted she could really handle that. Her eyes lit up as she lived vicariously through his experience.

"Holy shit." She leaned back in the creaky breakroom chair. "I need a cigarette."

Walker kept picturing Cameron's face, right up against his, as everything between them connected. Even though his feet hung off Cameron's bed and the sheets were barely Target-quality compared to his threadcount, he slept like a baby. And he got to wake up next to Cameron. That was the best part and what he remembered most from all of his experiences with Cameron. Those first few moments when Cameron was natural and exposed, before he suited up with his snark and the armor of who he was trying to be.

"Is this…this can't work, can it?" he asked.

"Sounds like it's working."

Walker smiled, mostly to humor her. He felt unease churn in his stomach.

"Stop that," Lucy said.

"Stop what?"

"What are you thinking?" She asked in a concerned tone.

He couldn't get anything past her. Lucy had a high-strength bullshit detector, honed from having to deal with four teenagers. She took the least amount of crap from the Radiance client.

She nodded at him to sit at a corner table. They had the break room to themselves, as they learned to hit it between coffee rushes.

"You like him," she said. It wasn't even a question.

"We crossed a line last night." He wasn't just talking about sex. "Lucy, we can't do this. He's fifteen years younger than me. I can't be falling for the guy."

"Enough!" she snapped. Walker inched back in his chair. "You've been mentioning his age ever since you first met him. My husband is seven years older than me, and we've been going strong for decades. Age is just a number, as long as that number is above eighteen."

"Which it is. It most definitely is."

"Then stop making it into such a big deal. Is he a good guy?"

Walker nodded.

"And you care about him?"

Walker nodded again.

Lucy rubbed his hand with that perfect amout of motherly warmth. "Then that's all that matters."

And Walker was smiling again, really smiling. His unease turned to butterflies in his stomach. He liked a guy who liked him back. It was such a simple concept, but so hard to find.

Φ

Walker let himself think about Cameron for the rest of the day. He dared to imagine them going on dates, meeting his friends and family, and having more sex again. It had been a while, a long while, since Walker had gotten any. When he drove past Browerton's campus, he kept his eyes peeled for Cameron, but no luck.

Walker bounded up the steps and rang the doorbell. He got to see Cameron this morning and now Hobie tonight. This could rank as one of his best days ever.

"Ron, my man! How's is going?"

Ron didn't know how to respond to such enthusiasm. "Hobie's just putting on his shoes."

"Fantastic!"

Walker crouched down and threw his arms wide open. Hobie's walk turned into a gallop as he sped straight into his father's hug. Walker loved how fresh his skin smelled, and it wasn't because of whatever organic soap Doug had him using. Speaking of Doug, he peered down at the twosome from the doorway.

"Thanks for having him ready on time," Walker said.

"Right." Doug eyed him suspiciously. "You seem very upbeat."

"I'm happy to see my son."

Doug hid an obvious frown and hung by the door. Walker wondered if Doug could tell that he'd been with Cameron. He probably knew him better than Lucy did. Well, Doug had Ron and his striped, lumpy sweater so he shouldn't be so unhappy.

"They scheduled Hobie's first soccer game," Doug said. "Are you on the email list?"

"Can you add me?" That stuff always went to Doug, but Walker was tired of having Doug be a conduit to his son's social life. "Actually, I'll get on myself."

"Try not to unleash your...friend on the instructors like at gymnastics."

"Cheer up, Doug," Walker said with a delightful grin. "We'll see you in two days."

When they got to the car, Hobie tugged on his dad's sleeve. "Dad, I have an awesome idea!"

Walker buckled him into the car seat, then buckled himself in, and they were off for some glorious father-son time.

"What's this glorious idea, Hobie?"

"A giant Thanksgiving!"

"In April?" Walker cocked an eyebrow at his son through the rearview mirror.

"No, Dad! Thanksgiving's in November. But we can have a giant Thanksgiving. We'll make pumpkin pie and stuffing."

"Together?" Walker loved playing along. "In the same pie?"

"Yuck! Dad, it's going to be great. We're going to make all this food."

"You mean I'm going to make all this food."

Hobie kept going, not answering any pesky logistics questions. "And we'll invite Cameron and his friends and make a turkey robot for Beerza."

Walker looked in the rearview mirror again. Hobie was glowing from his idea. He took a deep breath.

"Hobie, I don't think Cameron will be able to make it. You know, he has a family of his own."

"We can invite them, too."

"They live in Ohio. Remember I showed you where Ohio was on that life-size map?" They had hopped around a rug of the United States at a kid's store. Hobie bragged afterward that he visited all fifty states.

"Aren't they going to come here to see Cameron?"

"Cameron won't be here."

"But he lives here!" Hobie said.

"Not all the time." Walker pulled over to the side of the road. He turned to face his son. "Remember when we walked through that campus in town, and I told you that it's a sleepaway school for boys and girls to get really smart? Cameron is a student there, but this school only lasts for four years. Would you want your school to last forever?"

Hobie shrugged. His classes involved coloring and recess. That probably sounded awesome.

"This is Cameron's last year at the sleepaway school. In June, he's going to graduate and move to California. I don't know if he'll be able to come back to celebrate Thanksgiving with us."

Walker watched most of this sink in for Hobie.

"California is all the way on the other side of the rug," he said.

"I know." Walker hated this, hated seeing the look on his son's face. He'd take another year of changing diapers not to have to see this. "But actually, Cameron and his friends did say something to me about having Thanksgiving with us. You know, I think they will be here."

"They did?"

"They did! Now, I don't know if it's for sure. Thanksgiving is so far away. So we'll see what happens, okay?" Walker patted his son's leg, and turned it into a tickle. Hobie had no choice but to laugh, and that seemed to do the trick to lift the mood of the car.

Walker took him to a park to play on the swings. It was a warm, sunny day. It was actually spring, not just post-winter. Walker hoped this made Hobie forget all about Thanksgiving for a long while, and himself forget that he just outright lied to his son.

CHAPTER
TWENTY-THREE

Cameron

It had been two whole days since Cameron had seen Walker, and like an addict, he was starting to itch. He didn't know what was going on with him. Maybe there was some type of addictive chemical on Walker's lips, or other places. Ever since they had sex, Cameron couldn't stop thinking about him. And it was more than the usual daydreams here and there about Walker's eyes and smile. No, this was something deeper. Something embedded into his mind.

Walker wasn't making things easier by not coming into Starbucks for his usual coffee this week. Cameron feared that Walker was avoiding him. Perhaps it was karma for all the guys whose text messages he never returned after sex. He doubted the Puritans ever had to deal with this type of tension.

The last part of his shift was the worst. All the suits were already in their offices doing things that required wearing a suit. The morning rush was over. That gave

Cameron more time to think about the amazing sex he and Walker had, but the even more amazing morning waking up together. Cameron seemed to enjoy those times more than when they were at their hottest and heaviest. He really needed to pull himself together.

His brain seemed to be on a different wavelength, though, because it carried him to the west building instead of toward campus. He marveled at how office-like these office buildings were. All neutral colors and all business. Cameron felt his soul get crushed just a little.

Walker's floor was even worse. White walls, white fluorescent lighting, white rows of tables with computers. Yet despite all the white, it seemed nothing like heaven. More like a waiting room. There must have been well over 100 people on this floor, but you could hear a pin drop. Cameron didn't know a room full of so many people could be so silent.

"Cameron?" Walker approached him, his arms full of files and papers.

Cameron wanted to stare at that face for hours, but no. He had his own business to attend to in this office. He just couldn't remember what it was.

"How are things?" Cameron asked.

"Good."

"That's good." Cameron nodded. Quiet office people were looking at him. "That's grand, actually. I'm just wondering why you haven't been coming into Starbucks this week. My boss sent me up here to ask you. Because you're such a loyal customer, and he was worried that you suddenly didn't want to drink Starbucks anymore. Or that you found another Starbucks to frequent. And, you know, that would suck. Because of the loyalty aspect."

"I'm sorry if your boss was worried. We've been having early meetings here, and they've been bringing in breakfast. And Starbucks."

"My Starbucks?"

"I, I don't know. A Starbucks. Don't worry. I still want to frequent your Starbucks."

"Now is not the time for a sexual metaphor, Walker."

Walker blushed. He motioned for Cameron to follow him down the hall, past a row of cramped offices that overlooked other office buildings. A chubby Latina woman gave Cameron a goofy smile. They wound up in a conference room that had one wall painted cerulean to give it character, even though it was still just a conference room.

Walker shut the door. "What's going on?"

"I haven't heard from you all week. We could've hung out." Cameron couldn't get over how he sounded, but the words wouldn't stop. "I miss...ed seeing your face."

"I'm sorry. I've had Hobie this week, and those early meetings. And I didn't really know proper etiquette in this situation. It's been a while since I, well since I've been in this position." Walker stepped closer, and Cameron was able to smell him again and get a good whiff this time. That cologne and shaving cream. Cameron was going to melt.

"Well, I've never been in this position," Cameron said. He thought about it a little more, and yeah, still true. "I've never been in a relationship."

"So, we're in a relationship now?" Walker crossed his arms.

"No, I mean...we're hanging out together. You know, a lot. And I didn't kick you out of bed the morning after we slept together, which is something. And...shit. I think we're in a relationship." Now Cameron was speechless. *So that was how it happened? Relationships: the ultimate sneak attack.*

"For the record," Walker said, threading his fingers through Cameron's. "I missed you, too."

Cameron tilted his head back for a kiss. When their lips met, all the confusion and dumbfoundness that mashed around in Cameron's head vanished. Everything seemed clear.

He pulled Walker closer and felt the erection developing in his pants.

"Since we have the conference room to ourselves," Cameron said. His fingers danced on Walker's belt buckle.

Walker pulled away and pointed behind him at the clear glass wall that looked out on rows of desks. Some people looked up from their computers to gawk.

"Tonight," Walker whispered into his ear. Cameron could've come right then and there.

Φ

When Cameron arrived at Walker's condo, he could smell the food through the door. A warm pot roast marinating in the oven and some type of garlic mashed potato waited for him.

"Perfect timing!" Walker said as he took Cameron's coat. "The pot roast is just about done."

"Great. It smells wonderful." Cameron walked down the familiar hall.

"And the mashed potatoes came out really well."

"Awesome." And strolled into Walker's bedroom.

"Do you want a glass of wine?"

"No thanks." Cameron stripped off his shirt and unbuttoned his pants.

"I have beer if you want," Walker called from the kitchen.

"I'll pass." Cameron chucked his boxer-briefs onto the floor and stretched out across the bed. He gazed at his naked self.

It took Walker a few seconds to realize that Cameron wasn't coming back into the living room. He stopped at the entrance to his bedroom.

"Naked Twister time?" Walker asked.

"Naked Twister time."

The smile on Walker's face made him seem twenty-two again.

"Did you make sure to turn off the oven?" Cameron asked politely, stroking himself.

Walker turned into the Tazmanian Devil of nakedness, yanking off all his clothes in a whirr and climbing on top of Cameron. He was covered by Walker's warmth and loved the feeling of those hands exploring every part of him. They were doing the same things that Cameron had done with other guys, but something about being with Walker brought this to a higher level.

Probably that whole feelings-and-relationship thing.

Walker shifted further south and took Cameron's raging erection in his hot mouth. Cameron grabbed onto the worth-every-penny bedding. Walker's beard rubbed against Cameron's thighs. He watched Walker bob up and down as the room, the earth, the entire universe spun like a kaleidoscope. Just as Cameron thought he was about to shoot, Walker's mouth was off him.

He stumbled over to the closet. Cameron gave him a look through the mirror.

"I'm not leaving condoms and lube in a nightstand drawer that my six-year-old son can access."

"Fine with me." Cameron happily stared at Walker's tight ass and broad back as he pulled the necessary supplies from high up in the closet. Even just being away from him for these few seconds was making Cameron go into withdrawal. He didn't know how he made it two days. And then he wondered how he was going to make it once he moved to LA.

The thought was shuffled away as soon as Walker tugged Cameron to the edge of the bed and threw his legs over one shoulder. Cameron exhaled as Walker's thick cock slid inside him. Lust filled Walker's eyes, and it sure as hell filled Cameron's, too. His bicep bulged against Cameron's legs as he squeezed them harder and rammed into Cameron's opening.

And then they did something that Cameron had never done with anyone else during sex. They locked eyes, really locked eyes. Cameron could hear the clink of the lock locking and being unable to tear himself away. He didn't want to.

"Fuck!" Walker was getting close, Cameron could tell. And that made him get close. And it seemed like Walker could sense that he was getting close which made him get even closer.

"Fuck!" Cameron yelled. "Don't stop!"

Walker didn't. He spread Cameron's legs and plunged in even deeper, sending Cameron's back arching up in pleasure.

Cameron heaved in air but couldn't catch his breath. His heart raced as he hurtled toward an orgasm. Walker pulled out and stroked their cocks together, and they both emptied out across Cameron's chest.

Walker covered Cameron again, giving him warmth. Cameron kissed him softly, lips only. He ran a hand through Walker's beard. Words hung on his tongue. Big words.

But he wouldn't let himself say them. That was the orgasm talking, he thought.

Φ

Cameron's stomach rumbled with hunger as he showered. He hoped the pot roast and mashed potatoes didn't get too cold. They sounded so good right now.

"Your phone's been buzzing like crazy," Walker said as Cameron changed.

"Must be all my other boyfriends wondering where I am."

"Tell them to come over. I made way too much food."

Cameron pulled on his jeans and dug out his phone from the pocket. Two missed calls from a 310 area code. "That's Los Angeles," he said.

He dialed back the number.

"Arthur Brandt's office," an assistant said.

Cameron mouth went dry. He made sure he was dressed before continuing. "Hi. This is Cameron Buckley. I saw two missed calls—"

"One moment. I'll put you through. Arthur? You have Cameron Buckley."

"Cameron!" Arthur said. "What's up?"

"Not much. Just doing my thing, I guess." He didn't know how he should've answered that. He needed to be on.

"I have good news. The *Makeshift Coriander* script is close to being greenlit. We're going to make offers to some top actresses, one of whom was recently nominated for an Oscar."

"That's awesome!"

"Hopefully you'll be here as we put the movie into production."

"What?"

"I want you to be my new assistant."

Cameron sat on the bed. Wait, he was already sitting on the bed. His heart might have stopped beating. Nope, still ticking away.

"My old assistant got promoted to manager, and the two assistants I've had to replace him have been total shit. Millennials. No offense."

"None taken."

"Listen, I know you're super green, but I could tell by talking to you that you're smart, you're passionate, and you know your shit."

"Yes." Cameron didn't need to think on this. He thought it would take weeks or months of being in LA to become a development assistant at a hot network. The perfect job was thrown into his lap. "I'll be moving out to LA in September when my lease is up."

"September's not gonna work for me, dude. I need you to start ASAP."

"When you say ASAP, how soon is that? Tomorrow?"

"Ideally, yes. But I know that's not gonna work for you. I was able to get you two weeks."

"Two weeks? Arthur, please understand, I have a lease and classes and graduation and…" And a guy cooking him pot roast and mashed potatoes.

"I get it, Cameron. But you can work this all out. You don't need to walk in order to get your degree. Talk with your professors. Mackey will be cool with it. Listen, I'm going out on a limb vouching for you with HR. This is an amazing opportunity, and jobs like these don't open up that frequently."

"I know." Cameron tried to process this. It was like a rush of blood to the head.

"There is one thing. The studio has a policy in place that employees cannot work on side projects like films or screenplays. The president wants everyone to be completely focused on Mobius's projects. Plus it's a conflict of interest. If we are developinging a script that's happens to be similar to yours, it could open us up to lawsuits."

"I get it." Cameron sort of did. He'd heard about lawsuits in Hollywood about stolen ideas. Mobius didn't want the headache. The people working there, like Arthur, wanted to be there. They wanted to develop movies. *I do, too*, he told himself.

"There are assistants who've left Mobius and gotten agents on their own. They just couldn't do it while employed. But you seemed interested in development when we spoke. You knew your shit."

"Thanks."

"So, are you in or out?"

Cameron stared at himself in the mirror, deep in conversation with the voices in his head. He pictured himself in an office reading scripts, working with

Hollywood executives, watching scripts turn into actual movies that his friends and his mom and the people in high school he didn't talk to anymore could see in actual theaters.

"I'm in."

"Excellent!"

Arthur Brandt went on to say how excited he was to work with Cameron and how HR would be following up with him, but it was all white noise. Cameron looked into the mirror again and saw Walker standing by the door.

CHAPTER TWENTY-FOUR

Walker

"Walker, are you ready?"

Patricia scrolled through the Powerpoint presentation for the hundredth time. She read over each word carefully, as if their jobs depended on it. Well, they did. Walker and Lucy sat across from her, watching her pick apart their work.

"On slide eight, can you put the period inside the quotation marks? Actually, you know what? I'll just do it right now." Patricia peered at her screen. Her nose almost touched the glass. "I think the two boxes on this slide aren't the same size. The one on the left is a touch wider. Can you look into that?"

"Sure thing." Walker scribbled her comment in his notebook. His hand seemed to give up halfway through, like what was the point in writing or doing anything anymore.

A clean break.

Walker bristled at the phrase. Bones had a clean break, but they were still broken. You still did something to get them damaged.

"And Walker, you've triple-checked these spend and TRP numbers?"

"Oh, I only double-checked," he said as a joke. Patricia didn't find it funny.

"Can you please check one more time? We need this to be perfect."

Really? You don't say. As if that weren't the most obvious thing on the fucking planet.

"Okay. I will."

It wouldn't do any good. He could look at numbers all day today, but he wouldn't be able to fix anything or find any problems. Everything in his eye line was out of focus, all because of the clean break.

Walker didn't hear most of the conversation, just the "two weeks" part. Then Cameron looked at him through the mirror like a vision of death.

He knew this day was coming. Cameron always had LA on his mind. That was the place he was headed. But he thought they had more time than two weeks. Cameron said he couldn't push this Arthur guy, that he had to start immediately. Walker called bullshit. If they really wanted him, they would've worked with him. They would've let him attend his own damn graduation.

"I have to take this job. You know that."

"You don't have to take the first job you're offered. That's what I did with Berkwell."

"But this is an amazing opportunity."

"Is it? You're just going to be fetching coffee and answering someone's phone."

"It's starting at the bottom, learning the business from the ground up."

Walker remained by the door. A part of him saw relief in Cameron. Things were getting too serious between them, and this was the perfect chance to run.

"So do you still want dinner?" Walker asked, like an idiot.

"Can we talk about this?" Cameron got up and walked toward him. A smile quirked on his face. "I'm sorry. I'm excited. I'm…confused about this," he pointed at both of them. "But I'm excited. Can you please be just a little happy for me? This shouldn't be some big surprise to you. You knew from the start what my plans were."

"Your plans were to move in September, not April."

"I wasn't expecting this."

"Are you talking about the job or us?" Walker asked. He felt his insides turning to rocks. It was all about staying strong. He wished they could go back a half-hour when things were perfect.

"Let's just have dinner, okay?"

"Lucy, on this category slide, can you find a better way to phrase our market share situation? I don't want us to say that we've lost market share. We need to reframe it in a more positive way. 'The market has continued to expand as new competitors enter the field, diluting market share for all established players.' Something like that."

"Will do!" Lucy said. She gave Walker a supportive smile. He hadn't told her the news yet, but she knew how to read him.

"Oh, wait just one minute." Patricia ran her finger across the screen. "Our main competitors haven't lost share. How come they've kept share or even gained it, and we've lost it?" Patricia sighed for all to hear. "This is a major issue. The client is going to notice this the second we get to this slide. Walker, why wasn't this raised to my attention?"

"You knew that we'd been losing market share," he said. "Hence being put up for review."

"It looks so drastic on this chart."

"We can take out the chart."

"We need better reasoning for this disparity." She kept reading the slide over and over.

Lucy handed over a copy of our latest media plan. "We went dark last fall when the client cut our budget. Not running advertising for three months surely helped our competitors."

"I guess that's a start."

"I guess this is the end," Cameron had said. He hadn't touched his pot roast. Neither had Walker. This was the first thing either of them had said during dinner, and the words sliced through the silence.

"The end?" Walker shot back reflexively. "We still have two weeks."

"It's just going to be harder stretching it out. We need a clean break."

"What does that mean?" Walker took a healthy drink from his wine glass.

"I'm going to get my things together and go. And that will be that."

"Just like that? You're going to throw away these last few weeks."

"I'm not throwing them away. You don't think this is hard for me? It's hard, Walker. I think we should rip the Band-Aid off now, like you said."

Before you kissed me and changed everything! He had wanted to yell.

"It will hurt now, but it will save us all this anguish and heartache down the road. I mean, do you think we're going to do long-distance and Skype calls, and then you and Hobie can visit me during summer vacation? Let's be adults about this, Walker."

"Running away isn't the adult thing."

"I'm not running!"

"Two seconds after the condom came off, you had a job in place and said we had to end things."

Cameron pursed his lips. Direct hit. But Walker didn't feel any victory.

"You don't think you could find another entry level assistant job in September? You're willing to drop everything for this?"

"If I turn this opportunity down, I might not have another."

"And if you keep pushing people away, they won't come back."

Cameron stood up and washed off his plate in the sink. The clanging of the plate and silverware in the sink rang in Walker's ears. Cameron shoved his stuff into his backpack. Walker remained at the table. Even when Cameron opened the front door, Walker didn't move.

"Walker." Cameron waited at the front door. Walker knew he was waiting for a final hug. He was the adult here. He had to bring the civility, but he couldn't move from his chair.

"A clean break, right?" Walker said.

Cameron shut the door behind him. He closed it gently, but it slammed in Walker's mind.

"Any insight, Walker?"

Patricia and Lucy were looking at him. She still had that market share slide open on her screen. It was just numbers. Stupid, worthless numbers.

"Their creative fucking sucks," Walker said.

Patricia scooted back in her chair. "Excuse me?"

"That's why Radiance has lost market share. We've put their ads on the best TV shows and most-read magazines. But their advertising sucks. And their product sucks. I've read customer forums. People hate their product. They say it smells weird and is overpriced. Any losses that they've incurred are not our fault."

"Well, we can't tell them that, for obvious reasons," Patricia said.

"Why not? Maybe they'll appreciate honesty. It would save us the trouble of jumping through all of these hoops while their creative agency gets to sit back and relax." Walker tossed his notebook on the floor and walked around Patricia's office. "I need to stand up. I sit all day. I need to stand."

"Okay." Patricia was now treating him like a mental patient. He just wanted to stretch his legs.

"Maybe we should cut ties with Radiance. They're obviously looking for miracle workers. Once the numbers stop going in their favor, they decided to dump us. They aren't worth the trouble. Give them a fucking clean break."

"If that happens, we lose our jobs." Patricia stood up and pressed her hands onto her desk, staring him down. "Yes, clients are a pain in the ass. I'm not going to deny that. But that's the job."

Walker nodded and slumped back into his chair. For a second, he thought things would actually change. But this was like any other day for him. Just another blip. "Yep. That's the job."

CHAPTER TWENTY-FIVE

Cameron

Not even five minutes after Cameron officially accepted the job, Arthur emailed over a bunch of scripts for Cameron to read. Arthur's email was blowing up with agents wanting to get their clients in to pitch their scripts, and Cameron had to read through their samples to determine which ones were worth Arthur's valuable time. Cameron had to write coverage on all these scripts, which was basically a synopsis of the script and his thoughts on the writing.

One person was excited about his new job. His mom thought it sounded great, especially the part about him having a regular paycheck and benefits. Cameron's mom always acted supportive of his Hollywood dreams, but he knew that "My son the Hollywood film executive" had a better ring to it than "My son the aspiring screenwriter."

As if Cameron didn't have enough to do in these next two weeks. He took out his notebook and made a fresh, accelerated To-Do list.

1. Confirm with Porter and Grayson that I can move in early.
2. Go back home, pick up grandpa's beat-up Suburu.
3. Sell the rest of my furniture or give it away
4. Put up posting for subletter
5. Say goodbye to friends

There was one glaring omission from his list.
Walker.

Cameron hated how he left things between them, but he knew eventually they would all get over it. The wounds were fresh, but they would heal. That's what Cameron told himself about good-byes. He remembered saying good-bye to friends in high school and his mom when he left for Browerton. It was so tough. So many memories to look back on. Everything was so final and momentous. *This is the last lunch we'll ever have together. This is the last time I'll ever enter the front doors of high school. This is the final time Mom and I will eat breakfast together before school.* But once Cameron left, he didn't remember those times. He didn't look back fondly on the last this or last that. He remembered the normal, everyday times. As he began going through his closet to throw out things, he'd find a T-shirt he remembered wearing to a party once, or a wristband from a bar. Those were the times he would cherish. Not a crying hug. Goodbyes forced things to get serious, but they never withstood the test of time. Weren't the final episodes of most TV shows the worst anyway?

He had on an episode of *Modern Family*, the early seasons, in the background as he continued going through his stuff. He took pictures of things with sentimental value but no actual value, like a menu of Carmine's Pizza, which he and his freshmen roommates used to order from all the time. Two large trash bags were almost full, packed with old notebooks and papers and clothes that he wouldn't need in LA. A bag of bulky sweaters and jackets were heading to Goodwill.

The doorbell rang. Before he could stand up, the person pounded at the door. Cameron was dealing with one determined Craigslist buyer.

"Hi—"

But it wasn't a buyer for his dresser.

"I don't want us to do a clean break." Walker closed the door and marched into the living room, pacing around the coffee table. "I know it's going to be hard, but I need more time. I can't just pretend like I never met you."

Cameron's heart surged just getting to be in the same room again with Walker.

"I know it's abrupt," Cameron said. "But good-byes suck."

"Then let's not think of it like a good-bye. Let's not spend two weeks sending you off on a farewell tour."

"Good. Because I don't want that."

"I know. Those are so awkward. And you're going to do that with all of your other friends whether you want to or not."

"Henry wants us to do one last pub trivia." Cameron tried to talk him out of it. *We're roommates! We'll see each plenty of other times.* He was busy packing and getting ready for his trip. He didn't want to take a whole night for this when they had plenty of pub trivia memories already.

"Let's not do that to each other. I know you, Cameron. You hate good-byes. So let's just have this be two normal weeks. Normalish. I want us to go out on a high note." Walker pulled Cameron into a kiss. It would take Cameron some time to get over not being kissed like that again.

"Are you sure about this?" Cameron asked before kissing Walker again.

"Not entirely." Walker pecked his lips. "But I can't spend these next two weeks driving past Browerton, going to work, knowing that you're in the same town as me and I can't see you."

"What about Hobie? I keep picturing him running after my car, screaming my name, tears running down his puffy face."

"Are you picturing the scene from *Hope Floats*?"

"Maybe a little." Cameron kissed his nose.

"I'll have a talk with him."

"He'll probably forget all about me by the fall," Cameron said as a relief but really, the thought chilled him. "I'm still leaving in two weeks."

"I know."

"And we probably aren't going to do long distance. I mean, it's just not feasible."

"I know."

"This is still going to be tough in two weeks."

"Let's worry about that in two weeks then." Walker pushed them over to the couch. He cupped Cameron's cheek. They made out softly, slowly, savoring the small bits of time they had left. "We'll cry about it later."

Cameron wasn't sure if this was a good idea, but he was positive that he loved seeing Walker in front of him.

Maybe he could make an exception to his good-bye rule. Because technically, this wouldn't be a goodbye.

"So we're going to do an *Everybody Loves Raymond*," Cameron said.

"Huh?"

"*Everybody Loves Raymond*, the sitcom from the 2000s."

Walker rolled off Cameron. "Please tell me I'm not Brad Garrett in this scenario."

"They didn't do a 'final' episode. Their last episode was a normal, run-of-the-mill *Raymond*. No big changes. No characters moving or getting married or having babies. They didn't want to get sentimental and sappy."

"So we're *Everybody Loves Raymond*?"

Cameron nodded, proud of his off-the-cuff TV metaphors. He pounced on his boyfriend, for two more weeks anyway. His hands massaged Walker's chest and traveled south.

Then the doorbell rang again. No door pounding this time.

"Crap."

"Who is that?" Walker asked.

"This guy buying my bedroom furniture off Craigslist."

"You're selling everything?" Walker sat up.

"My life is a firesale." Cameron shrugged. He kissed Walker's ear. "Maybe we can pick up once he leaves."

"I need to get home. And anyway, you got me thinking about Doris Roberts now, so I doubt I'll get an erection for the rest of the night."

Φ

Professor Mackey smiled at her desk and motioned for Cameron to come inside her office. She placed her red pen atop her piles of papers. Other students' scripts awaited feedback.

"I have some good news." Cameron told her about the job and the quick turnaround.

"Cameron, that's great!" She stood up and gave him a hug, but Cameron sensed she wasn't 100 percent on board. He felt a part of her hold back.

"How will it work with me missing the last few weeks of class?"

"The only thing left is your final script. I can accept it via email. I'm looking forward to reading it." She sat back down in her chair and tapped the pile of papers on her desk. "Intro to Screenwriting."

"I'm afraid to ask what reading all those are like. I have to write coverage for Arthur, but at least I can be brutally honest in my opinion."

The edges of her mouth crinkled with laughter. "It can be a challenge," she said diplomatically. "But every once in a while, I come across a writer with raw talent, and that makes the job all worth it."

He still couldn't fully accept that she was talking about him. He never stopped being scared to show someone his writing. A part of him kept thinking it was a fluke, and he wondered if all writers felt that way.

"You'll see it when you read more scripts for him," she said. "You'll read some junk, a lot of stuff that's fine and that works, and then a few scripts that grab you and announce in big letters that you're reading good writing. You'll know it. A gut feeling, and it'll light you up inside."

There was no way she was still talking about him, he thought. She was a professional screenwriter who knew other professional screenwriters. She knew actual good writing. Cameron only managed to beat very low expectations.

Cameron wiggled in his chair. "I don't know how much writing I'll be doing. Mobius has this policy where employees can't write on the side. They can't pursue agents while working there."

She cocked her head to the side. "Wow. Things have gotten stricter since I was in the business. Everyone hates when their assistant wants to write or act because they'll never be as committed to the job, but I haven't heard of a studio doing this. How can they enforce a No Writing rule? Will they bug your apartment?"

Cameron wasn't sure, but he wasn't going to play chicken with a multi-billion-dollar company.

Mackey laughed at the rule. "Don't worry about it. You just keep working on your samples on your own time."

"I won't have time to write. Arthur was saying that it's more than a full-time job. The assistant tasks, the script reading, the networking. I have to focus on those things."

"Don't take your eye off the bigger picture," she said.

Ever since he spoke to Arthur, Cameron had been thinking about working on a studio lot and being right in the thick of the movie business. Their bigger pictures looked different.

"I don't know. Development seems interesting, and I'd get to work with writers."

"Or you can be one."

Cameron laughed at the thought of trying to make it as a writer in Hollywood. Writing in Starbucks. Peddling his scripts to anyone who will read. Hanging your career hopes on luck.

"No offense, Professor Mackey, but you read a few script assignments of mine. I don't think that means I should try to make a living at it."

"Cameron, I've read a lot of assignments over my decade as a professor. I've waded through a lot of shit, to be quite honest. I know when I see raw talent." Mackey leaned back in her chair and examined Cameron. He felt the hot interrogation lights. "Where is this coming from? You were so excited about screenwriting. Don't let Arthur scare you."

"He's not."

"If you want to write, you should write. Maybe this isn't the right opportunity for you."

Cameron was tired of other people thinking they knew what was best for him. He was running to something, not away. "Development could be a lot of fun. Arthur really enjoys it. It sounds cool."

"Why do you want to spend your life critiquing other people's work rather than working on your own?"

Cameron felt his ears getting red. "Like you?"

Mackey bolted out of her chair and sat at the edge of her desk. He had never seen her this animated. Her air of cool thinned out. "People in development look cool. They have expense accounts, fancy offices, and the ability to say yes or no. But deep down, they're all people who don't have the power to create. The good ones actually like working with writers and producers, and they know how to nurture talent, but most of them are wannabes. Too scared to make the leap, or they inherently knew that they weren't good enough. You don't want to turn into that."

Cameron did the obligatory head nod whenever adults went off on one of their weird theories. Perhaps Mackey was jealous that he was moving to LA, and she was regretting her decision to leave the game for teaching in Pennsylvania.

"It's your choice, and development can be an exciting area of the business." Mackey looked him square in the eye. He gulped back a lump. "But don't stop writing, Cameron."

CHAPTER TWENTY-SIX

Walker

"Think of it as one long party. We're going to send off Cameron in style, you know? Remember that huge party we had for your Aunt Lara when she moved all the way to England? There was cake, and music, and you got to play Frisbee with your cousins in her backyard."

Hobie blinked at him and tried to pick his nose. Walker pulled his fingers away.

"It's going to be fun! And yeah, we'll be sad to see him go, but we're going to have such a good time, too."

"What's an assistant?" Hobie asked.

"It's someone who organizes an important person's life," Walker said, confusing him even more. "It's an important job."

"How long is he going to be on the other side of the rug?"

Walker didn't have the heart to say forever. Forever sounded like a black hole of time. "For a long time."

Hobie's face sank like the Titanic. That was a double-edged sword with kids. Their feelings were always easy to read.

"He doesn't want to stay here?"

"No. He's crazy, right?" Walker elbowed him, but Hobie wasn't laughing. "California has the ocean."

"There are sharks in the ocean!"

"We'll tell him to be careful before he leaves."

Hobie rolled a Lego piece around in his hand. "Why does Cameron want to go so far away?"

"Because he wants to pursue his dream."

"What does that mean?"

Walker tried to figure out an explanation. He wrapped his arm around Hobie and pulled him close. "One day, when you're older, you're going to find something in this world that gives you more happiness than anything else you could imagine. More than a thousand birthday cakes. It'll light you up inside and make you excited to wake up in the morning. How do you feel when you play with Legos?"

"I love it."

"You love playing with Legos more than anything. What if you could play with Legos all day? Would you move far away to do it?"

Hobie stared at the ceiling, deep in thought. His lips squiggled around. "I guess so. As long as I had ice cream breaks, too."

"Then that's your dream. That's what Cameron's doing. He has a chance to play with Legos all day long, by the ocean."

"Away from the sharks?"

"Far away from the sharks. He wishes he didn't have to move to California to play Legos, but we'll all still be

friends. We can talk on the phone or Skype with him."
Walker doubted that would happen. Cameron seemed like
a person who truly left a place. "What do you think?"

Hobie acted like he understood, but how could he
make sense of all this? *Welcome to growing up,* Walker
thought.

"What's your dream?" Hobie asked him.

Walker didn't have the heart to feed him bullshit.
What a simple, but loaded question. That's how kids
operated. He kissed his son on the head and breathed in his
fresh smell. "You, kiddo. You're my dream."

Φ

Although he'd promised Cameron not to treat these
next two weeks like a good-bye tour, he couldn't help
getting sentimental. At least this wasn't too overt. They
were watching *The Incredibles* and eating pizza.

Hobie mimicked the action happening on screen with
his Legos. He had trotted out his creations to the living
room. Lego spaceships swooped through the air.

"Hey Cameron, want to help Monte save King
Dandelion from Smort? Smort planned his attack to be the
new King Dandelion." Hobie handed Cameron one of his
ships, but Cameron was glued to his iPad reading yet
another script.

Walker nudged him, breaking him from his trance.

"I'm going to watch you play, Hobie. Okay? I have all
this homework to do. Isn't homework the worst?"

"For homework, my teacher had us draw a picture of
our favorite stuffed animal."

"Well, trust me kid. It's all downhill from there." And

back Cameron went to his iPad. He scribbled notes in his notebook. Walker couldn't decipher them.

"Are you even watching the movie?" Hobie asked him.

"Yep."

Walker put a hand over the iPad. "Could you maybe do your reading later?"

"I have a buttload of scripts to read and write coverage on for Arthur."

"Your job hasn't started yet."

"It kinda has."

"Are you getting paid to do all this reading?"

Cameron shook his head in a very "Parents just don't understand" way. "That's not how it works."

"How much is a buttload?" Hobie giggled because no matter what the answer was, he got to say butt.

Walker pointed at the TV. "Your favorite part's coming up." Hobie turned away from them. "Tell him you'll start on this once you get out there."

"He's taking a chance on me. I need to prove myself."

"Can you prove yourself tomorrow?" This was not how it was supposed to go in Walker's head. They were supposed to have a great two weeks, but it seemed like Cameron was already in Los Angeles.

"Let me just finish this script." Cameron rubbed his leg, but it didn't feel like a sweet gesture.

Walker put his arm around Cameron, but Cameron didn't shift any closer to him. He was deep in some crappy script.

"Hey Cameron, watch this!"

"I'm watching," Cameron said without looking up, almost as if he were talking in his sleep.

Hobie *tap-tap-tap-tapped* at Cameron's knee.

"I'm watching."

"No, you're not." More tapping. Hobie's eyes bulged into freakish globes as he stared at Cameron. Walker enjoyed his son doing that to someone else for a change.

"Just give me one second, Hobie."

"One second's up."

"Then I need 133 seconds."

"I can't count that high up. You gotta see this, Cameron!" His tapping got more desperate.

Walker knew Cameron was waiting for him to jump in and pull the ultimate Dad card. But a part of him was inside Hobie tapping at that knee. Cameron wasn't gone yet. *He couldn't just ignore us.*

"Hobie, please!"

Hobie pressed his palm right on the iPad screen. Walker realized after tonight, Cameron might never come over again. It was time to play the Dad card.

"Okay." Cameron shut his iPad and slipped it between the couch cushions before Walker could speak up. "Show me whatcha got."

Hobie zoomed a Lego person through three Lego walls in a row. "My Lego people have superpowers. They can bust through walls!"

"Just like *The Incredibles*?" Cameron asked.

Hobie nodded enthusiastically.

"That is so cool! What if Smort had developed super evil stength and could throw a dragon through a building?" Cameron got on the floor with Hobie and spent a good chunk of the movie helping him stage his next action sequence. They built up elaborate, but fragile, buildings with lots of windows and floors, structures that appreared imposing but would crumble at the slightest hit. It reminded Walker of relationships and how quickly they fell apart.

Cameron didn't look back at his iPad once. Walker got a warm feeling heating up his chest as he watched them play and laugh. It felt like home.

"Ready?" Cameron asked Hobie.

Hobie launched the dragon action figure into the Lego building, and it crumbled and shattered on impact. They threw their hands up and cheered.

Soon after, they rejoined Walker on the couch for the last part of the movie. It was a tight squeeze, but that was the best way to enjoy couchtime. All together, not spread apart.

"Cameron, are you still coming to my soccer game?"

"You know it."

Hobie fell asleep on Cameron's lap before the end of the movie, and Cameron rested his head on Walker's shoulder. That warm feeling now spread through his body, like he was wrapped in towels fresh from the dryer.

"Thanks for playing with him," Walker said.

"It was a lousy script anyway." Cameron smoothed out Hobie's hair. The kid didn't flinch. If only they could stay like this forever. All of the complications of age and distance and custody didn't exist on this couch.

He heard the lulling murmur of Cameron's faint snore in sync with Hobie's. Everything seemed to click into its proper place, and Walker hugged this moment tight to his chest. He embedded it deep in his memory.

"Don't go," Walker whispered into Cameron's ear. He didn't know if Cameron heard him, but he hoped some piece of the universe heard his wish.

CHAPTER
TWENTY-SEVEN

Cameron

There was one bright side to leaving Browerton early. Cameron got to skip graduation. He was never looking forward to all the pomp and circumstance. First off, there were two graduation ceremonies he would have had to attend: for the whole school, then his individual college. That meant two long ceremonies with two speakers giving two kinds of *Chicken Soup for the Soul* advice. Not to mention the senior socials, special events, and one awkward dinner with his extended family where he would try explaining for the umpteenth time what a Hollywood assistant does. He just wanted to get his diploma and move on.

He thought his new job had let him avoid graduation stuff, but Henry had other plans. Cameron read an email Henry had sent around for "A Very Cameron Graduation" that he planned to throw on the front lawn of their apartment building in a few days. Being a producer, Henry knew how to put on a production. Cameron was already dreading it. He looked at who was CC'd. Cameron couldn't figure out how Henry knew everyone's email addresses. He was observant, that one.

Cameron dialed up his mom. "Hey, you can ignore the email you just received from Henry."

"What? Wait, I haven't seen it yet. Let me check...oh, a graduation ceremony! That sounds wonderful!"

He rubbed his temples.

"It's not a real ceremony. Henry's going to make me wear a kimono, throw some confetti, and hand me a rolled-up takeout menu."

"I'm still coming." That was his mother. Stubborn as anything. Cameron should've reverse-psychologied her and told her that she had to come.

"Okay, then. That's like six hours of driving for you round trip."

"I was going to make the trek out there for your actual graduation anyway. At least now hotels will be cheaper."

"You don't have to get a...great!" It was no use.

"Will that guy and his son be there?"

Cameron tensed in his dining room chair. He had already sold off his desk and office chair.

"Walker and Hobie, Mom."

"So you're still seeing him?"

"It's...I'm...we're enjoying the time we have left together, then it's over."

"You don't sound convinced," she said.

Cameron rubbed his hand through his hair. He didn't want to have this conversation and face his mom's litany of questions. He didn't have easy answers here.

"What is it, sweetie? Let's talk." That was what his mom always said when he was growing up. It was just the two of them, and they needed to communicate. Their little family would never suvive if they kept things from each other. Cameron wanted to honor the value of those two words, and in his growing confusion, he needed to talk to his mother.

"Mom, I don't know if I should've accepted this job. That whole no writing thing is weird, don't you think?"

"I understand where they're coming from legally. It's a CYA. And they want their employees to be loyal. You can always do this job for a while and see if you like it. Writing will always be there. Who knows? Development may suit you."

The thought of not writing for "a while" made him itch. He remembered how he felt when his fingers pounded the keys. He hoped development would provide that same type of high. *It'll be an education*, he told himself.

"You don't think having to move next week is very abrupt?"

"Arthur's not going to hold this job for you."

"There will be other jobs."

"You don't know that."

"My plan was to move out in September."

There was a noticeable pause that echoed in the phone line. Cameron wished he knew what she was thinking.

"I don't know if you will," she said softly. "If you spend more time with Walker, it's only going to be harder to leave."

She had a point. Infinite Mom Wisdom struck again.

"Maybe I wouldn't leave." The thought had been brewing in his mind quietly for days, and it felt good to say it out loud.

"You have to leave, Cameron!" His mom rarely yelled at him. It shook him up, made his throat go dry. "I don't want this guy to hold you back. I've done everything in my life to get you to this point, and it wasn't to watch you make the same wrong choice I did."

"Me?" His throat made sandpaper feel like mud.

"No. No, sweetie. You've been my saving grace. When I was your age, I stupidly followed my heart, not my dreams. You were too young to remember, but before your dad walked out, things were pretty awful. Your dad and I would get into fights every night. Screaming until our voices were raw. When he left, I told myself that I would give you the chances that I didn't have."

"Did he just really walk out?" Cameron was so quiet he didn't know if anyone heard him.

"Yes. He put a note under your sippy cup because he knew I'd find it there."

"What did it say?"

"I stopped reading it after 'Please don't hate me.' There wasn't a valuable word in there."

Fucking asshole, Cameron thought. He hated that he shared that man's DNA. But something inside Cameron couldn't make him hate his father completely. Some unbreakable, inescapable father-son connection. That damn DNA. It really pissed him off.

"But I was lucky," his mom said. "Without you, I wouldn't have gotten through it. You were such an easy kid. You never gave me any trouble. I just put on a movie for you on the TV, and cried it out in my bedroom."

"I remember the TV in our old place. It had a fat back, and the green paint was peeling off the power button." That's all Cameron remembered from those years. A set of tears rolled down his cheeks. His memory was filled with old movies, but no recollection of his mother's misery or his parents fighting.

"That's why you are meant to be in Los Angeles," she said. "You love movies, always have. This is your dream, Cameron."

It was also her dream, he thought. She'd get to see her son become a hotshot executive. She'd done so much for him, more than he would ever know.

"Walker will understand. If he's a good man, he won't try holding you back."

Φ

Cameron showed up at Hobie's soccer game sometime during the second half. He was hesitant about coming, but Hobie asked him personally, and he just couldn't say no to that kid. He would've made a terrible stepdad, letting Hobie get away with anything. Just thinking about the word stepdad made him pause on the grass. Vagina sounded more natural coming out of his mouth than stepdad.

Parents crowded the sidelines. They brought folding chairs or sat on blankets and ate snacks, turning the game into a picnic. The more competitive parents stood next to the coach and yelled instructions at their kids. Walker sat on his coat. Cameron squatted next to him.

"Hey," he said tentatively.

"You made it!" Walker stretched out his coat to make more room. He had none of the tenseness that Cameron seemed to possess. "We're glad you came."

He nudged at the field. Hobie played defense, which consisted of ripping out grass while his team's offense was busy downfield. He looked up, and flapped his arm back and forth at Cameron.

"Cameron! Cameron!" Hobie screamed from the field. "I kicked the ball all the way down, and the offense person got it and kicked it into the goal!"

"Hobie!" Doug hissed from the sidelines and pointed a firm arm downfield. He looked over his shoulder at Cameron. He was wearing sunglasses, but Cameron had an inkling that a glare was waiting for him under those shades.

Cameron waved and smiled to be polite, but Doug returned to the business at hand.

"It sounds like he's doing well out there," Cameron said.

"He likes kicking the ball. Doesn't matter to whom. That goal assist was more of a happy accident than my son's planned strategy."

"At least he's having fun. That's the most important thing."

"I think so," Walker said before rolling his eyes at the intense parents on the sidelines.

Doug clapped his hands to get Hobie's attention. "Hobie, the ball's coming. Be prepared. Remember what we practiced."

"Well, now I understand helicopter parenting," Cameron said.

Walker snaked his fingers through Cameron's. He loved the way his fingers felt on his hand. He was going to miss this easy connection.

"Hey, what did we say? No tears until later," Walker whispered.

Cameron reached up and felt droplets at his eyes. He couldn't remember the last time he burst into spontaneous tears that didn't result from a fight or a funeral. He wiped them away. *Well, that was embarrassing.*

He let himself enjoy holding hands with Walker. It was like a mini hug contained to his hand. They watched Hobie kick the ball to the outskirts of the field, where it rolled out of bounds. Once the ball made its way back to offense, Doug sidled up to their spot on the grass.

"Nice to see you again, Cameron."

He released his hand from Walker and shook Doug's cold palm. "I didn't know you were coaching the team, Doug."

Doug tensed for a second. His sunglasses made it seem like he was scowling at Cameron all the time, which might've been accurate.

"I'm just a parent invested in his child's activities." His head swiveled to Walker, whose relaxed demeanor was a thing of the past.

Cameron offered to make room on the coat, but Doug preferred to look down at them.

"Are you excited about graduating? Do you know what they have planned for senior week yet?" Somehow, everything Doug said came out like a personal dig. He had that natural bitchy quality to him that came easily to gay men and the British. "It's an exciting time. It seems like forever ago. Although, I guess it was for Walker and me."

"I won't be here for that. I got a job in LA. So lucky for you, I'll be out of your hairplugs in a week."

Doug felt his hair reflexively. It was all real, for now. "You're really going?"

"I am."

The snarky smile slipped from Doug's face. He seemed to be taking the news in, and he glanced at the soccer field.

"That's very exciting." He whipped his head back to the adult area, and Cameron felt something much more serious than a bitchy look emanate off Doug. "Cameron, after today's game, you should say goodbye to Hobie for good."

"Excuse me?" Walker asked.

Cameron massaged his arm to calm him down. "I still have a week, Doug."

"Don't make it any harder on him. Just say your goodbyes now, and then I don't want you to see my son again."

"Our son, and you don't get to make that call," Walker growled.

"The more he sees Cameron now, the more it's going to hurt later."

"Cameron and I already talked about this."

"You never discussed it with me, Walker. Like you said, he's our son. How do you think Hobie is going to feel? You're spending all this time with him, and then you just go."

"We're all going to hurt later, but that doesn't mean we can't enjoy the time we have left." Walker shot Cameron a look that showed just how much hurt was underneath those eyes. Hurt due to Cameron. "Hobie can see Cameron as much as he wants until he leaves."

"Until he leaves," Doug repeated and gestured at Cameron. "You initiated this relationship, which I learned to accept no matter how unorthodox it was." Every word sounded strained from Doug's mouth. "You built this relationship with Hobie, and just as fast, you're taking it away."

"Taking it away?" Cameron glanced at Walker for backup, but he was in his own world. "Do you have these requirements of every person your son comes into contact with? What about if someone dies? I don't want to hurt Hobie, but people come and go. It's a part of the world, and he's going to learn that sooner or later. You can't control every aspect of Hobie's life."

Doug crossed his arms and returned to calm. "I don't know why you want to prolong this. You have no intention of staying in Hobie's life. Just leave now while you have the chance."

"That's bullshit and you know it," Cameron said.

"Watch your mouth. This is a children's soccer game."

"I'm not just going to disappear."

Doug aimed a fuck you smile straight at him. "You really think so? You think once you're busy at your job, and with your new friends, and fully settled into your new life, that you're going to have time for them? Unlike you, I've been through the whole graduation thing. I've had friends who moved to LA or New York or Chicago or London, and we all promised that we'd keep in touch." He shook his head. The condescension dripped from his gaping pores. "You can guess how that went."

"People not wanting to keep in touch with you? Shocker." But Cameron couldn't enjoy the victory because he knew on some level Doug was right.

"I may not know you that well, Cameron, but from what I've gathered, you seem like someone who leaves no trace once he's gone. You have fun with people, pick at their fabric without letting them pick at yours, and then you're gone."

"Don't psychoanalyze me."

"Just go, Cameron. This is what you want. An easy out."

"Doug, shut up." Walker stood up and soon towered over both of them. His eyes burned into his ex.

"Don't you tell me to shut up."

"DOUG, SHUT THE FUCK UP!" Walker yelled. Parents from the folding chairs and sidelines swiveled their heads. Doug's face reddened at the attention. So did Cameron's. Walker was already a deep red.

"I beg your pardon," Doug spat out.

"This is my life. Not yours. Stop acting like you always know what's best for Hobie, because you don't. You do what's best for you and your image, and OUR SON is just along for the ride.

"Cameron and I love each other, and whatever happens next, we're going to figure it out. We'll do what's best for Hobie. You don't get to decide jack shit."

Did he just say he loved me? Cameron's stomach twisted in knots.

Walker stepped closer to Doug, who looked visibly shaken. It didn't give Cameron the satisfaction he thought it would. "Get the hell off your high horse, and leave us the fuck alone."

"Dad?" Hobie called out from the field. He wasn't the only one watching. An opposing player kicked a ball between his legs, then scored.

It took Hobie a few seconds to realize what happened, and he started crying. The coach joined their conversation.

"Can you gentlemen take this to the parking lot? This is not the time or place."

"It's okay. I'm going," Cameron said. He was already running to the street. Before Walker could interject, he was gone, no trace of him left on the field.

CHAPTER
TWENTY-EIGHT

Walker

Walker worked late that night to show Patricia he was
serious about this job. He knew he was on thin ice after his
outburst, right when she needed them all to be at their
most buttoned up. If it were possible, she sent him more
emails.

Subject: Weekly Spend Report

Subject: Slide six

Subject: You triple-checked all numbers, right?

**Subject: Did you see the new Pantene
commercial last night?**

It could be worse, he reminded himself. He could be
making minimum wage or doing backbreaking work. Or
both. They were called the golden handcuffs for a reason.
On some level, you never wanted to take them off. But
when he thought of people he knew, they liked what they

did. Doug loved being a psychiatrist. Cameron was moving across the country to pursue his love of movies. Where did Walker miss the boat?

Graduation was weeks away, but already the campus was covered with decorations. Cap-and-gown paraphenalia blanketed lampposts, sides of buildings, and even the sidewalk.

Not much had changed since Walker was a senior. He remembered snippets of graduation. The bus rides to senior week events, although not the actual events. The photo albums they made. Picking up his robe and tassel. His mind couldn't place specific events, but rather the overall feeling of hope and excitement that stirred him up.

He had so much promise. That's what graduation was, one big promise. A celebration of one half of your life ending, and the whole other half beginning. Numerically, it didn't line up, but it was the end of what you knew: school, classwork, that routine gone in favor of working.

He drove by kids writing "Congrats Graduates" in chalk on the sidewalk. His friends had done that outside of his and Doug's apartment. They had woken up the day of graduation to find the front steps of their building covered in multi-colored well wishes.

All of the graduating seniors had congregated in the stadium before the ceremony. Taking pictures, sharing hugs. It was a sea of green and white robes. Doug and Walker had an impromptu make out session behind a curtain. Those were the days when Doug lusted over Walker, and kissed him like he never wanted to let go.

"We're graduating, Walker," Doug said, nose brushing against his lips.

"We are? Huh, so that's what this robe is for."

"Is it weird that it doesn't feel as momentous as it should? Maybe it'll feel more important when I look back. I'm just hungry right now." Doug left no moment unanalyzed.

"You didn't bring a snack with you?" Walker broke off half of his granola bar and handed it to his boyfriend.

"What would I do without you?"

Walker rested his forehead against Doug's. "Starve."

"I'm happy I get to take this step with you," Doug said.

"It's just the first of many."

Doug bit off half of his half of the granola bar. Walker didn't stop hugging him. Doug had the perfect body to hug. Short, compact, soft but not flabby.

"Maybe one day we'll have a house," Doug said. "And then...who knows. Maybe we could even have a family."

"And then who knows." He kissed Doug. He never got tired of those lips.

"Forever."

"Forever," Walker said back.

"Forever," Walker said to himself in the car. He was living his forever, and it dragged.

Φ

It was Ron who dropped off Hobie off the following night. Doug and Walker didn't say anything to each at the soccer game after Cameron left. Doug hated the negative attention, and Walker wanted to be left alone.

"Why were you and dad fighting?" Hobie asked him.

"Sometimes grownups fight, Hobie." Walker said it firmly enough so Hobie knew not to follow-up his question.

Truth was, he couldn't think of an answer, not one suitable for a kid. His anger had spewed out like a fleeting high that left a long trail of regret. He knew he was going to hear from Doug eventually. Doug always had to have the final word.

"He's still mad, I take it," Walker said to Ron jokingly after Hobie ran inside. Ron didn't bite.

"Some of the other parents…they'd feel more comfortable if just one parent were at the games from now on," Ron said politely. But there was no nice way to say you'd been ostracized from a group of snobby housewives.

He figured Doug would find him when he had something to say. When they fought as a couple, Doug would write him long emails detailing his feelings, or give him mini-speeches in the kitchen. Maybe this was part of growing up for him. Learning to take a step back.

That night, Cameron came over for dinner and Lego time. He gave them a status update with his move. All he had left was a mattress and two neat piles of clothes on top of a box. He made it sound like an adventure to Hobie, but Walker just thought of emptiness.

Hobie barely made it through dinner before he ran to his room, inviting Cameron along for Lego time.

"I'll be there in a minute. I just need to talk to your dad about something. Get all the pieces ready."

Hobie nodded like his head was detached and was off.

"Look, I'm sorry for causing that scene at the soccer game. I shouldn't have gone. It was a total overstep."

Walker rubbed his shoulders and kissed him on the lips, feeling goosebumps in his toes.

"Or not, apparently."

"That'd been brewing between Doug and I for a while. You were not the cause." Walker found the framed picture of his cartoon on the fireplace. He held it, wishing it could hurtle him back to the past. "We were supposed to go to New York. That was the plan. I got a job at an ad agency, but Doug got rejected from NYU for graduate school."

Cameron smiled at that.

"He got into Browerton's psych master's program, though."

"So you stayed." Cameron nodded. "His decision?"

"I stayed to be with him. He kept saying that I should go, that I was meant to be in New York, but I knew Doug. It was classic reverse psychology. He was testing me, I knew he was. But I loved him." Walker remembered when he moved the last box out of their house. The silence between them lasted longer than their relationship. Fifteen years, over like that. "We were going to be together forever. And then he broke my heart."

Cameron slid his arms around Walker's waist, and Walker let his warmth cocoon him. "He's not worth having a broken heart over."

Walker humored him with a smile. Cameron didn't realize that it was so much more complicated than that.

The two of them absconded to Hobie's room. Cameron and Hobie had been working on his medieval space opera over these past few visits. Walker brought them sodas and marveled at the Lego creations sprawled across his son's floor. None of them remotely followed the instructions on the box. They were straight out of Hobie's mind, and he felt like he understood his son more through Legos than anything else.

"Pretty impressive," Walker said. He sat on the bed.

Hobie launched into a whole presentation. He sucked in a huge breath before starting. "So this is the spaceship castle. It's owned by King Dandelion. His wife Queen Spacedragon lives in this tiny plane that has eight wings so it can go eight times as fast."

"King Dandelion doesn't realize that his wife is plotting a coup with his supposedly trustful guard Smort," Cameron said with equal excitement. "She's going to cut the brakes on the spaceship so that it crashes into this village. But the problem is, the night before the mission, she realizes she still loves him. Just as Monte, the other, loyal guard, catches onto their plan and plots his own plan to kill the queen."

Hobie nodded along, even though he probably didn't understand a word of that. He just wanted to crash a spaceship castle into a village.

"That all sounds great! Maybe don't include a murder plotline with a six-year-old, though?" Walker said, in that put-on encouraging dad voice that Hobie was too young to notice.

"I see your point. Hey Hobie, Monte is plotting to throw the queen in a space jail now. Can you construct a supercool space prison where we can hold her?"

Hobie gave him a thumbs up with confidence.

Walker didn't care what the plot was; he loved seeing his son so happy in his house. Hobie would run from the car into his house now, instead of having to be prodded. And it was all because of Cameron. Walker worried that he was the glue holding everything together, and soon he would be gone.

He let them play for a few more minutes before announcing it was time for bed.

"Toothpaste zombie time!" Hobie yelled. He raced Cameron to the bathroom. They showed Walker their foaming mouths, but Walker didn't smile back. A pang of sadness sucker punched him, then stuck to his ribs and pulled him down. He had to sit back down on Hobie's bed.

Cameron brought Hobie back into his room, and they tucked him in for sleep.

"Why do I have to sleep if I'm not tired?" Hobie protested.

"Are you sure you're not tired?" Cameron asked knowingly. "You've been working on the largest medieval space omnibus in history tonight. Even I'm..." Cameron yawned out the rest of his remark.

Hobie caught his contagious yawn.

"Close your eyes, and we'll see what happens," Walker said.

"Sounds like a date I once had sophomore year." Cameron clamped his hand over his mouth.

"I don't get it."

"Go to sleep, Hobie," Walker said. The scene was too cute, and he knew it. But his chest wouldn't stop aching, and he had to swallow back a lump.

They shut off the light.

"Cameron?" Hobie called out, a groggy, squeaky voice in the dark.

Walker and Cameron hung by the door.

"Yeah?"

"I don't want you to move to Los Angeles."

Cameron looked to Walker for an appropriate response. Walker wanted him to be on his own for this one.

"I'm going to miss you, Hobie. But I promise I'll visit, and we'll Skype. I'm going to be the development executive covering the King Dandelion saga."

"Go to bed, buddy. We'll talk in the morning." Walker closed the door.

He marched to his bedroom, didn't wait for Cameron. He undressed into his pajama bottoms. His throat dried up like a sponge in the sun.

"He'll be okay," Cameron said, a little bit statement and a little bit question.

Walker faced the window. Cameron's reflection looked back at him. "Hobie and I aren't going to go to your mock graduation. In the morning, you should say your final goodbye."

Cameron's reflection didn't move. He was waiting for Walker to face him. You didn't throw down a decision like that without eye contact.

"Hobie and I?" Cameron asked.

The pain continued to weigh him down. *Doug was right.* He would never say those words aloud, but they bellowed in his head.

"Hearing him ask you to stay tonight broke my heart. It's only going to get worse." Walker paced in front of his mirrored closet doors. "And let's be honest. You're not going to visit or Skype."

"So Doug was right?"

"Don't say that."

"You're the one saying that."

"Because it's true!" Walker burst out. "What do you always say? No looking back?"

Cameron glanced down for a second. Walker was right, and he knew it.

"Let's not do this. Let's watch a movie and cool down." Cameron pulled out his phone and opened the Netflix app.

"Why do you always do that? Watching something won't fix this. This problem isn't going away with a jaunty score." Walker pointed at his phone. "That shit just makes you numb. Did it help to have the TV on when your dad walked out?"

"Fuck you!" His voice wobbled with emotion. All of Cameron's cool faded away. "I'm not used to this, okay? I didn't plan for my first real relationship to be with a guy with a 401k and a son. This started as a fling. We both said this was going to be a fling."

"Things change."

"I know!" Cameron did his best to keep his voice down, but Walker could tell it was a losing battle. "We'll find a way to stay in touch."

"I don't want to stay in touch." Walker said those words like they were a slur. Staying in touch was for classroom acquaintances, people you wanted to network with in the future. "I love you, Cameron."

He searched Cameron's eyes for an answer, but there was so much going on behind his baby blues, so many conflicting feelings.

"I'm not ready to be a desperate housewife! I'm twenty-two!"

"Something like this doesn't come along every day. I've been in love and I've been married, but I've *never* felt anything like what we have. You've changed my life, Cameron. And I know underneath your sarcasm and Hollywood hopes, you're scared. Scared that you feel it, too."

"My parents felt it, too. And then my dad left."

"Is that going to be you?"

Cameron's eyes bulged. It was a low blow comparing him to his dad, but Walker couldn't stop what came out of his mouth. His heart had the controls.

Cameron knelt on the bed so he was eye level with Walker. "I've had this plan, this dream, since I was a kid. It's been my passion, and everything I've done to push myself and excel has been because of this dream." He grabbed Walker's cheeks, rubbed a finger over his beard. "I love you, Walker. But I love my dream, too. No matter what I choose, I'll have to wonder 'What if,' and you don't realize how hard that is."

"Your dream is to write. You can do that from anywhere. You think being this guy's assistant is a golden ticket, but it's just a job. You don't know this yet because you've never had a real job, but they're all the same. You'll love your job for the first few months, but then it'll get boring or rote or your awesome co-workers stop being awesome. Soon, you start to see a job for what it really is: a way to make money and pass the time."

Cameron seemed taken aback by the statement, but he'd learn eventually.

"If you really think that, then why are you still at your job? I never hear you applying anyplace new."

"I have a son to look out for."

"Will you stop it!" Fury lit up Camron's face. "Stop using Hobie as an excuse. Don't say shit like 'Hobie and I can't come to graduation.' Just say what you really feel: *you* don't want to go because it'll be too hard on *you*." He slid off the bed and put his shoes back on. "Newsflash, Walker: There are lots of people who love their jobs. You had a dream, and you still have the talent to achieve it. But you made your choices. Now let me make mine."

Walker's jaw tightened in anger. He didn't know what to say back. Somehow, saying that Cameron didn't understand didn't ring true.

"I think I'm going to go," Cameron said. His eyes darted to Hobie's room. He stared at the closed door with an intensity that kept Walker frozen in place. Anger reddened his whole face. He took a tentative step forward.

"He's asleep. Don't wake him."

They stared each other down for a second before Cameron relented. He charged into the kitchen and took out a notepad and pen from a drawer. Tears fell down Cameron's face, and Walker felt like they couldn't all be for him. Cameron scribbled away on the pad. He held it up to his face and read it to himself. He heaved in a breath and glared at the note, like it was the Voldemort of notes.

He tore it up. Walker felt the slashes of the paper ripping. Cameron let the pieces fall to the floor. He barged down the hall and left, leaving Walker sitting on his bed in his quiet condo.

CHAPTER TWENTY-NINE

Cameron

Cameron stared at himself in the bathroom mirror. The long, white graduation robe billowed out around him. Now he knew what he'd look like obese. He placed the matching cap on his head and straightened the tassel.

Whoa.

It might have been a mock graduation, but in that moment, the realness shocked Cameron. The last time he wore a cap and gown was high school graduation, but he had wanted that to end just as soon as it began. Once he got through that graduation, he would be done with high school and onto the next chapter of his life. He knew he would come to Browerton and find people just as passionate and knowledgeable about film as he.

No looking back.

He heard sniffles off to the side. There was his mom, watching him. She already had a tissue in hand, and she dabbed at her eyes.

"It's a mock graduation," he reminded her.

"I don't care. You better get used to this," she waved her hand at her face. "I'm letting the waterworks run free today."

She wasn't much of a crier, so it was an odd sight to Cameron. His mom always worked hard to put on a happy face. As he got older, Cameron got good at picking out the genuine smiles. Like the one she had on now.

"So what's exactly going on today?" she asked.

Henry jogged over, a phone in one hand and decorations in the other. "It'll be a cozy graduation ceremony in the front lawn of our building. I've arranged for a special commencement speaker, then Cameron will get his diploma, then we'll eat lunch. Very short, very sweet."

"Wow." Cameron couldn't believe how legit all of this sounded and that Henry went to all this effort. He even got Cameron a robe from the theater wardrobe department. "Thanks for doing all this, Henry."

Henry didn't look at him, and gave off a minor late winter chill. He ripped off a square of toilet paper for his mom to dab at her eyes. It seemed like everything was going to make her cry today.

"We still have a little bit of time before the festivities start," Cameron said. "I have to write coverage on a pair of scripts for Arthur."

Arthur wrote him a congrats email on his graduation and attached two scripts. Cameron wished he could have had a small break, but in this moment, he appreciated having something to take his mind off the festivities of today. Among other things.

He hoped that despite how he left things, Walker would show up.

Wishful thinking.

"I just want to say again how proud I am of you. Of everything you've accomplished and will accomplish. This job with Arthur is only the first step." She brushed his hair out of his face in one familiar swoop.

"Are you sure you'll be okay with me so far away?"

"I'll be fine. I've been fine these past four years."

"But Browerton is only a three-hour drive from home. I hate to think I'm leaving you behind."

"Think of it as giving me a reason to get out of the cold during the winter." His mom smoothed out the wrinkles in his robe. "You're leaving nobody behind."

She stared up at him. He was now taller, but she would always be bigger. The one in charge.

"Now, I know you have scripts to read. Want me to make a Starbucks run for you before everyone gets here?"

"Like my assistant?" He kissed her on the cheek and gave her some money for coffee, which he knew she wouldn't use.

Cameron took off the robe and sat on his mattress with iPad in hand. Henry was buzzing around the apartment getting everything ready.

"Hey Henry, do you need help with anything?" He called from his room.

Henry walked inside and gawked at the emptiness. "Whoa."

"Do you need help with anything?"

"Nope."

"Is everything okay?"

Henry tightened his lips. He knocked on the wall. "I'm going to miss you."

"Not you, too." Cameron laughed to himself. "I can't

take any more tears today. It's not a real graduation."

"Cameron, would it kill you to be just a little sentimental?" Henry yelled.

"Only if you stop acting like the human embodiment of Green Day's 'Time of your Life'."

"Is this even a little hard for you?" Henry asked. "Do you give like the tiniest shit about leaving? Or were we all just speedbumps you drove over on your way to Hollywood?"

"We're all going to graduate eventually, Henry. This'll be you next year. It's a part of life."

"This came out of nowhere. Two weeks ago, we were eating pizza and drinking beer and talking about going to Revolution this summer. It's the end of our world as we know it, but you feel fine."

"You really enjoy that '80s dance floor at Revolution, don't you?" Cameron smiled at this joke, but not Henry. He wasn't used to such a serious Henry. That wasn't their thing. Cameron stood up from the bed, which was hard to do when all you have is a mattress. "You want this to be like the end of *Steel Magnolias,* me a crying mess? That's a movie *and* a play, so it works for both of us."

"You're acting like none of this means anything to you! In a few days, your college career will be over. This is the last time we'll all be able to meet up at McFly's because we feel like it. This is the last time where our whole social network will be on the same campus. This is the last time you can burst into my room to ask me a random question about V-neck versus crew neck. Now we'll have to make time to talk to each other and book flights to hang out. And you're being so fucking cavalier about everything. Don't you realize that people will miss you? You're not the only who has to say good-bye."

Everything Henry said was like someone kicking open a door and letting the sunlight in. Cameron needed to adjust to the brightness. He wasn't used to this, having non-family members care so much about him.

"I'm sorry," he said. "I'll never compare you to a Green Day song again."

"Don't make a joke out of this. Please." Henry sighed. "Don't push me away."

"I'm not."

"Because you do that. You have this moat of humor. And casual sex."

"How do you know me so well?"

"Because you're my best friend, asshole."

"I'm going to miss you," Cameron said, and he meant it. He wasn't saying it to be nice this time. He had the lump in his throat as proof. It was a good moment, but it also hurt like hell.

"I love you."

"I love you, too." Cameron hugged Henry tight. "Platonically, of course."

Henry smacked him in the stomach. "Just read your damn scripts."

Φ

There was not much to mock about this mock graduation. Henry had amassed enough people to fill up the hodgepodge of folding chairs he scrounged up and organized in the front lawn. Green and white balloons dotted the tops of chairs on the aisle. And there was an actual platform with an actual podium.

Cameron looked on in amazement, and a touch of something else. He really did have great friends.

"You ready?" Henry asked. They stood in the lobby of his building. "I'll cue up the procession music."

"I am seriously impressed." Cameron pulled him into a spontaneous hug. "Thank you."

They held each other a few seconds. So much to say but words couldn't cover the expanse of this friendship. But they knew. They both knew.

"Don't forget about us little people." Henry wasn't entirely joking.

"I'm sorry. What was your name again? Hugo?"

"Get out there." He pushed Cameron toward the door and cued up the music.

It was the traditional, lame graduation music. Yet it wasn't lame now that Cameron was graduating to it. As soon as he stepped onto the lawn, people applauded and cheered him onto the stage. It was a wonderful feeling to be loved. He scanned the crowd, but there was no sign of Walker.

He did a double take at the speaker. Professor Mackey sat next to him with a typed-out speech. *Damn, Henry was good.*

Henry took to the podium. "Today, we are celebrating a graduating class of one. Cameron Aldous Buckley made the most of his four years at Browerton. He attended classes and parties in equal measure. He made a great group of friends and an even greater group of enemies. He learned to love cheap beer."

The audience howled with laughter. Cameron turned a mortified shade of red.

"And now, our honorary speaker. She wrote that

movie that we all were obsessed with in junior high. Professor Elizabeth Mackey."

A light applause accompanied Mackey's ascent to the podium. Cameron clapped louder and encouraged those in attendance to do the same. Mackey sure deserved it. The second she hit that podium, she owned the entire courtyard.

"Cameron Buckley. I've only known you a short time, but I'm grateful that I got to have you as my student. You have the talent, intelligence, and ambition to go far in Hollywood. That, we already know.

"It's scary when you enter the real world. It's like turning off the highway in the middle of nowhere. Maybe there's another road, or a dirt road, or nothing at all. But it's up to you to forge your own path. You can ask for advice, but ultimately, it's your road. And the good thing about this road is that it can go in any direction you want. You can turn left, turn right, turn around, get off the road completely onto another dirt road. All that freedom is scary, frankly. But eventually, you'll look in the rearview mirror and marvel at this amazing journey you built from nothing. Enjoy the journey. Enjoy the confusion. Enjoy making mistakes. That's how the best roads are built."

She spoke with an urgency Cameron was not expecting. He was suddenly very aware of his heart beating, but he didn't know why the speech was affecting him this way.

"Good luck, Cameron. Follow your own road." Henry handed her the rolled-up diploma. Cameron crossed to her, did the grab diploma/handshake movement that was surprisingly complicated, and smiled for the cameras. His friends and his mom cheered him on. They wished him well.

"Congratulations to our graduate," Mackey said. "Cameron Buckley."

Cameron stood on the stage and soaked in the standing ovation. He looked out at this community that had sprung up around him, all people who cared about him. He wiped a tear from his cheek. This was supposed to be a stupid, funny "graduation."

But there was one person missing from the crowd. Cameron searched and searched. No Walker lingering in the back. His community didn't feel complete.

"Okay, everyone!" Henry was at the podium. "There's lunch upstairs in our apartment." He rubbed Cameron's shoulder. "You need to turn your tassel to the left. You've graduated, man."

Φ

His kitchen was tight with guests milling about and pouring their own drinks. It seemed that graduation ceremonies, no matter how real or fake, always brought out the worst of the weather. This spring day had switched places with a dog day of summer. Stifling humidity coated the apartment in a mist of sweat. Cameron took off his robe. He wore gym shorts and a T-shirt underneath.

"Don't judge. This thing is like wearing a plastic bag." Cameron tossed the robe to Henry, who put it back in its proper garment bag.

People brought up folding chairs from the courtyard and jockeyed for a seat near the air conditioner. Greg and Ethan fanned each other.

"I wish this could've been the real graduation," Greg said. "Did you hear who the commencement speaker is this year? That good ole Christian senator who was caught sexting his male interns."

"I'm sorry I'm missing it," Cameron said. "Except not at all. When do you start Teach for America?"

"September. So we still have some time." Greg squeezed Ethan's knee.

"And you're okay with him going?" Cameron asked Ethan.

"Of course." Ethan didn't seem to understand the question. Then again, Greg was only going to be a three-hour drive away in Philadelphia. Not a four-hour flight. "I'll miss him, but we'll make it work."

"Or die trying." Greg grabbed chips from Ethan's plate.

"And when I go off to law school in a few years, we'll keep making it work."

"You're so sure about that?" Cameron asked.

"Yeah," Greg said. He gave Ethan a look that was indecipherable to Cameron or anyone else who wasn't Ethan. But Cameron felt the love between them, and he knew that they truly would make it work.

"Will you stop eating off my plate? Get your own chips!" Ethan covered his plate.

"They don't taste as good when I get them."

"Get a room," Cameron said. "Or a library."

Ethan turned ghost white. Cameron loved doing that.

Professor Mackey approached him with her big purse in hand.

"You're going?"

"I have my daughter's ballet recital. Can we talk privately?"

Cameron led them out to the back terrace. It was still

hot, but at least they could catch a light breeze now and then.

"I didn't want to just mail this to you." She handed him his screenplay. Cameron was impressed at the weight of it in his hand. He wrote this.

On top was an A-plus.

"You probably give these to all your students," he said of the grade.

"I haven't given one of those out in three years."

Cameron rubbed his finger over the grade. He hadn't received an A-plus since elementary school. "I won't tell Robert."

She smoothed her hand over the top page. "Robert's parents have called me asking why their brilliant and gifted son is getting a B on all his assignments. I told them I was being generous and hung up." She shrugged and leaned back against the railing like a boss. "The power of tenure."

"You might have just insulted a future Oscar-winning screenwriter."

She didn't seem to care. "I sound like a broken record, but you have talent. If you keep at it, you can make a go at being a professional screenwriter."

He had to laugh at that. Cameron Buckley, Professional Screenwriter. Cameron Buckley, Studio Exec sounded more realistic. "I've been wondering this whole time. Why didn't you stay? You wrote a hit movie. You could've…"

"Done more than grade screenwriting assignments?"

"Been successful."

Her face tightened at the remark, and Cameron wished he could take it back. Or at least pad it.

Or not. He remained defiant. Damn it, Mackey had talent. "Do you know how many people dream of being a screenwriter? I've read so many scripts, most of them by writers who will never achieve the type of success you had. You were on this path to be the next Callie Khouri or Diablo Cody."

"One A-plus, and you think you run the joint." Her tone stayed light, but he detected an edge to her voice. "Shortly after my movie came out, my mother-in-law got very sick. My husband kept coming back here to take care of her. After our first daughter was born, we decided to move back permanently. It was a tough decision at the time. A very tough decision. I mean, we were living in Brentwood! I told him we would rent around here for a year first and see how we liked it. Turns out we loved it."

"You don't miss working in Hollywood? You don't miss writing scripts?"

"Sometimes, I do think about what could've happened if I'd stuck with it, but I know that ultimately, it wasn't the place for me. And I never stopped writing. I actually got into writing children's books, since I read so many with my kids. I just landed a literary agent."

"Congrats!"

"We'll see what happens." She showed Cameron a picture of her family on her phone. Three kids, all with matching red hair. "It's funny."

"What is?" Cameron asked.

"If you had told me at twenty-two where I'd be at forty-two, I never would've believed you. I would've laughed in your face. A professor mother of three living in the middle of Pennsylvania? But that's the fun part of life. There are plenty who stay on the path, and I still keep in touch with them. They kept pursuing their dreams, and now they're executives, producers, writers, actors. Many of them have families, too. My husband went to medical school right out of undergrad and still practices today. And then there's people like me, who let life take some crazy twists and turns."

Cameron held his script against his stomach. His throat went dry as his mind scrambled with thoughts. "Are you happy?"

"I am." She had to think about it. "But it's a different kind of happy."

He pictured mornings he and Walker laid in bed with Hobie about to bust the door down. It was a different type of happy he experienced, too. He felt accomplished and proud when he secured the job with Arthur. But there was an everyday joy that coated his life when he spent time with Walker and his son. It wasn't the happy moment that came with a career victories, rather a general feeling that was so stealth, he hadn't realized it until now.

"What if I don't want to move to Los Angeles?" He couldn't believe the words left his mouth, but they didn't sound as scary aloud. "What if I make the wrong choice?"

"Then it's just another twist in your path." She hugged him with a mom hug perfected over three children. "Keep in touch, Cameron."

CHAPTER THIRTY

Walker

"I'm really okay, Lucy." Walker pushed away the oversized cupcake from his keyboard. She nudged it back with her finger.

"It's okay to eat your feelings."

Walker was not going to get away from this cupcake-free. They always cheered each other up with food. "Let's both eat my feelings."

He sliced the cupcake in half with a plastic knife and scooted the larger half over to Lucy.

"Talk to me," she said before taking a bite. Lucy pretended she was always on a diet until half a cupcake was put in her way.

"There's still a puddle of Hobie tears on my bedspread." Walker didn't know the protocol for telling Hobie that Cameron was gone from their lives. He told him the truth, that Cameron had to leave early. "But he didn't even say good-bye!" Hobie had whimpered through tears. That hit Walker the most.

"He'll be okay. This is just the initial shock," Lucy said. "Kids are resilient. My kids survived burying all four grandparents who they were close with."

"He's not dead, Lucy," Walker said, and the look she gave him reminded that Cameron wasn't coming back either.

Walker dug into his treat, and his knees wobbled at the deliciousness. "This cupcake is amazing."

"I got it from Dollop. It's a really sweet lady who owns it. For how much longer, I don't know."

He licked his fingers. Sweets hadn't been as delicious to him these last few years. All the sugar went to his head. He was told that's what happens when people get older. Yet another downside to aging.

But this cupcake was a grand exception.

"What do you mean, you don't know how much longer?"

"We chatted in the store, and she says business is not doing too well. The Duncannon cupcake craze is over, it seems."

He thought back to her atrocious billboard he saw outside Cherry Stem. That probably cost her more than a pretty penny. What a waste.

Walker heard the familiar ping of a new email in his inbox.

Subject: Can you come into my office?

"I'm being summoned by Patricia." Walker savored the last bite of his cupcake half.

266

Patricia typed an email on her computer while reading another one on her phone. She held up a "one minute" finger. Walker took a seat.

The pen in his hand began doodling an ad for Dollop's oversized cupcakes. That could be their hook. *A woman jumping out of a cupcake at a bachelor party? Probably not the right audience, but still funny.* He laughed at his sketch.

"Sorry about that." Patricia put down her phone. Walker put down his pen. "Can you shut the door?"

Walker immediately went on high alert. He felt a *plunk* inside him, like a rock dropping into a glass of water. Closed-door meetings were never a good sign.

He did as instructed and sat back down.

"Our presentation to the client is in two days. As you know, this is more than important. It's make-or-break for us. I need to be sure your head is in the game."

"It is."

"Your work hasn't been at your previous level of quality these past few weeks, right when I need you to be more focused than ever."

Patricia was using corporate-approved nice speak to make this sound as pleasant as could be, but it still stung. Walker hated letting this job get the better of him.

"What do you mean?"

"Well, that market share issue. You should've been on top of that. We couldn't go into a presentation that openly told the client that because of us, they were losing money."

"It's not our fault, though. They have lousy commercials and a lousy product."

"We can't say that. It might be true, but that's not our job. You're an associate director. You should know this."

Patricia's chair squeaked as she leaned back. She played with a pen cap. Even though she had an office and was the consummate professional, she still seemed nervous, like she wasn't totally used to being the boss yet. "And it's not just that issue. You don't seem to be paying attention in meetings. I see you, staring off, or doodling."

Her eyes traveled to his notebook. He snapped it shut.

"I know you don't want to be here." The bluntness got Walker's full attention. "I'm sure you'd rather be somewhere else. But you are here, Walker, and you're paid quite nicely for it. And when you're in this office and sitting at that desk, I expect you put in maximum effort."

"Okay."

But she wasn't done. "If we are able to save the Radiance account, I want to be sure I have the best team in place moving forward."

Another *plunk*. Walker pressed his notebook shut tighter until his fingers hurt. "Does that include me?"

"I don't know."

Walker clamped his lips shut to stop them from trembling. He didn't even like this job, but he pictured not having it. The condo, the car payments, Hobie.

"I just had some personal issues come up, but my head is clearly in the game, I promise."

As he left her office, he felt the golden handcuffs chafe against his wrists.

Φ

Walker found himself getting angrier the more he drove. It built up like water in a dam. It was because of Doug that he was in these golden handcuffs, in a job he hated, in a life he didn't plan for at all. This wasn't how things were supposed to go. Walker wanted to hit the gas pedal and rocket to over 100 miles per hour and keep driving until the world blurred.

He rang the doorbell to pick up his son, and sure enough, Ron answered.

"Hey, Walker. Hobie's just finishing up a bath." Ron opened the door further. Even though it was a nice night, Walker came inside. He knew Doug was keeping himself locked away in the bathroom with Hobie to avoid him. Doug liked to hold grudges.

But so can I.

Walker bypassed Ron and charged up the stairs. Ron tried to catch him.

"It'll be just a few minutes more," Ron said, his eyes pleading.

Poor Ron. He was perfect for Doug because he didn't fight back. Walker used to play that role well. He had lost his fight after years with Doug. He had gotten used to being told he was wrong. But he was right. He knew it. He felt it in his bones. Doug had to be put in his place.

He was going to be the obnoxious twenty-two-year-old so unbelievably sure of himself.

He reached the top of the stairs and beelined to the closed door with light flooding out underneath. The sounds of Hobie splashing echoed down the hall.

"Ron," he swiveled around and held out his hand. "I got this."

Ron seemed to give him a good luck nod and retreated downstairs to his PBS special.

Walker opened the bathroom door without knocking. Hobie played with Legos in the soapy bathtub while Doug sat on the toilet with a towel on his lap. He bolted up as soon as he saw who was at the door.

"Dad!"

"Hey, buddy."

"I thought you were waiting downstairs. We're almost done," Doug said with a hint of worry.

"My time with Hobie started sixty seconds ago, technically." Walker hopped up onto the sink counter to sit, which he knew made Doug boil with rage. "I think Ron should help Hobie get dressed and packed up. We need to talk."

"About what?" Doug crossed his arms.

"Something you did." Walker eyed his son, who was no longer playing with Legos. There was a much more entertaining show to watch. He didn't need the past dragged out in front of Hobie. That was something he and Doug could agree on easily.

Doug called for Ron, who joined them in the hall seconds later. Doug cast daggers at his husband, the failed gatekeeper. He led Walker into their bedroom, which had double doors at the end of the hall. It was almost as big as their whole senior year apartment.

"What do you want, Walker?"

"I want to talk about graduation."

"Cameron's?"

"Ours."

"I could ask my mother to mail me her VHS copy from her camcorder." Doug kept his distance from Walker, which wasn't hard in a room this size. Was this all Doug wanted? A big house, a rich husband, and a life that existed just to make others envious?

"I got that job in New York, and I turned it down for you. You gave me that puppy dog look and told me you loved me. I loved you, and you played me."

"I never made you stay. You made that decision yourself." Doug's calm tone only caused more rage to build up in Walker.

"You had me wrapped around your finger and knew what buttons to push. I put my life on hold so we could be together. I did it all for you, and then you left to live happily ever after in your castle." He gestured to the McMansion Monstrosity surrounding them.

"Where is this coming from?"

"You manipulated me!" Walker yelled. To hell if Hobie heard. He should hear this. "Then you cast me aside like the fucking heartless human being you are. I gave up my future for you!"

Doug wiped off his not-amused smirk and put on his game face. He still knew how to fight. They both did. It was like riding a bike for them.

"I won't let you do this again," Doug said.

"Do what?"

"Rewrite history."

"We both know what happened. I got the job in New York. You got rejected from NYU and wanted to stay here. So I stayed." Walker's hands slicked with sweat. His heart pounded in his ears. The ceiling fan lapping above them wasn't helping.

"Is that how you think of me? That I'm this evil mastermind?" Doug shook his head. "You made your own choices. You ruined your own future. And if anyone was used in this relationship, it was me."

Walker busted out laughing, a real ha-ha-fuck-you laugh that he hoped Doug felt in his chest. Doug stared at him like a child having a tantrum.

"That's rich, Doug."

"You sat on accepting that job offer for weeks. You hemmed and hawed about whether you wanted to move to New York."

"I was waiting to hear about you."

"Bullshit. You were scared. And you used me as an excuse." Doug scowled and looked out the window.

Walker stayed back. "What the hell are you talking about?"

"You were too scared to go to New York. When you got the job offer, you panicked. I saw it flicker in your eyes." He turned to Walker and stared him square in the eye. All of his psycho, prissy bullshit was stripped away. All the armor he had put up around himself fell to the ground. "You were scared to pursue your dream because what if you couldn't cut it in New York? What if you couldn't be the celebrity cartoonist you were on campus? So why try, when you could just give up."

"I thought we were going to be together forever."

"Stop it!" Doug screamed. "Stop putting this on me. I even said we could try long distance. Remember we talked about it in the coffee shop in the Borders?"

And there they were, years ago. Walker sipped on his coffee while Doug opted for green tea.

"When you turned down the job in New York, I thought you did it because you loved me." Tears sprung from his eyes as he shook his head no. "I was an easy out."

Walker hadn't seen this face in years. He wanted to comfort Doug, even though they were still fighting.

"You were a fucking coward, Walker. You use people as excuses. You think you're being noble, but you're just scared to take any kind of risk. You used me as an excuse to stay behind. You used Hobie as an excuse to stay at a job you've hated for years. You used your little senior boytoy as an excuse not to enter the real dating world."

"You shut your mouth about Cameron. He is twice the guy you'll ever be."

"At least Cameron knows how to go after what he wants." Doug heaved in breaths. Walker had never seen him so angry, so primal. "You use people as shields and then blame them when things don't go your way. I spent years trying to make it work while you did nothing. It wasn't easy being married to a guy who resented you when it wasn't your fault."

Walker sat on the bed, feeling like he got punched in the gut. Doug yanked open one of the bedroom doors.

"Get out of my house," Doug said with eerie calm.

After a few deep breaths, Walker was ready to go downstairs. He caught himself in the mirror. The lines on his forehead, the beginning droop of his cheeks. He hated what he saw. Everything.

Ron and Hobie watched TV. It didn't seem like they heard anything.

"Ready, buddy?"

Hobie nodded. "Can you carry my bag, dad?"

As they walked out of the house, Walker's feelings for Doug hardened into hatred. He turned around to say goodnight, but Doug had already slammed the door shut.

CHAPTER THIRTY-ONE

Cameron

Cameron gazed at the wood floors and white walls of his bedroom. So much had happened in this place, and memories played against the bare wall like a projector. All the times he and his friends hung out in his living room, drinking and eating and talking, seemed unimportant at the time. But they codified into potent memories.

Cameron did one final sweep of his apartment. Shoved in the back of a kitchen drawer was a note to himself. *Get detergent.* He actually remembered trudging out to the supermarket in a rainstorm to pick some up—avoiding a guy he'd hooked up with who stood behind him in line. That was the epitome of Cameron. A responsible adult and complete interpersonal mess at the same time.

He locked up behind him and slipped his keys under the doormat for Henry. His mom offered to cover the rest of his rent unless Henry found a subletter. And just like that, Cameron no longer lived in Duncannon, Pennsylvania.

A random passerby would never guess Cameron was leaving town. He only packed two large suitcases, which sat in his trunk. As a graduation gift, his grandpa gave him his old car, a Suburu nearly as old as Cameron. He had sold, donated, or trashed everything else. He would start fresh in LA and take an IKEA trip his first available weekend. New stuff for a new apartment. Cameron looked forward to the clean slate.

He sat in his car, key in the ignition, but he couldn't turn it on. Something didn't feel right. The clean slate didn't feel appropriate. He was ready to leave high school and his hometown in the rearview mirror. He had no problem letting it go. But not Browerton, not the life he'd made here.

It was finally here. The future.

"This is what you want," he said to himself in the side mirror.

The car roared to life. Cameron drove down Susquehanna Avenue, waving goodbye to Browerton's campus. He passed by these buildings thousands of times in his college career, and he took a moment to really look at them, not just treat them as background scenery on a soundstage.

And the campus was behind him. It felt weird, like he officially crossed over to adult now. Cameron waited at a stop light and turned on the radio. Music would clear his mind.

"You're listening to Nineties at Nine," said the DJ, who desperately tried to sound cool. "Next up is a jam any '90s kid can rap the lyrics to. Straight off the *Dangerous Minds* soundtrack…"

The opening bars to "Gangsta's Paradise" came on,

and Cameron nearly lost his shit. He cranked the volume all the way up and rolled his windows all the way down. He mimicked Walker's horrible dancing from the club and bounced in his seat. He mumbled along to the rap portion as best he could and was dying in anticipation for the chorus.

In three...two...one...

Cameron sang the lyrics at the tippy top of his lungs. He sang at his windshield. He beeped his horn at no one, just to be heard.

He made the first right turn available and pulled into a strip mall parking lot. Cameron burst out of his car, the radio still blaring, and danced. Right then, right there. Maybe people gawked at him, but he didn't care. He squatted down down down then leaped up to the sky at the chorus and sang even louder than before. He was out of breath but not out of sheer energy.

He found himself making up a dance routine during the bridge. Step-two-three-fouring to the left, waving his hand wildly. It was better than any choreographed dance in the history of existence, or *Glee*.

A tubby security guard jogged across the parking lot. Cameron got into his car and bolted. He realized why this car trip didn't feel right. He had to make one last stop.

Φ

He walked through the maze of the white circle of hell until he found Walker in the breakroom talking to his friend Lucy over second-rate coffee.

Walker's coffee nearly fell out of his hand. He looked like he saw a ghost. Maybe that's what Cameron was for him now.

"Hey," Cameron said lightly. "Can we talk?"

"I'll catch up with you later," Lucy said to Walker. She gave Cameron a sweet nod on her way out.

"I thought you were already on the road."

"Aren't we all on some type of road?"

Walker ushered him to the elevator, and they found a bench outside Cameron's old Starbucks. Where they first met.

"What's going on?" Walker asked—he looked bruised and tired. Cameron wanted to hug him, but got the sense he should keep his distance.

Cameron looked down and gathered his thoughts, his courage, his strength. "I'm staying."

"What?"

"I want to be with you." Cameron's heart felt lighter just saying the words freely. "I love you."

"What about LA?"

"They'll be there. But right now, I want to be here, with you and Hobie. I like this life we have." Cameron slipped his fingers through Walker's. "I want to give this a chance and see what happens."

Walker nodded, which wasn't the exact response Cameron anticipated.

"I could move into your condo." Cameron breathed in the fresh air. "Maybe this is my path, you know? I never expected it, but I'm glad fate brought me here, to you. Man, do I sound corny."

Walker kept his fingers still, no reciprocating. He gazed at his office building.

"This is the part where we kiss with tears in our eyes," Cameron said. His attempt at a joke crashed and burned.

"Walker?"

"You're scared," he said to the building. "You think this is what you want, but it's not." When he finally looked Cameron's way, his expression was as fixed as marble.

"I thought a lot about this."

"Have you? You've wanted LA ever since I met you and way before that."

He didn't have a quick rebuttal. He did want LA, but he wanted this more. "Things change."

"On the day you're supposed to move?"

Cameron grabbed his chin. He needed to see the Walker that was still in there. Not this spokesperson. "We can make this work."

"No, we can't." Walker pushed away Cameron's hand. "I'm not going to hold you back."

"You won't. I'm making this choice on my own." Cameron didn't think he'd have to try this hard. He thought by now, Walker would've swooped him up in his arms.

Walker pulled him into a hug. Cameron breathed in his lingering shaving cream scent. Everything seemed too final in this moment.

"You're not staying here," Walker said softly. His eyes burned with feelings his mouth wouldn't say. "You're going to get in your car, drive across the country, and make something happen in LA."

This wasn't the plan. This wasn't the moment they were supposed to share. Walker's hands felt alien on his skin.

Cameron yanked himself away. "I don't get it."

"Did you really think we would be together? We

weren't thinking clearly." Walker seemed to be saying that as much to himself as Cameron. He had never seen Walker so angry, so red. "We had fun. We had some great sex. That's all it was."

"You don't mean that." Tears beaded at Cameron's eyes. He knew Walker didn't believe that. *He couldn't.* But the words still hurt.

"You were supposed to leave." Walker glared at him. "So leave."

"This isn't you." Cameron couldn't breathe. He was standing on a cliff, ready to jump. He thought Walker would catch him, but now.... "I'm scared. You're scared, too. We can be scared together and figure this out. I feel it, Walker. I love you."

Walker grabbed his arms and pushed Cameron up against a tree. He tried to act cold, but he was failing. His eyes burned with a barely contained fire. "Whether you stay or you go, we're breaking up. So if I were you, I would go. I gotta get back to work."

He let go, turned around, and headed back inside without so much as a backward glance.

No looking back.

Cameron wiped his eyes. That would be the final set of tears he would cry over that man. He returned to his vehicle, just as he'd left it. He peeled out of the parking lot. He didn't look around as he drove through the rest of Duncannon. He kept his eyes on the road ahead. Once he got to the interstate, everything would be better. His life here would crystallize into memories. Scabs would form. Wounds would heal. By the time he reached California, Browerton and Walker would be firmly in the past.

CHAPTER THIRTY-TWO

Walker

Walker didn't want to wake up. If he woke up, he would have to sit up. If he sat up, he would have to look at himself in his mirrored closet door. And he wasn't ready for that.

He sucked it up and trudged through his morning routine. His brain shifted to autopilot. He didn't realize he was brushing his teeth until he was spitting into the sink. Clothes found their way onto his body. It was another morning before work. Same routine, same blips. Maybe zombies had the right idea. No thinking. No feeling. Just eating and destroying everything around you.

He made himself a cup of coffee in his fancy Keurig machine. His fancy appliances and chic furniture surrounded him, yet it all seemed empty. He had accumulated such nice things. That was all they were. Things. What had he sacrificed for them?

That's what an adult does. He sacrifices. Yet Walker didn't understand why sacrificing had to suck so much.

He poured the coffee down the sink.

I did the right thing. I couldn't hold him back. He had told himself that repeatedly for the first few days, but soon he stopped wanting to remind himself of what happened. The things he said. The way he acted. *I did the right thing* didn't seem to cut it.

His stomach dipped below sea level when he drove past campus. College students strolled on the sidewalk. They all reminded him of Cameron. Young, confident, full of energy.

He found himself in his office building's lobby. His routine carried him along. Walker pressed the button, but skipped the elevator that came. And the next one. He had to push himself into the next elevator, like when he made Hobie eat all of his broccoli.

Walker sucked in a breath before the elevator doors opened.

"Thank goodness it's Friday!" A fellow elevator rider said to him. *What difference did it make?* Next week, the grind would start all over again.

He hobbled to his desk, when it hit him that he didn't drink coffee this morning. He put his bag under his chair.

It was just him and his computer for the next eight hours. More time for him to think about Cameron and to force himself to not think about Cameron, which would only lead him to replay the events of last week in his head again.

"Walker." Patricia was at his side. He jumped back in surprise.

"Morning, Patricia." He shoved his phone into his pocket. "Thank goodness it's Friday!"

"Same to you! Can we talk?" She nudged her head to her office.

He followed behind her. Lucy sat in her usual chair by the window. She looked just as confused and nervous as him.

"I don't have good news," Patricia said, before breaking out in a smile. "I have excellent news. The Radiance client loved our pitch. Loved it! They called me this morning and said how much they regretted putting us up for review. They were impressed by the level of detail and strategy that we presented, which no other agency could even touch."

Patricia beamed, and Lucy was not far behind her. Walker felt an immediate pit in his stomach.

"So we're safe?" Lucy asked.

"We're never safe, but we saved the account."

"I'm so relieved because I really didn't want to update my résumé." Lucy cackled for all to hear. She didn't love the job like Patricia, but she had a big family and liked her non-blip routine.

Walker wanted to celebrate with them. He made himself smile, but that pit of dread did not leave his stomach. It weighed him down like an anchor dropped in the sea.

This is good news. Be happy, dammit! His body wouldn't listen, and the pit seemed to grow.

Patricia swiveled back and forth in her chair. She was a kid on Christmas morning. "That presentation was thorough and flawless, and this would not have happened without your hard work. You guys did a phenomenal job, and I'm keeping our team intact to keep working on

Radiance." She turned her gaze to Walker and gave him a nod.

But Walker didn't breathe a sigh of relief. In fact, breathing became more difficult.

"So what happens now?" Lucy asked.

"Like I said, we're not safe. We wowed them with our new direction, and now we have to carry it out. We have to be more on-the-ball than ever before. We may have won back the business, but we still have to earn it. For the most part, though, things will go back to normal."

Normal. The word slapped Walker across the face. His routine wasn't changing. The weeks of unease and nervousness and scrambling and worrying had all been reduced to a blip.

"He's still in shock." Lucy elbowed him in the arm. "Smile, Walker. We have jobs!"

Walker smiled like a good employee. The golden handcuffs squeezed his wrists.

"Because of working on the review, I know we're behind with planning for the fourth quarter. Walker, put together a draft of the media plan and create briefs for our digital, TV, and print buyers. Plus see if they have any cross-promotional opportunities still available that they believe can generate substantial ROI. Can you get that to me by Tuesday? It's a tight timeline, but we can't show the client that we've let anything drop during these past few weeks."

He pictured Cameron living his dream, reading scripts on his iPad with a smile on his face, because he wanted to, because his passion wasn't just "what ifs" rolling around in his mind. Not because it was merely paying the bills.

"Walker?"

What am I doing here? He thought to himself.

"What did you say?" Patricia asked. Lucy gawked at him, too.

Perhaps he actually said that out loud.

"Right. I'll get on that right away," he said.

Patricia didn't seem convinced, but completely ignored the comment. It was as if Walker flubbed a line in a play, yet the show had to go on.

"Lucy, I want us to redo our reporting. Now that I know what they're most sensitive about, we can recalibrate reporting to address those concerns."

"You got it." Lucy diligently took notes. She was a master actress.

"I'll put some time on your calendar to discuss this in more detail. Walker, let's have a meeting this afternoon to go over your strategy for the media plan."

"What am I doing here?" Walker asked himself again, this time he didn't whisper it.

"Do you have someplace else to be?" Patricia asked.

"Not here." He said it without thinking, but it was a load off his chest. He instantly felt better, even though he just dug himself deeper.

"Excuse me?"

Cameron was right. Life didn't end at thirty-six. His fingertips tingled with vitality, with life worth living.

"This is not the place for me."

"I see. Is there another account you'd want to transfer to?"

Walker shook his head no.

"I've tried, but I will never care about this job like you do." He might have been unmotivated at his job, but a part of him admired Patricia's drive and work ethic. She knew she was in the right place. This was her dream. "I've learned a lot from you, but I need to move on. I will email you my letter of resignation when I get back to my desk."

She struggled for an answer. Walker enjoyed watching her get thrown off balance. Lucy's face was bleached with shock, but she had a hint of her supportive smile somewhere in there.

"If that's how you'd like to proceed, okay then. Do you have another job lined up?"

He shook his head no, throwing her for another loop.

"Are you at least giving two weeks notice?"

"Yes." Walker envisioned leaving in a blaze of glory, some triumphant *Jerry Maguire* moment. But Patricia and his co-workers didn't deserve that. They weren't terrible people, and all things considered, this wasn't a terrible office. It just felt that way when you knew you were meant to be someplace else.

Patricia held out her hand, and he shook it. "Well then, good luck."

"Thank you." Walker could tap dance right now. He knew the fear and uncertainty would sink in and gnaw at him soon, but he let himself take in this moment when the world seemed infinite and full of new paths and possibilities.

As he ambled back to his desk, he felt his wrists. They were free.

CHAPTER THIRTY-THREE

Cameron

From one empty room to another. Cameron pulled his suitcases into the corner of his new bedroom. He looked out the narrow window. It faced an alley, but in the distance, he could make out a lone palm tree.

His new roommates knocked at his door. Neon green sunglasses sat atop Grayson's bleach blond hair, and his waifish figure had muscle definition to it, which he showed off by walking around the apartment shirtless. Unlike Grayson, Porter had brown, wavy hair and was shedding the last of his college weight judging by his one-size-too-snug polo.

"Welcome to the West Coast." Grayson pulled Cameron into a handshake-hug. "How do you feel?"

"Tired." Cameron had made great time driving across the country. It involved him missing most historical landmarks, although he did pass a sign for the Grand Canyon, which was close enough. When he was seventy, he would RV through America and take in the sites.

"How was the drive?" Porter asked.

"Long. It didn't help that I hit a bad stretch of traffic on ten."

"It's The Ten." Grayson shook his head while reading his phone. "People in LA take their highways seriously. The Ten, The Four-Oh-Five, The One-Ten, The One-Oh-One, The Five."

Cameron made a mental note. He stared at the emptiness and realized something. "I don't have a bed to sleep on."

"Don't worry. I have an air mattress. And by the looks of it, Grayson may not be spending the night here, so his bed will be free." Porter read over Grayson's shoulder. "Which dick pic have you fallen in love with today?"

Grayson pushed him away. "In his profile, he says that he likes Shakespeare."

"Methinks the lady doth go on Grindr too much."

Cameron laughed. This apartment would never be boring.

"So when do you start work?" Grayson asked, putting away his phone for what would probably be a short recess.

"Tomorrow. In Century City, I believe. Off Pico."

"That's Century City or West LA. They all blend into each other," Porter said, leaning against the doorway. "I'm not far in West Hollywood."

"I work at this bar in Venice," Grayson said. "It's great for auditioning, very flexible, and close to my gym. And I meet a lot of interesting characters. I've perfected my Australian accent after working there. How about another shrimp on the barbie? Digiridoo, mate."

"Nice."

It sounded more like Brooklyn than Down Under, but

Cameron wasn't going to mess up his living situation. Henry had told him several times how fragile actors could be.

"How's Browerton doing?" Grayson asked.

"It's the same as you left it, I'm sure."

Grayson snuck stolen glances at his own abs, which were impressive.

"Do you want to go to the beach?" Porter asked. "We'll celebrate your arrival."

"The beach? But it's 4:30. When does it close?"

"Never." Grayson laughed, at Cameron and at a message that pinged on his phone. "We're not going to lay out. Just walk around. You know we're only a few blocks away."

"I know." Cameron glimpsed the lone palm tree again. He was in Los Freaking Angeles. "I've never been to the ocean."

Grayson and Porter did a double take. "Never?"

"Never ever."

"We need to do something about that," Porter said. "Put on your flip-flops and meet us in the living room in five."

Cameron rummaged through his suitcase for flip flops. He pulled them out from the bottom of his largest bag, naturally. Out with them came a Browerton pennant.

He stared at it for a good, long while. Memories surged through his mind.

"You ready?" Grayson called from the living room.

"Yep." Cameron let it fall onto his suitcase and joined his new roommates.

The breeze wafting off the ocean rustled Cameron's hair. The temperature was that sweet spot that people set their thermostats to, but this was natural. Cameron wished he'd brought a hoodie like Grayson, who wore a fitted one opened over a striped tank top. Pennsylvania only had this weather one day a year for two hours. Blink and it was gone, replaced by heat, humidity, or bitter cold.

On the walk over, Cameron told them the story of how he got to know Arthur Brandt and how luck and timing were on his side.

"We'll be working together then!" Porter said, putting on his sunglasses. "I'm Brian Mendelbaum's assistant. He's an agent at CAA. Arlo Falconer is developing a movie with Arthur."

"Arlo Falconer?" Cameron could feel his eyes bulge from his face. "I'll be working tangentially with Arlo Falconer?"

"Don't worry. He's really chill. He was asking me about Costco the other day. He's thinking about getting a membership."

"He makes $20 million a picture. Why is he shopping at Costco?"

"For the discounts. Obviously," Porter said.

"I think Arlo Falconer is gay," Grayson declared. "Just a feeling." He returned to texting someone on his phone.

"You think everyone is gay." Porter returned back to Cameron. "You'll be hearing from me a lot in these next few weeks. I'll set up drinks with you and a few other assistants once you get settled."

"Porter's going to be the next Jerry Bruckheimer," Grayson said. "Only gay."

"*Top Gun* was plenty homosexual," Porter said. "And Captain Jack Sparrow was practically a drag queen."

They walked down Santa Monica Boulevard and

passed cute, trendy shops and moms pushing the latest hi-tech strollers. The streets and sidewalks were clean and looked new. A row of palm trees shielded the horizon. Cameron couldn't believe he got to live here year-round.

"It sucks that you have to miss graduation," Porter said. "Senior Week is a blast. You basically own the campus for a week."

Cameron shrugged it off. It couldn't compare to working on a Hollywood backlot. "I couldn't pass up this opportunity."

"You said all your good-byes, too?"

"Yeah." A pang of sadness flicked at his chest, but then he let the sunshine suck out all his pain. The future awaited.

When they crossed Ocean Avenue, Cameron caught his first true glimpse of the Pacific Ocean, stretching out until it met the sky. People dotted the beach and a few boats dotted the water. That's all they were. Dots on this magnificent canvas.

Cameron's eyes didn't want to blink.

"Shall we?" Grayson asked.

Cameron galloped down the wooden stairs to the beach. He kicked off his flip-flops and buried his feet in the cool sand.

"Holy shit," Cameron said. "We can just walk on?"

"Yeah." Grayson seemed amused by him. "It's a free country."

Cameron ran for the water. His feet bounced through the sand, and he darted into the water up to his ankles.

"Crap, that's cold!" He jumped up to the shore. "Is it always that cold?"

"Yep. It's a big ocean. I don't think the sun's strong

enough to heat it up," Porter said.

Waves crashed on the shore. Real waves. Not the puny hiccups that Cameron had experienced on the Susquehanna River.

He couldn't believe he was here. On a new coast. The scrappy kid from small-town Ohio stared out at the vast, expansive ocean. He thought of his mother and everything she had wanted to accomplish.

As the next wave touched down, Cameron dashed back into the water, ignoring the cold. He was up to his knees. The bottoms of his shorts dipped against the tide. He breathed in the salty smell of the sea.

He tossed his roommates his wallet and phone, and on the next wave, he dunked himself under. The drama from Browerton washed off him. When he came back up, he was reborn.

Φ

Cameron had never been this close to an Oscar statue. Mobius Pictures won a Best Picture Oscar a few years back, and the trophy sat in a glass case in the center of the lobby. A tall, wiry man with wiry glasses and a mop of thinning hair exited the elevator and greeted Cameron.

"I'm Brad."

"Cameron."

"You ready?" Brad told him he was Arthur's assistant before he got promoted. He directed him to the elevator. He pressed the button for the tenth floor.

"I read some of the coverage you've been doing for Arthur's scripts. You really loved *Makeshift Coriander*."

"That script is amazing," Cameron said. "It's dark,

complex. I've never seen a movie like it. I can't wait to see the actress they cast for Helena."

"Arlo Falconer has expressed interest in playing the president, so the script is getting tweaked slightly to accommodate him."

"Intersting." That wasn't whom Cameron imagined to play the president. Arlo Falconer was known for his comedies, beloved in Browerton's frat row. "The president doesn't have a large role in the script. I'm surprised he'd want to do it."

"Well, we're doing some very minor tweaks on the script to beef up his character's arc. Arlo is a huge draw, especially for young male audiences."

The doors opened on a movie lover's paradise. Posters for Mobius movies past and present lined both sides of the hallway. Desks sitting outside executives' offices bustled with activity. People on calls, typing up emails, chatting with their co-workers. This was the real world, right in Cameron's face.

Brad stopped at the second-to-last desk in the row. There sat a computer with basic office supplies on a desk, a small file cabinet, and a shelf against the wall. "This is your new home."

Cameron ran his fingers along the desk. He had his very own desk, his own mini-office. *This is so cool.*

"You'll meet with HR in an hour, and they'll go through all the paperwork and insurance stuff. But let's talk responsibilities."

"Answering phones, reading scripts, setting up emails," Cameron rattled off, proud of his already existing knowledge.

"Right. Your main job as an assistant is to make your

boss look as good as possible at all times. Everything you do needs to come back to that." Brad leaned in. "But also don't forget about yourself."

He gestured for Cameron to sit in his new office chair, and Brad sat on the desk.

"This town is all about relationships. In this position, people will want to talk to you. Use that. Set up drinks with assistants you talk to on the phone or over email. Build that network, build those relationships. That's how people rise up in this business."

"My roommate is an assistant at CAA. His boss represents Arlo Falconer."

"You're living with Porter?" Brad smiled and nodded. "Very cool."

The phone rang. Cameron froze. His first Hollywood phone call. He couldn't screw this up. Brad reached up and picked up the line.

"Arthur Brandt's office...Alan! What's up?...He's in a meeting, but I'll leave word. No, I really will leave word." Brad hung up. "That was Alan Septor. He's this nobody agent who keeps trying to schedule a lunch with Arthur. Arthur obviously has more important things to do, but he doesn't want to flat-out reject the guy. He could rep a big-time writer or get a job at a real agency one day. And then he might be valuable. I keep them playing permanent phone tag."

"Got it," Cameron said. It seemed that relationships in this town worked a lot like dating, where people were too nice to be outright mean and hoped you got the hint.

"Technically, the hours here are nine-to-seven. But that's only half your job. When I was an assistant, I worked nine-to-seven, then met another assistant for drinks after work, then read scripts when I got home. Crashed around midnight, woke up, went to the gym, came to work and did it all over again. Nobody gets ahead working standard hours. Always be hustling. Is there a girlfriend or boyfriend back in Iowa?"

Cameron pictured Walker. He didn't want to, but that was the first thing that flashed into his mind at the mention of boyfriend. It was in the past.

"Boyfriend, Pennsylvania, and no," Cameron answered resolutely.

"Good. I dumped my college girlfriend within three months of my first assistant job. It was too much. Some people do manage it, but it's tough."

Arthur stormed down the hall in a crisp blazer and jeans. He stopped at Cameron's desk and slapped Brad on the shoulder.

"Has he scared you away yet, Cameron?"

"He tried, but failed miserably."

Arthur's death grip handshake nearly crushed Cameron's knuckles.

"Welcome aboard," Arthur said with a blazing smile. "Now let's roll some calls."

He went into his office and shut the door. Cameron's eyes darted to Brad, who laughed reassuringly at his newbieness.

Brad rested a comforting hand on Cameron's shoulder. "Let's roll some calls."

CHAPTER THIRTY-FOUR

Walker

Walker was the first car in the pick-up line at school. He'd perfected the science of getting to the school early enough to grab this honor. One of the benefits of being unemployed. Walker would worry about what to do next with his life later. Those fears and concerns and second-guesssings faded away as soon as he watched his son run to his car.

A picture flopped in Hobie's hand. "I drew this today, Dad! It's a picture of a bunny rabbit and a rabbi."

Walker examined the piece of art. Hobie was telling the truth. A human-sized pink rabbit sat on a park bench with a man dressed in a khakis and button-down shirt wearing a prayer shawl and yarmulkah.

"How do you know a rabbi? Are you thinking of converting?"

"Jason's dad is a rabbi. He's really nice and knows a lot about baseball. They can't watch TV on Saturdays but *Dad*, they get presents eight days in a row at Christmas."

"It's Hanukkah for them."

"Is that the Jewish word for Christmas?"

"Sure." Walker buckled Hobie into his seat. He drove them to Doug and Ron's house. The whole trip, Hobie regaled him with tales of his school day. He remembered the tiniest details like picking dried glue off the Elmer's Glue nozzle. Walker listened like they were folktales around a campfire. He enjoyed hearing the minutia rather than getting a watered-down recap once a week.

Not working had some perks.

Ron answered the door in tight biking shorts that would never leave Walker's memory, unfortunately.

"Hey, Hobie! How was school?" He scooped him up in a hug.

"Great!"

"Your stepson is studying to become a rabbi."

"Mazel Tov!" Ron said.

"Bless you!" Hobie replied.

He put him down, and Hobie ran into the house.

"Walker, are you able to drop Hobie off at soccer practice tomorrow? I have a meeting I know is going to run long."

"Definitely!" *Look up, look up.*

"Thanks. I appreciate it."

"And I appreciate this," Walker said. "Letting me pick up Hobie from school and drive him to practice on your days."

Ron peered around to make sure nobody was watching them. This was their secret. Doug didn't know. Ever since their epic fight, he wasn't speaking to Walker at all. He was picking up Hobie promptly from Walker's house and dropping him off not a second earlier than he had to as directed by the courts. Ron was their intermediary, and he gave a nod that acknowledged the awkwardness but reminded Walker that Doug knew how to hold a grudge.

They shared a look of understanding.

"I'm happy to do it," Ron said, and Walker gave him an appreciative nod. "I hope you guys patch things up soon, for Hobie's sake. He asked Doug the other night why he hates you."

"What did Doug say?"

"He of course denied it and said it was part of adult feelings. He's waiting for you to apologize."

Walker didn't want to apologize to Doug. He didn't want to give him that satisfaction, even if he wasn't proud of how things went down

"You really don't mind shuttling Hobie back and forth like this?" Ron asked.

"No. I'll take whatever extra time I can get with him." Walker and Ron said their goodbyes. Walker got a mistaken, unfortunate glimpse of the bicycle shorts again, and he knew he would never be able to unsee it.

Φ

Walker searched online for jobs while Hobie played in his room. It was June 1. *I will have a new job by the end of the month*, Walker promised himself. So far, it wasn't looking too hot.

He scanned the listings for other project management jobs, but whenever he clicked on a listing to view a job description, a red light flashed in his mind. *Abort, abort.* None of these jobs seemed interesting. He could see through their HR-approved language. He knew what *multi-*

tasking, can-do attitude, good communication skills, and *a self-starter* really meant. It was all a trap.

But he also needed a job. Because he quit, he couldn't file for unemployment. He had savings, but he watched his bank account dwindle thanks to everyday, innocuous things like gas and bills and food. He took a deep breath. He reminded himself that on some level, he knew what he was doing when he quit. He recalled the high he felt, the sense of clarity and excitement that fueled him.

I did the right thing, he told himself. It was time for a new beginning.

His job search was cut short when he heard sniffles coming from Hobie's bedroom.

"Hobie, what's wrong?"

Hobie sat on his bed, glaring at his Legos sprawled on the floor.

"It's all wrong." Hobie used his whole hand to wipe away tears. "King Dandelion can't drive the spaceship and I can't remember if Smort or Monte were the good or bad guys and my space jail for Queen Spacedragon is so stupid!"

Hobie tossed his space jail into the Lego bin where it broke apart. Walker kneeled next to his son. He used his shirt to clean off his cheeks. "It's okay. It's okay."

"It's not okay!" Hobie's head was hot. "The story is ruined!"

"It's not ruined. Stories can be whatever you want them to be."

"No they can't! Cameron and I came up with a story, and I can't remember it."

Walker picked up the spaceship set and brought it close to them. "Why don't you take a good look and see what you can remember."

"I can't! Cameron knew the whole story, and I can't do it like him!"

He threw the spaceship set against the wall, and it crumbled into little pieces.

"Hey! No throwing!"

"It's all stupid!!" Hobie was as red as one of his Legos. He heaved in sobs. He kicked his Legos and collapsed onto his bed, kicking the mattress.

Walker wondered if he should call Cameron. Cameron hated him, but he'd want to help Hobie. He took out his phone. Hobie's muffled crying hung in the air.

We don't need him, Walker told himself. He fixed his gaze at Hobie, face shoved into a pillow. Then he turned to the Legos with steely determination blazing in his eyes.

Hobie wound up crying himself to sleep. When he awoke from his nap, Walker was still on the floor hunched over the Legos.

"What is that?" Hobie asked.

"Spaceship castles were part of the old story. So I decided to make a Pirate Spaceship." Walker held up the Lego Pirate ship. The top half was covered pod-like in Lego car windshields. Two big engines were affixed to the bottom.

Hobie marveled at the creation.

"Monte knows how to drive a Pirate Spaceship." Walker picked up who he thought was Monte. "He used to live on an island. He and King Dandelion can escape together. Smort wants to learn how to drive the Pirate

Spaceship, but Monte doesn't know if he's ready for such an important mission."

"Pirate Spaceship," Hobie whispered. He handled it with extra care, as if it were a family heirloom. "What about Queen Spacedragon?"

"You tell me. It's your story, too."

The corners of Hobie's lips quirked up. "They need to go find her."

Walker spotted a Lego Queen under a discarded sock. He hid it in his hands. "Monte told me the Queen might be out there." He pointed outside the room.

"Really?"

"They have to go find her."

Walker jumped up and used his multi-second head start to hide the Queen behind a leg on the ottoman. He and Hobie raced around the condo, the Pirate Spaceship buzzing in his son's little hand. They threw pillows off the couch, flapped through old magazines, searched under Walker's comforter.

"Hey, are you hiding her?" Hobie asked.

Walker gave a guilty shrug. He barricaded himself into a pillow fort constructed from his West Elm couch cushions and chenille throw.

"You'll never get me!" He teased.

Hobie jumped over the fort into his dad's lap. Walker couldn't tell whose heart was beating faster, who was breathing harder, who was laughing loudest. Everything combined into a cacophony of silliness. Hobie rolled to the ground.

"Aha!" He snatched the Queen from her hiding place.

"You got me." Walker was prone on the carpet, arms and legs stretched out like a lazy snow angel. The condo was a complete mess. It was wonderful.

Hobie sat on his chest, giggling. "I like you this way."

"What way?"

"When I watched *Snow White*, you always reminded me of Grumpy. But now you're like Happy. Happy's my favorite."

"Me too." Walker grabbed his son in a hug, then tickled him.

Φ

Hobie ran to Walker's car after school, first in the pick-up line again. He surprised his son with a surprise trip to the movies. The theater was playing a special showing of *The LEGO Movie*.

"There's a whole movie about Legos?" Hobie asked, his eyes saucer-wide.

"There is, my child. There is."

Hobie bounced in his seat all the way there. Walker did too, but the concealed adult version.

Outside the theater, they waited in line with other families. Walker recognized the quiet building next store as the club he went to with Cameron a million years ago. He thought back on dancing like an idiot for all the too-cool twentysomethings to see. He remembered Cameron smiling at him. Being with Cameron ignited a spark within him that he couldn't recapture. He glanced up, and sure enough, the terrible cupcake billboard was still there. Cameron was so impressed with his doodling skills that night.

Cameron's gone, he told himself.

Hobie tugged at his hand.

"They're letting us inside, Dad."

A huge gap separated them from the kids in front.

"Let's go then."

After the movie, Hobie and Walker strolled around downtown. Hobie recounted the entire movie to Walker, which differed greatly from the actual plot.

They found themselves in front of Dollop, and Hobie asked if he could have a cupcake. Walker knew that most of it would wind up on his shirt or the ground. "We'll split one," he said.

"But I want my own!"

"You had popcorn and Reese's Pieces at the movies." He was going to be at full sugar high by the time Walker dropped him off at Doug's. A smile cracked his lips.

Dollop was a pastel colored paradise. Magenta chairs and yellow tables and mint green walls. The woman behind the counter had all the pep of a kindergarten teacher. Walker recognized her as the woman from the billboard.

"We'll take a Cookie Dough cupcake," Walker said. Hobie gave him the thumbs up. He stared at said cupcake in the display window.

"That's my favorite!" The woman said.

"I'm sure you say that about what everyone orders."

She gave a humoring laugh and put the cupcake on a plate for them. She even split it down the middle for them. Inside was a ball of cookie dough.

"So this is your shop?" Walker asked. "I recognized you."

"It is. Today is our six month anniversary."

"Congratulations. How's business going?"

Her pep faded as the hard, adult truth of business interrupted. "It's okay. I think people are still finding the store."

A worry line creased her forehead.

"Word of mouth and all that." She went back to smiling, but it wasn't the same as before. Walker realized he and Hobie were the only customers in the store.

"Have you thought about switching up that billboard that's across from the movie theater?"

"I got a great rate on it, and it's in such a good location."

"It is, but is it helping?" Walker asked.

She looked around the empty store.

"Dad." Hobie pointed at the cupcake just out of reach.

"Here, go sit at that table." Walker handed him the cupcake and directed him to the closest seat. "Don't eat my half."

"I won't!"

Walker watched him in the window's reflection. "I think the billboard is prime real estate, but maybe you should switch up your campaign. What does your advertising agency say?"

"Oh, I don't have an agency. I know the guy who owns the billboard, and my friend and I designed the artwork," she said with pride.

The wheels turned in his head. He was on his own sugar high. "I think a fresh, dynamic piece of creative could help you out. What if you did something like this?" Walker took a napkin and a pen next to the register and doodled an exact replica of the design he showed Cameron. It flowed out of him without any strain on his memory.

Not even his daily coffee could give him an energy boost like this.

"That's so cool!" The woman held it up to her face for a better examination. "And you just thought of this?"

"For a while. I've seen your billboard a lot. It's in an effective spot. It just needs to be effective, in my opinion."

She placed the napkin on the counter but kept staring at it. "I love this design."

"You could even run it during the preview reel at the movie theater. They run lots of static advertisements. Get people thinking about a post-movie treat even before the film has begun."

"Wow. You're good." She held up the napkin. "Can you create this for me? Like as a real billboard? We can discuss your fee, of course."

"My fee?" Walker thought of a photographer and graphic artist that he worked with on a Radiance execution a while back. They were all freelance, all hungry for work. Everything was falling into place faster than he could process. "Right. My fee."

Walker threw out a number, which she negotiated down to a still comfortable amount. His mouth hung open slightly.

"I'm looking forward to working with you. I'll email you tonight," Walker said. They shook on it. And just like that, Walker was no longer out of work.

CHAPTER
THIRTY-FIVE

Cameron

"Let's roll some calls," Arthur said, breezing by Cameron's desk en route to his office. Cameron quickly figured out what rolling calls meant. Arthur and Cameron would get on the same phone line and call back (or not) all the people who tried Arthur while he was out. Cameron already had on his headset and waited for Arthur to settle into his office. He pulled up the phone sheet of everyone who called so far.

The phone clicked in Cameron's headset. Arthur was on the line. Assistants listened in on all of their bosses' phone calls in order to take notes and chime in while needed.

"You ready?" Cameron asked.

"Let's do this," Arthur said with his usual gusto.

"First we have Aileen Marshall. I told her you were swamped and would try to connect with her next week. But don't worry because I knew that she's going on a two-week African safari starting this weekend. So you won't be hearing from her until the end of June."

"Yes. Perfect." Cameron heard Arthur clap his hands in his office. "Next!"

"Next, we have Mary Joyner. She replaced Adam at Imperative."

"What do we think?"

"She has this new writer she really wants you to meet with. Fresh out of Yale. I read his stuff, and it's good. Out there, but it has a voice."

"Can you send me—"

"Coverage and the script were emailed to you two days ago, but I can resend if you don't want to sift through your inbox."

"That's fine. Remind me to read this script, and I'll see if I call her back."

Cameron made a note on his calendar.

"Next we have Brian Mendelbaum." Cameron was already dialing his number before Arthur said yes.

"Hi, I have Arthur Brandt calling for Brian Mendelbaum."

"One moment," Porter said. They both had on their professional, for-the-boss voices. Cameron grinned at his computer screen, and he figured Porter was doing the same. "Brian, I have Arthur Brandt calling."

"Dude!" Brian shouted into the phone.

"Dude!" Arthur shouted even louder. They talked about how drunk they got last weekend and Arthur's ex-girlfriend and Chipotle burritos.

Cameron put himself on mute and half-listened for when they jumped back to business. He scanned that script from the Yale graduate that was sitting on his screen. *I*

could write better than this, he thought. Although he
hadn't written since he arrived in LA. Adjusting to life as
an assistant sapped him of energy by the end of the day.
And technically, per his agreement with Mobius, he wasn't
supposed to be writing at all.

I've hit my dudebro threshold of tolerance, Porter
texted him.

*Just pretend they're Muppets. It makes it much more
entertaining.*

*Are you going to that networking speed dating thing
tonight?*

Might as well. These events all blended together, and
many of the people going were not useful contacts. But
Cameron reminded himself that any networking was good.
Also, you never knew where these people would be in five
years, or even five days. He met a guy at one mixer who
was unemployed and sleeping on a friend's couch. He
chewed his ear off, and Cameron couldn't escape him. But
then the next week, he was hired as a development
assistant at HBO.

That's what excited Cameron the most about the
industry. Your luck could change at any minute.

It won't be terrible, he texted Porter. *We can get
through it.*

*I don't even like regular speed dating! I have to tell
you about this awful date I went on last night, btw...*

Save it for tonight. There's an open bar.

*Perfect! How about you? Any dates worth talking
about?*

Nope.

You need to get out there, Cameron.

Too busy. This time, it wasn't an excuse. Between work, reading, networking events, drinks, the gym, Cameron didn't have time for romance. He welcomed the distractions.

"So dude, let's talk *Makeshift*," Brian said. Cameron's brain snapped to attention. He positioned his fingers on the keyboard, ready to take notes. "Arlo liked the script changes, but feels like they could do more with his character. He wants more sexual tension with the Helena character. Like what if they fall in love?"

Sexual tension and love with an assassin? Cameron texted Porter. *That's not the point of the movie AT ALL.*

"I like that, dude," Arthur said. Arthur seemed to like all of Arlo Falconer's ideas. Or he liked that the man's last six films topped $100 million at the box office. "An assassin chef who falls for the president. So it's like *The American President* meets Rachael Ray. But like a fuckable Rachael Ray."

"Exactly!" Brian shouted.

A fuckable Rachael Ray? Cameron texted Porter.

It could work, Porter texted back.

The screenwriter will never go for this. Cameron had spoken to Malcolm Richards twice on the phone and both times came away with a chill. He was a British playwright who used his accent to intimidating effect.

"Cameron, type up an email to send to Malcolm's agent regarding these changes," Arthur said.

"Including the 'fuckable Rachael Ray' part?"

"Better to leave that out."

"So how's Arthur treating you, Cameron?" Brian asked.

"Terribly."

They howled with laughter. Cameron took a sitting bow at his desk.

"He's awesome," Arthur said. "I can't believe he's only been on this desk for a month. He skipped his college graduation to work for me."

"That's dedication," Brian said.

More laughs, but none from Cameron this time. It did sound a little crazy when he heard it aloud.

"You still got the diploma, right?"

"Yeah, Bri, he still got it," Arthur said.

"That's all that counts. The rest is just bullshit."

Φ

Before Cameron went inside to the networking event, he sat in his car and scrolled through Instagram. His timeline was stacked with graduation pics. Friends in robes, shots of the commencement speaker, arty pictures of the cap on the ground. Classmates and acquaintances and real friends still in Duncannon, celebrating the culmination of their college careers. He got a lump in his throat. He knew it was all meaningless pomp and circumstance, but it still looked fun.

And then, because he wasn't sufficiently bummed, he looked up Walker on Facebook. He was one of the few people who kept his profile viewable to the entire public. His profile said he was no longer at the Berkwell Agency. He posted a picture at a cupcake place that looked familiar, but Cameron couldn't place it.

Working on my first solo ad campaign and having the time of my life.

Cameron reread it. Maybe he got another job. He wanted to text Walker and get the details. He hated being so close to the loop, yet out of it.

He put away his phone.

Inside the bar, the tables were arranged in an O-shape. A ring of chairs lined the outside, and a ring was inside. Cameron grabbed a nametag and a drink. He waved and said hi to other assistants he knew. Each time he went to an event, he knew more. People he didn't know flocked to him when they saw his nametag.

Cameron Buckley
Assistant—Mobius Pictures

He got pretty good at finding decent people. They were the ones who were genuinely interested in what you said and didn't immediately ask you if there were openings at Mobius.

Porter found him and clinked glasses.

"You're drinking wine tonight?" He asked. "That's new."

Cameron looked down at his drink.

"There's an open bar." He sipped on his vodka soda.

"I know." The wine in his hand soothed him. "What was your college graduation like?"

Porter was caught mid-sip. "It was so hot that day. I was sweating under my robe. My mom and dad avoided eye contact with each other over dinner. And then I got wasted with my friends." He placed a comforting hand on his shoulder. "Cameron, graduation is one of those things people make a big deal out of that isn't so big. It's a ceremony and an uncomfortable dinner. And I partied with my friends plenty before and after that weekend."

He appreciated Porter's concern, but it didn't help. Graduation did seem like a big deal, although everything seemed ten times more momentous when viewing it on social media.

"You're here now," he said, like he was rescued. "Aren't you having fun?"

"I am."

"Good. So drink that wine and get ready for lots of awkward convos."

They took seats on the inner circle so they wouldn't have to move. One assistant after another sat down and chatted up Cameron. It was a montage of faces and namedropping, the same conversation looping over and over.

"I'm an assistant over at Paramount."

"I'm second assistant to the president of the network."

"What do you think is going to be the breakout movie at Telluride?"

"I heard he's reupping his deal at the network and is developing a reboot of *Ally McBeal*. It could go straight to series."

"I'm on the lot, too. We should totally do drinks."

"I heard they're getting tossed off the project and the studio is bringing in new people."

"So Ryan Gosling came into the office yesterday…"

Cameron could run down the hot writers and hot projects and the execs ankling their posts to start their own shingles. He knew how to have those conversations.

But he didn't have the energy to care at that moment. He wanted to look at more pictures from graduation.

"So you're at Mobius," the next guy said. He had the generic cuteness of a failed congressional candidate. "I'm at Popcorn Pictures. I work for Alvin Baylor. We just bought the rights to the Stairmaster and are fasttracking it for a fall production start date."

Cameron's head perked up from his wineglass. "Did you just say the Stairmaster? Like the exercise machine?"

The guy nodded with pride. "It's perfect. It's a well-known property popular with men and women. It has a straightforward name. And nobody's thought of it."

"How are you making a movie out of the Stairmaster?"

"Alvin had the genius idea to make it like *Transformers*, where the Stairmaster and other exercise equipment are actually an alien species sent down to help humankind defeat its greatest evil."

"Trans fats?"

Sarcasm did not penetrate this guy's excitement. "We haven't pinned down a villain yet. But Alvin scooped up the rights to the Thighmaster, the NordicTrack, and a brand of spinning bikes. He's planning to do it *Avengers*-style: Big ensemble pictures with standalone films in between for each supermachine." The assistant shook his head in delight. "It's brilliant."

Cameron tried to wrap his mind around watching a film about a superhero Stairmaster. If a sequel to *Mad Max* could become an Oscar-winning movie, he supposed anything was possible. "What's the script like? Is it tongue-in-like or serious?"

"We don't have a script yet. We're in the process of finding writers to slap something together."

"I don't know who'd want to write that," Cameron said.

"We've already got interest from agents. A-list writers are pounding at our door. It's going to be one of the hottest script assignments in town."

"Really?" Something about that seemed so depressing, yet so Hollywood. Cameron had reached his industry smalltalk threshold. "Are you single?"

"Um...I am."

"Were you always single?"

The assistant looked at the speed networking leader, who counted the seconds on her clock. "I had a girlfriend for a year. We both started in the mailroom at Gersh. She's now a manager of casting at Fox."

"What happened?"

"Well, she worked for a talent agent and got to know a bunch of casting directors and assistants. She got an assistant job to the head of casting for Fox and got promoted six months ago."

"I mean with the relationship."

"Oh. It's personal. Do you think Mobius will push into scripted television?"

"Is personal so bad?"

The assistant shrugged his shoulders. His networking game face began slipping off. "We both got too busy. This town can take a lot out of you."

"I'm starting to understand."

"It was amicable. We bump into each other all the time. Alvin has a project in development at Fox."

The Boldness. Cameron read the script. In his coverage, he bemoaned the underdeveloped female characters.

"Did you have a girlfriend in college?" Cameron asked.

The assistant shook his finger. "I get it. How long have you been out here?"

"A month."

He laughed, but Cameron didn't get the joke.

"What's her name?"

"His name," Cameron corrected. "Doesn't matter."

"We all had someone back home. Don't worry. He'll be a distant memory soon."

The bell rang.

Φ

Cameron sat in his car after the mixer and let himself sober up. All these assistants had left places and people, and they were doing fine. Cameron couldn't let himself get unglued over a picture. He was still in transition.

He stared himself down in the rearview mirror. "No," he said.

But the urge remained. He gripped the steering wheel. "No," he said louder.

Walker pushed you away.

He strummed his fingers on the wheel. "Once. Just once. You do this once, and you don't do it again."

Cameron pulled out his phone and watched a video of Walker and Hobie. The three of them played soccer in a field on campus. Walker helped Hobie work on his dribbling while Cameron cheered them on from behind the camera. Cameron's heart wanted to surge out of his chest. Walker's voice was like a hug. He looked over his shoulder at Cameron and winked. Cameron was there, in the field with them now. He could smell the cut grass and Walker's cologne and feel Walker's hand reach out to him while Hobie giggled and bounced the ball on his knee.

He watched the video to the very last second. His fingers touched Walker's face on the screen. He could feel the prickly hairs of his beard.

Cameron deleted the video from his phone. In less than a second, it was gone.

CHAPTER THIRTY-SIX

Walker

Walker had the shortest morning commute ever. Twenty steps to his kitchen table, which was taken over by his computer, printer, files, and design mock-ups. He could see traces of the glass surface underneath. He made himself a cup of coffee while checking his email. It wasn't like the morning email check at his old job. There were no emails to dread here. Only opportunity. He didn't mind the more high-maintenance clients. They were his problems to solve. No bureaucracy. No micro-managing. Walker breathed deeper. What was that in the air?

Freedom.

The fear he had about quitting his job and not having that safety net drove him, pushed him harder, spun his creative wheels.

"Clancy," he said to his newest client, owner of a new BBQ joint. "We can work on this. Tell me what you don't like, and I can create a new spec."

"I....I don't know. It just isn't Ribs & Co."

Walker could tell he was nervous. He'd gotten used to nervous clients. They didn't have deep pockets like Radiance. They were going out on a limb hiring Walker because their businesses were just as fragile as his.

He stood up and paced in his kitchen. "I get it. That was a first draft. I'll take your feedback and go back to the drawing board, literally."

"I know you're still kind of new at this, Walker. I know you haven't done a restaurant. It's different from a bakery."

"It is, and it isn't. I've done campaigns for a hardware store and a community theater's fall production. I know how to make campaigns unique."

"It's just not what I thought of when I thought of Ribs & Co."

"Let's talk this out, Clancy." Walker was on his tiptoes. His body was wired and springy like he just went for a morning run. "Just start saying whatever comes to your mind. I'll write it down and work some magic."

"Well, I wanted it to remind people of a family barbeque but nicer. And Texas, but not desert Texas. Kind of like cowboy but not too cowboy. I don't want people making fun of it." Walker scribbled away on a notepad. "It's a place where you can take the family, but also go with some friends after work."

"I got it. Like an Applebee's vibe, but for ribs. Real ribs."

"Not Applebee's!"

"Right. But it's the same place you can go on a Sunday night with the family or a Tuesday night to blow off steam. Either way, you know you're getting ribs." Walker wrote down that last sentence. It could be a great slogan. "Listen Clancy, I'm going to work on some ideas. I'll scan and email them to you tonight. And if you think there's something there, great. We can mold it into an amazing campaign. But if I'm still not getting it, we can part ways. No hard feelings. I want you to be happy. This is your baby."

"Sounds like a plan. I appreciate it, Walker. What was that?"

A clang and crash echoed through the kitchen. Hobie stood next to an open cupboard and a broken bowl.

"Just my assistant," Walker said with a smile. "I'll send you those mockups by end of day."

"Can I have breakfast?" Hobie asked.

After he made his son breakfast, they got ready for a playdate in the park with Melinda and her daughter. Walker got dressed in shorts and a T-shirt. He loved that he would wear this on a Wednesday. He checked on Hobie in the bathroom.

"You almost re…." He watched his son make a foamy beast mouth in the mirror.

A pang of sadness hit his chest. It always happened like this. Life would be just fine, and then these moments from the past snuck up on him. It was like those summer rainstorms that left just as quickly as they came.

Walker snapped out of it and cleaned off his son.

"You shouldn't do that anymore. It's too messy."

Φ

Walker sketched out ideas for Ribs & Co. while watching his son and Sophie play. Melinda came back to the bench with two iced coffees for them. Now that he had time for playdates, Walker had gotten to know the parents of Hobie's friends and classmates. He was no longer seen as the Dull Dad (a name some of the parents had actually given him).

"Hey Dad, watch!" Hobie yelled from the top tower of the jungle gym. And Walker did, happily and easily. Hobie slid down the slide on his stomach, covering his shirt in a racing stripe of dirt.

"I have the best laundry detergent," Melinda said. "It gets out everything, and it's hypoallergenic."

She gave Sophie the eye, and her daughter didn't dare copy Hobie.

"How's business?" Melinda asked.

"It's going. Still bumpy, but going." Not as much money as his old job yet, but Walker believed if he kept at it, that would soon change. "I'll have more time once school starts up next week."

"I can't believe they're going to be full-time." Melinda didn't seem as thrilled as Walker, probably because she dreaded having nothing to do for those extra thirty hours a week. "I loved the campaign you did for Dollop. I got cupcakes for my mother-in-law's birthday there."

"That's what I love to hear. Hey Hobie, you are not going down that slide on your stomach again." Walker stopped his son just as he was about to slide. He stared him down until he sat on his butt and went down the normal way.

"You're even stricter than Doug," she said. "Are you guys still…"

"Not talking? Pretty much." Walker laughed it off, even though it stung him deep down. Even during the worse of the divorce, he and Doug never went this long without speaking.

Melinda scooted closer to him. He noticed just how meticulously parted down the middle her hair was. Literally none out of place.

"So Walker, I know we're not this type of friends, but I couldn't resist. There's this lawyer at my brother's firm that I think would be perfect for you. His name is Ryan. He's tall, handsome, smart. A really great guy."

She pulled up a picture on her phone, and sure enough, he was everything she described. Ryan wasn't some Ralph Lauren model. He had his imperfections like a toothy smile and some wrinkles around his eyes, but that only made him cuter. Walker found him to be objectively attractive, what anyone would describe as a catch.

"He's great with my kids. Fantastic sense of humor. He does very well," she said under her breath.

"How old is he?"

"Forty."

"Wow." Then Walker remembered he was only four years younger.

"He was really impressed with your work."

"You've already told him about me?"

"In passing," she said with a sly smile that people get whenever they try to play matchmaker. "What do you think?"

He looked at the picture again. The man knew how to fill out a suit.

"I appreciate it, Melinda. I really do, but I'm not looking to date right now. I have my hands full with the business and Hobie."

"Ryan works hard, too. And he's on the hospital board. People make it work. You just have to want to find the time."

He handed her phone back. "I know. I just want to focus on the business for now."

She seemed to peer right inside him, straight through his layer of bullshit. "Are you still hung up on that boy?"

"No." Walker watched his son climb across the monkey bars. "I'm just not looking to date now."

"I don't think you'll find better than Ryan." She shoved her phone into her purse. Melinda was not used to any type of rejection.

Φ

Walker picked up some of that hypoallergenic detergent en route to dropping off Hobie. He kept glancing at his son in the rearview mirror, who made funny faces at him. *Life was good.* He was allowed to think it without jinxing himself.

But was it true?

Doug opened the door and stopped Hobie from running inside. His eyes went straight to the strained shirt. "Hobie, you shouldn't go down the slide on your stomach."

That was directed as much to Walker as Hobie. Melinda must've given him a full download as soon as they parted ways.

"I got this detergent that Melinda recommended. It'll be a distant memory."

Doug nodded and prepared to close the door. Walker stepped inside.

"Can we talk?"

Hobie ran upstairs to his room. Walker wondered if those words were a trigger for him to get out of the line of fire. He appreciated how much of a trooper his son has been. He was lucky, and he knew it.

"We need to fix this," Walker said. "For Hobie's sake."

Doug sat on the arm of the couch.

Walker sucked in a breath. "I was in a bad place that night I stormed in here." This wasn't easy, but it felt right. He kept going. "You were right. I was scared to go to New York. I've been scared for too much of my life, and you didn't deserve to get sucked into that. But I loved you, and I cared about you."

And for the first time all summer, Doug unclenched. They seemed to be equally taken aback by Walker's honesty.

Doug picked at a loose string on his pillow. "I liked it."

Walker's ears perked up.

"I liked thinking that you stayed for me. It was romantic in the beginning, but then it became stressful. I knew you weren't happy for a long time." Doug slumped into the couch. "That I wasn't making you happy."

He put a tentative hand on Doug's shoulder.

"I think we were two people who found each other at the wrong time," Doug said.

Walker squatted down to get eye level with him. "I don't regret it. Because one amazing thing came out of it." He nudged his head upstairs.

They smiled at each other with pride. They had a great son. Walker saw the Doug that swept him away all those years ago. They would always have a connection, a shared history.

"I'm sorry I cheated on you. I hurt you."

"We hurt each other."

"I used to hate you for taking those years from me,"

Doug said. They glanced in the mirror. They weren't in their twenties anymore, that was for sure. "But if I hadn't been with you and then not been with you, I wouldn't have found Ron."

Doug didn't let the past hold him back, Walker realized. He moved forward. Walker wondered how many years he wasted trying to go backward.

"You and Ron work well together. Although please tell him to stop wearing those bicycle shorts."

Doug nodded in agreement. "You should call Cameron."

"You're serious." Walker stood up, wondering if this was a trick. "Why would I do that?"

"Because you love him."

"It was a fling. A fling with an expiration date."

"You and I both know that's not true. You should fight for him." Doug smiled, and he was his young and carefree twenty-year-old self for a second.

"He's happy in LA."

"Remember how happy people used to think we were?"

They knew how to pose for the camera. Doug was a master of curating their life online.

"Why are you doing this? You hated Cameron! You pushed him away!"

"Because you looked at him in a way you never looked at me."

Walker sat next to his ex on the couch. They'd spent too long fighting a battle with no winners.

"Give him a call, Walker. You deserve to be happy."

Then Walker did something he hadn't done in years. He hugged Doug goodbye.

CHAPTER THIRTY-SEVEN

Cameron

Cameron sat in his car for a few seconds before going into work. His phone buzzed with an email from Arthur. He used his email like Post-it notes. Any random thought he had got sent to Cameron and catalogued for future use. He stopped using the subject line.

(No subject)

Set up a lunch with me and Renee Alvarez. The Grill. Or what about Deus Ex? Been wanting to try that place.

(No subject)

Make a list of directors for potential Civil War zombie project.

Cameron answered at all hours and at breakneck speed. He wanted to prove he was the best assistant Arthur ever hired, so great that he would get promoted. He didn't know when he started to think about how to get promoted. That was what all assistants talked about. Moving up was the name of the game. Cameron tried to play along. Arthur had called him one of the best assistants he'd ever had, but it didn't feel like the accomplishment he thought it would.

He shook his head. He wasn't thinking clearly. *That damn voicemail.*

Cameron walked across the lot, past a shoot for one of their movies, through the lobby, up the elevator, down the hall to his cubicle. None of it felt as majestic as it had his first day. It was Thursday. Another day at the office.

The alcohol from last night swooshed around in his head. Was it a mixer? Drinks with a producer's assistant? *Did it matter?*

Of course it did, he told himself. The honeymoon was over, but he was still doing what he wanted to be doing. *I'm living the dream. I'm making movies.*

Or, assisting people who are making movies.

His phone burned a hole in his pocket.

Ever since he deleted that video of Walker and Hobie, he hadn't looked at another picture of them. He and Henry gchatted a few days ago, but he made sure not to ask Henry about them.

Maybe Walker just wants to see how you're doing, Henry messaged him.

He can check my Instagram, if he ever joins. I met Neil Patrick Harris. I'm doing great.

Cameron went about his day, which was calmer since Arthur was at a doctor's appointment. He read scripts, logged them, opened and responded to email. He took note of how much of his day was about playing tetris with

Arthur's schedule. Shuffling around meetings. He knew what an assistant's job entailed, but seeing it in motion—organizing someone else's day—seemed depressing. He was spending his life living someone else's, but not getting to enjoy the good parts.

In a quiet moment, he pulled out a legal pad and began writing out a scene about the inanity of his job. The dialogue flowed through his fingers, and this dormant part of his brain awakened. All he had written in the past few months were emails. Before he knew it, over an hour had passed. His inbox was full of emails. He threw the pad in his drawer as soon as he heard Arthur's footsteps.

"How was the doctor's appointment?" Cameron asked.

"Fine." Arthur seemed taken aback by the question, as if it were too personal. He checked the physical mail. "What's my day looking like?"

"You have a call with Malcolm Richards in fifteen minutes, then a lunch at Deus Ex, a pitch meeting with this writing team Caplan and Turngrove at three, and a department meeting at four. And a reminder that your nephew's birthday is next week. Let me know what you want me to order."

"What are six-year-olds into?"

"Lego," Cameron said. *One six-year-old in particular.*

"That'll work." Arthur handed him mail Cameron could chuck. "Bump the pitch meeting to three-thirty. That way they won't run over. And get Malcolm Richards on the phone now."

Cameron did as ordered, all with a smile on his face. "Hi, Malcolm. I have Arthur Brandt calling."

He put his line on mute while Arthur and Malcolm exchanged pleasantries.

"Listen, Malcolm. The studio absolutely loves *Makeshift*, and so does Arlo. He's intent on making this his next movie."

"That's fantastic! I'm excited to see him tackle a gritty drama."

"He's a great actor. But about that," Arthur said. Cameron could hear the fake smile through the phone line. "Since we have Arlo Falconer on board, we're thinking it's best to lighten the tone of this script and play to his comedic side. He's on a comedy streak, and we and Arlo both agree this script has major comedic potential."

"Sure," Malcolm said hesitantly.

"Arlo wants the president character to be front-and-center, instead of Helena. So we need to shift the focus of the story. I was talking with him and other execs on my team, and we think this shift would work best through a romantic lens. The president falls in love with the White House chef."

"Um, okay. I can add a romantic subplot, I think."

"Well, we don't want it to be a subplot. That should be the main arc of the story. Arlo's president character adjusting to life in the wacky Oval Office and falling in love with his in-house chef."

"I don't see how I could fit in the assassin storyline."

"We absolutely love the assassin storyline and Helena's backstory. But the thing is, we don't think it would play well with these changes. We're taking the material in a new direction, so you can go ahead and drop that whole plotline, and drop the struggles with her daughter and ex-husband. She's just a chef who's unlucky in love. So it'd be like *Notting Hill* meets *The American President*, but with Arlo's signature brand of humor."

Cameron's eyes bulged. He saw his reflection in his computer screen and imagined Malcolm's was similar. He didn't get how this script that everybody loved was devolving into dreck.

"But what about the grittiness and Helena's character arc?" Malcolm asked. "This is a dark character study, not some trite romantic comedy."

"Scripts evolve in development. That's part of the creative process."

"There's nothing creative about this!"

"This is moviemaking, Malcolm." Arthur remained aggressively pleasant, like a salesperson desperate to make a sale. "You should be excited. The biggest comedy star wants to make your movie."

"This is not my movie. I spent two years crafting this script. You're turning Helena into a generic love interest. That's not *Makeshift Coriander*!"

"About that," Arthur said. "*Makeshift Coriander* doesn't really go with the new direction we're taking. Marketing was batting around new titles, and we're going to go with *Steve of the Union*. And we're going to change the president's name to Steve."

"Are you kidding me? What have you done to my script?" Malcolm yelled. "You said you loved it and didn't want to change a word. You said it was Oscar-quality. Now you want to make it another Arlo Falconer piece of shit comedy?"

"Malcolm, this is the movie business. You think you're the first writer to get his precious script changed? We bought this script and can do what we want with it. If you don't like it, we can bring in new writers. Your choice."

Malcolm didn't say anything back. Arthur poked his head out to check that Cameron hadn't accidentally dropped the call.

"Malcolm, buddy? You there?" Arthur asked.

"When do you need the revisions by?" Malcolm sounded hollowed out, sufficiently pummeled into submission.

When the call ended, Cameron tried going back to answering email, but he couldn't focus. He pulled up the *Makeshift* script, scrolled to a random page, and marveled at the sharp dialogue and tight scenes. He didn't get it.

He knocked at Arthur's office door. Arthur was watching music videos on YouTube.

"Some call, right?" Arthur said.

"I thought you liked the *Makeshift* script," Cameron said. He felt hurt for Malcolm.

"I do. This is development. It's my job to take great scripts and turn them into successful movies. A movie like *Makeshift Coriander* would've flopped at the box office. We saved it."

"We savaged it."

Arthur shot out of his chair. His eyes narrowed into black bullets. Cameron's heart stopped for a moment.

"You've been on my desk for a few months and you think you know better than me? We're not running a fucking charity here. The movies we develop need to turn a profit."

"You loved the *Makeshift* script, and you let Arlo steamroll it."

"Because Arlo will give us a hit movie. Cameron, you are here to listen, not speak. Right now, you are my assistant. Your job is making sure my calendar is how I want, making sure I have the files I need when I need them, and making sure I have a coffee in my hand when I ask for it!" Arthur threw a disposable coffee cup past Cameron's head. It exploded against the wall and coffee splattered onto the floor.

Cameron froze in place. A part of him wondered if he'd make it out of here alive.

"Relax, Cameron. There was barely any coffee in there. Call maintenance and get this cleaned up."

Cameron returned to his desk. People went about their business around him, pretending they didn't hear a word, but he felt the spotlight was on him.

Another assistant, once she was done rolling calls with her boss, came by with a glass of water for Cameron. "Don't worry about it. We've all been yelled at. Welcome to the club."

Cameron took a sip. "Some club."

She told him that this would be forgotten by lunch. "And Arthur wasn't really that angry. Trust me, I've seen him angry."

Cameron didn't feel reassured.

He left his post and went to the bathroom. He chose the last stall and pushed the tears out. They were blocked at first, but soon they came pouring. He yanked out his phone.

That damn voicemail. That was why he was off his game today. He listened to it again.

"Hey Cameron. It's Walker. I just...I just wanted to see how you're doing, how you're enjoying Hollywood. And...I need to tell you something, but I don't want to say it all on a voicemail. Give me a call."

What did he have to tell me? Cameron wondered. Fury heated up his head. If Walker wanted to hear from him, fine. Cameron called him back. He wanted to get this over with and move on with his life.

"Hey," Walker said.

"Hi, Walker. I got your message. What's up?"

"Not much. I quit my job."

"What?" Cameron yelped out.

"I did." Walker sounded relaxed, or maybe that's how the rest of the world was compared to life in the industry. "I started my own business designing ads. It's doing okay. We'll see how it goes."

"Good for you."

"I have to thank you," Walker said. "You motivated me to make the jump. You went out there to pursue your dream, and you made me see it wasn't too late to pursue mine."

"I'm glad." Cameron clenched his jaw.

"How are you doing out there? Are you writing?"

"Life is great here. Walker, why did you call?" Cameron could hear the asshole tone in his voice, but his emotions had taken over this conversation as soon as he dialed. "Because you walked away. You called me a fling and walked away. That was the last memory I have of Browerton, of us. Your back."

"I hated every word I said that day. I didn't want to hold you back."

"You weren't going to hold me back," Cameron said coldly.

Silence took over the line. Cameron wanted to hear his voice again.

"What did you have to tell me?" He asked. "In your voicemail, you said you needed to tell me something."

More silence. Cameron rubbed his hair.

"Walker?"

"I still love you," Walker said. "And I miss you, Cameron."

Cameron wiped away a tear.

"Do you miss me?" Walker asked.

"Five seconds ago you said you didn't want to hold me back."

"I know."

"I love it here."

"You didn't answer my question, Cameron. Do you miss me?"

Cameron sunk against the stall wall. "It's only been like four months. We're still healing." Although Cameron realized they'd now been apart longer than they were together. Why did it still feel so fresh and painful for him?

"Cameron…"

"Just give it time, Walker. I have to get back to my desk."

"We had something, Cameron."

Cameron gripped the phone tighter, hoping that maybe he could feel a hair from Walker's beard rustle in the connection.

"We had a moment in time. And it passed." Cameron slipped his phone in his pocket.

He cried a little more. He dabbed his tears on toilet paper. A minute later, he was ready to get back to work and show Arthur Brandt how great an assistant he could be. He would show his boss, and himself, how much he wanted this.

CHAPTER THIRTY-EIGHT

Walker

Walker hadn't been back to The Complex since he quit. He had flashes of post-traumatic stress from his old job as he crossed the parking lot. He wished he hadn't wasted so many years at his old job. He couldn't get that time back. The first breeze of fall flitted in the air.

He waited for Lucy in the Starbucks in the north building. A different Starbucks untarnished with memories of Cameron. Lucy waved with both hands and practically ran over to Walker.

"It's so good to see you!" She said while hugging him. She pulled away and blatantly checked him out. "You look great. Being CEO of your own company has its perks."

"I'm not at CEO yet. Just a humble business owner, but thank you." Because of his more flexible schedule, and because he wasn't stuck inside a cubicle every day, Walker had developed a golden tan. He was more active throughout the day. Now that Hobie was in school, he could go to the gym when it was empty. It was like his old college body was back, albeit with more effort and less hair.

"I wanted to scream at work when I saw the online ad for Ribs & Co. Did you design their menus, too?"

"Guilty. The client's even talking about doing a commercial, and he wants me to create it. I've never written or directed anything before in my life!"

"You'll be great! So you love working for yourself?"

Walker nodded and nodded. "It's scary knowing that everything rests on my shoulders, but also exhilarating."

Lucy examined him again, but this time seemed to be checking out something deeper than a tan. "It suits you well."

They ordered drinks and grabbed one of the few empty tables by the window. The large oak tree outside had some orange and red leaves hidden in the green. Lucy proceeded to give Walker all the requisite office gossip. He had this small hope that everything fell apart once he left, but reality was not as satisfying.

"The new you is so boring!"Lucy rolled her eyes. "She's nice, but she has no personality and only wants to talk about work. She and Patricia get along fabulously."

"How is Patricia?"

"She's doing her Patricia thing."

"Sounds about right."

Lucy swirled her coffee stick in her drink and raised an eyebrow at Walker.

"What?" He asked.

"So your career is flourishing. But how about your love life?"

"Wow. Subtlety is so not your forte."

"I want to know. We may not be working together, but I still need to live vicariously through you."

"It's...pretty much nonexistent." Walker gave a hapless shrug. Lucy and her husband probably had a better sex life than him at the moment, a thought he never wanted to think about again.

"I'm just busy with the business," he added. "I'm going to concentrate on that for a while."

She shot him a look. "You and I both know that's complete bullshit."

He was taken aback by her honesty and cursing. The usual jolliness of her words evaporated.

"I may not have to report to an office everyday, but I'm putting in tons of hours building this thing up. I don't know, I'm just not in a place to date right now."

"You're just saying that because that college student broke your heart."

"He didn't break...that was months ago."

"You need to move on."

But what if he didn't want to? Their phone call last month did not go as he planned, but he sensed a glimmer of something that he couldn't let go of so fast.

"You need both, a career and a person that you love," Lucy said. "I don't love my job. It is what it is. I don't hate it, but it's not my passion. But it allows me to get home to my family every night at a decent hour. And that's my life's passion."

"Not all of us have four wonderful kids and a wonderful husband."

"Oh, they drive me crazy, but I couldn't imagine life without them. It can be scary, but exhilarating," she said with a knowing smile.

"You want me to give up my business to find the man of my dreams?"

"No. The business and personal life will never be in perfect harmony, but err toward the personal. When you find people you love, who love you back, you hold onto them. Hence why I dragged you out here for coffee."

Φ

Walker drove around after meeting Lucy, no destination in mind. Streets whizzed past. He hadn't done this since he was a teenager. His new business filled him with joy, but it didn't fill him completely. There was a pocket of emptiness, right around his heart. He tried. He tried to win Cameron back, but the kid had Hollywood on the brain.

He wound up driving past the Browerton campus. New students and their overprotective parents roamed the sidewalks with maps. Kids helped each other move boxes into the dorms. That was the weird thing about the fall. It had only been five months since Cameron left, but school starting up made it feel like a whole year had passed.

Walker pulled over and found a space on a street where upperclassmen knew to park because it wasn't permit only. After all this time, not everything had changed. He strolled into the heart of campus. He could walk these paths with his eyes closed. They were imprinted onto his brain.

Students buzzed around him. Meeting up. Taping flyers to the sidewalk. Handing out flyers on the street. Nothing but future and potential lay ahead of them. And ahead of Walker, too. The Future was relative, he realized.

His feet had taken him to the library. It was extra quiet inside. Nobody had homework yet. He remembered taking Cameron here eons ago. Walker dipped into the Time Machine Hallway and strolled down the stone floor to Waring Library. He pulled open the giant double doors and breathed in its musty smell.

This place was all memories, past and present. There he was with Doug, sneaking a quick makeout session away from their straight comrades by the records. There was Cameron leaning against a pole, hanging on Walker's every word. Walker closed his eyes and let himself get possessed by memories. They were so close, but just out of reach.

No trip to the music library would be complete without a trip to the musical theater bookcase. Walker squatted down and pushed back the shelf. He found his and Doug's heart. It would be there forever, a time capsule of those years. They weren't wasted. They were but one road in his path, filled with good times and bad.

But then he saw a new one just as he was about to stand up. It stuck out for its freshness compared to the years-old etchings around it.

C.B. + W.R.

Walker ran his fingers over the letters. He had trouble breathing, and his heart was going a mile a minute. He traced his fingers in the C, then in the B.

"Well, damn," he said. "You really do love me."

CHAPTER THIRTY-NINE

Cameron

Cameron lay in bed, staring at the ceiling. He'd been up for half the night already and was waiting for the sun to catch up with him. Last night, he'd had drinks with an assistant. They went through the same motions. The same conversations. But listening to this assistant, Cameron had been struck by how much the guy cared, genuinely cared. He listed off projects his boss was working on. He discussed industry gossip about whose head was on the chopping block. His eyes blazed with passion. Passion that Cameron thought he had.

That passion dimmed each time he went to the movies, when he saw terrible films that had once been great screenplays. He also saw the first poster for *Stairmaster: The Movie*, starring Daniel Day-Lewis as the voice of Stairmaster, coming Memorial Day weekend. When he greeted writers coming in to pitch Arthur their latest project, he viewed them with a mix of pity and jealousy. Their beautiful words were about to be ripped apart, but at least they had the chance to share them.

He called his mom, who answered sprightly. It was nine a.m. where she lived, and she probably got plenty of sleep.

"Cameron, you're calling so early."

"I wanted to catch you."

"What's wrong? Let's talk."

It was always those simple questions that tripped him up. "It's...tough." Just talking to her unleashed something within him. "My boss hates me."

"Oh, he does not."

"Let's see: He barely talks to me, unless it's to ask me to do something. When he sees me reading scripts, he asks if he's not keeping me busy enough." But Arthur would never say any of this, Cameron knew. His passive-aggressiveness was on par with most sorority girls.

"Being an assistant is hard, but it will all be worth it," his mom said.

"How?"

"You're smart and you'll rise at Mobius fast."

That didn't sound appetizing to Cameron. And when he thought about it, it never did.

"I don't like going to work," he said, like an addict admitting a relapse. "I lie in bed and try to psyche myself up."

"You can tough it out, Cam. See, when you moved out there, you thought you were living your dream. But you're not. Your dream is to be a development executive. Not an assistant. And that will take time. Years." Years as Arthur's assistant. Cameron's stomach turned again. "You're still in the process of reaching your dream. It's all part of the plan."

"That's not my dream, Mom. I want to write!" It was like coming out all over again. Cameron rubbed at his headache. It was a perpetual throbbing, either from the stress or the drinking. "Your plans changed when you had me. Did you regret that?"

"I....no. I love you, Cameron. You're the best thing that's ever happened to me."

"And yet I wasn't part of the plan."

She didn't respond for a while.

"I miss him," Cameron closed his eyes and pictured being in Walker's arms, smelling his skin, feeling his warmth. He'd been doing that a bunch since their phone call. It was the only thing that could make his headache go away.

"You've just hit a rough patch. Things will improve."

"I hope so."

"Walker and Hobie are in the past where they belong," his mom said. "Just focus on your future."

Cameron hung up and got ready for another day of work.

Φ

At the office, Cameron waited for the coffee machine to be free. An assistant bounced in and picked up her full mug.

"Another day at the grind!" She said with a smile, like that was a good thing. Maybe it was for some people.

Cameron placed his mug under the machine and programmed in his coffee of choice. He turned around and Brad stood by the fridge.

"Hey, Cameron! Do you have a minute?" Brad asked,

a serious tone coating his voice.

"Sure." He looked back at his coffee but decided it could wait.

Cameron followed Brad into Arthur's office. Arthur sat behind his desk glaring at Cameron. A blonde woman from human resources stood by the window.

"What's going on?" Cameron asked.

Arthur pulled out Cameron's legal pad. His screenplay scribblings blazed on the top page. Cameron gulped back an *oh shit* lump.

"Interior, Sunrise Pictures, day," Arthur read from the page. "Arnold Grant, thirty, wildly cocky as he is wildly insecure, struts down the hall hoping that people think he is prom king. He is the epitome of trying too hard."

Arthur chucked the pad onto his desk. Cameron shrunk like a pile of snow in the sun.

The HR woman stepped forward. "Cameron, when you accepted the job offer at Mobius Pictures, you agreed not to partake in any writing endeavors. We do this to avoid any potential copyright issues or conflict-of-interest."

"That was just something I jotted down during a work lull," Cameron said. He was on the stand, fighting for his life. He glanced behind him at Brad, whom he knew wasn't going to help him.

"It's against policy," Arthur said, stifling a smile. "When I offered you the job, I asked if you still wanted to write, and you said no."

Cameron thought back to that night when Arthur called, when Walker was just one room away. That was forever ago, a different person ago. Cameron had a moment of mental clarity, one of those rare opportunities that you had to pursue no matter the inconvenient timing.

"I did say no. And I lied. To you and to me. Because I was scared." He was hearing himself for the first time. "So I ran."

"What are you talking about?"

And he was back in Arthur's office, three sets of eyes staring at him like he was speaking a foreign language.

"Unfortunately, this writing does constitute a breach of your employment agreement," the woman said. "We're going to have to terminate your employment with Mobius effective immediately."

"Terminate? For this?" Cameron asked.

Arthur pushed the pad back to Cameron. "It looks like a good script. I wouldn't want to savage it."

Cameron was escorted back to his desk flanked by security guards. He picked up his bag. This time, nobody pretended they were busy. All eyes were on him. He kept his head down until he got in the elevator. *And that's a wrap on my Hollywood dreams.*

Φ

Cameron dug his toes into the warm sand. He dangled his loafers off his fingers. Santa Monica beach was empty for a weekday afternoon. He had the sand, the ocean, the horizon all to himself. He let the breeze flow through his hair.

Grains of sand meshed themselves into his slacks as he plopped down on the beach. He watched the waves crash against the shore. It was the sound people listened to for meditation, live and just for him. And it helped. Cameron relaxed. He would worry about his job prospects and the future sometime tomorrow.

"Shouldn't you be at work?" A voice behind him asked.

Every hair on his neck stood up. It had to be a dream.

"What are you doing here?" Cameron asked. He didn't want to blink.

Walker squatted beside him. "What are *you* doing here?"

"I asked you first."

"I went to your apartment, and your roommate Grayson said you were at work. He suggested I come here to wait since I've never been to the Pacific Ocean. I was walking along the beach, contemplating just what I would say to you tonight, and then…" He gestured to Cameron.

"Here I am."

"There you are." Walker had a twinkle in his brown eyes. It was a beacon of light for Cameron. "Did work let off early?"

"Something like that." The details weren't worth sharing, not now. Everything revolving around the film industry seemed so trivial compared against this moment. "What were you going to tell me?"

"I was still in the middle of contemplating." Walker stopped joking. His face flushed with emotion, and he grabbed hold of Cameron's hand. "Letting you leave was the easy way out. I let you go because I was scared, scared of what would happen if you stayed and we tried to make this work. I've passed up many different roads in my life because of fear. But I want to go on this new path with you. I know I'm asking you to give up a lot, but…"

"But what?"

Walker pushed Cameron's dangling hair out of his face. "I love you. I miss you. And I want to give us a real chance."

Cameron caressed Walker's hand and stared out at the ocean. He thought of everything that led him to this point. All the passion and hard work and script reading and wild chances and Lego storylines and wine and meeting scheduling. Even when he tried to follow his dream, life kept interfering.

"I don't want to stop you from living the life you want, but now you have all the information." Walker gazed into Cameron's eyes, completely unguarded. "And thank you."

"For what?"

"For asking me to help you with trivia that night. For making me come alive."

"You made me come alive, too. You and Hobie. I'd been closed off for...well, my entire life."

Their fingers locked together. Cameron had never considered believing in fate before, but now he'd have to reconsider.

The waning sun twinkled in Walker's eyes. "C.B. plus W.R. When did you write that?"

"After you kissed me in the closet. It was wishful thinking."

"Sometimes, wishes come true." Their lips met in a soft kiss that quickly turned passionate. It resuscitated a part of Cameron that he didn't want to ignore again. The drooping red rays of sunlight flashed over the horizon. Cameron had been told about the sunsets here, but he never got to sit back and experience one. Colors mashed together as if on an artist's palette.

He leaned his head against Walker's shoulder as the sun slipped beneath the sea.

CHAPTER FORTY

Walker

Walker checked himself for the fifth time in the mirror. He wanted to make sure his shirt was perfectly pressed and beard properly trimmed. He had booked a dinner reservation for him and Cameron that night at a fancy restaurant in Malibu. After the beach, Cameron had gone back to his apartment where he was going to talk to his roommates about moving out. Walker spent that time buying a brand new, super expensive outfit at some trendy boutique on Melrose Avenue. He wanted to look perfect for Cameron.

He noticed a pair of dastardly grey hairs. That was his cue that time was almost up. We only got one go-around, and we had to make it count. And he was. He felt life and love coursing through his veins.

Walker took the elevator down to the lobby. Cameron sat on a chaise next to a fireplace. He wanted to throw him backward and take him right there.

"You look amazing," Cameron said.

"So do you." Walker lost his breath. There was Cameron. In front of him. All his. "I made a reservation at this restaurant called Nobu. The concierge said it's unbelievable, and we might even see some celebrities."

Cameron nodded, only half-interested. His muscles peeked out from his gray sweater. "Sounds great. How's your room?"

"Great. I got upgraded to a view of the ocean. Now I get why people want to live here."

"I want to see." Cameron walked past him to the elevator. They both got in. Cameron had a familiar mischievous glint in his eye. "What time is our reservation?"

"Seven."

"We have some time," Cameron said. The elevator dinged to Walker's floor. "What's your room number?"

"618."

Cameron walked down the long hallway. He took off his sweater somewhere by 606. He unbuckled his belt while passing 611. Unzipped the fly at 612. And kicked off his shoes at 617. Walker dutifully gathered up the clothes.

"Do you have the key card?" he asked nonchalantly.

Walker slid it into the slot. The green light was like fireworks to him.

As soon as they stepped inside, their human selves went to sleep and animal selves sprang to life. Lips were on lips, kissing as if they were trying to solve the energy crisis. Walker tasted Cameron's breath, felt his warm tongue enter his mouth. Every scent and taste and touch of Cameron only revved his engines harder.

Cameron's hands tangled in Walker's hair. They rubbed at his beard. Walker kissed his lips, his nose, his cheeks, his eyebrow. There was no part of Cameron he didn't want to claim.

"I missed you," Walker heaved out.

"I missed you more."

Walker yanked Cameron's jeans to the floor. His tongue slid down the curves of Cameron's chest and abs like an expert skier, licking his tight skin. Cameron let out a gutteral moan. Walker continued south.

He gripped Cameron's raging erection and gave it a few strokes, getting to hear that moan again, that music to his eyes. He licked Cameron's cock from tip to base, taking in his sweaty taste, making Cameorn beg for more. He jammed Cameron's dick all the way in his mouth. Cameron held onto the door handle for balance. His own cock was about to rip through his designer pants.

They stumbled over to the bed, neither letting go of the other. Cameron pushed Walker down. He climbed on top and unbuttoned Walker's shirt, then undid his pants. In a flash, they were both naked, their warm bodies in a tight embrace.

"Mind if I take the lead this time?" Cameron asked.

Walker nodded yes, excited for the new experience. Doug had always preferred to be a bossy bottom. *I do not want to think about Doug right now.* "I want to do this with you," he said to Cameron.

"Then do this we shall." Cameron kissed his neck. Walker pointed him to the condoms and lube he'd picked up after the beach.

"Did you stretch today?" Cameron asked with a wink.

"Fuck you and yes," Walker said. He didn't care how sore his lower back would be tomorrow.

Cameron threw Walker's legs in the air and spat on his hole. His tongue swirled around his opening. Walker grabbed onto the bedframe and gasped in breath. He felt like his body was going to spontaneously combust. Cameron slipped a finger inside, and perhaps he already was on fire. Heat encased his body, made hairs stand up on his arm.

"You ready?" Cameron asked.

Walker nodded yes.

It felt much different than a finger. Thicker, fuller, more determined. Walker felt himself opening up. Cameron leaned over him. His sweaty strands of hair hung in his eyes.

"You're not so bad at Naked Twister," Cameron said.

"I learn from the best," Walker heaved out in short breaths, punctuated by Cameron's thrusting.

Their lips brushed over each other's. Cameron gave him a penetrating stare. Walker could hear their souls clicking into place together. He moaned like the walls were soundproof.

"I love you," Cameron said.

"I love you."

Walker slapped Cameron's pert ass, and pushed him in deeper. They were cheek-to-cheek, exhaling against each other's ears. Walker held him closer. He never wanted to let go. Cameron grabbed Walker's thighs and pummeled his ass with his motivated cock. Walker felt each jab, inching him closer and closer to exploding. Sweat slipped down the sides of his head.

There were no words. Just each other.

Cameron grunted with orgasm while still inside him. Walker felt the extra heat in his core. Cameron's stomach rubbed against his cock, getting him rock hard.

Cameron wiped a hand across his sweaty forehead and used the improvised lubrication to stroke Walker. He balanced himself over Walker with one hand, his tricep flexing in support. His other hand jerked off Walker's thick cock. Walker writhed around on the bed, grunting in pleasure. He shot his load up onto Cameron's glistening chest. Cameron collapsed atop him. Walker wrapped his arms around this guy who had upended his world. He could stay here forever.

But it wasn't forever. They really did have dinner reservations. Cameron and Walker showered and got redressed.

"I should've just invited you straight up here," Walker said while putting on his boxers. "I never learn."

"You never do." Cameron strutted out of the bathroom in just a towel. Walker had never been more jealous of a piece of fabric. Droplets of water beaded his biceps.

"So since you're looking for a job, I may have an opportunity for you," Walker said. He zipped up his pants.

"I'm listening."

"My business is expanding. I'm going to need a copywriting partner. I have the sketches, but I need the words."

Cameron lay on the bed. "Go on."

"You'd be a partner, fifty-fifty. We can work on entire design concepts. One of my clients even wants to do TV commercials."

Cameron got on his knees on the bed and threw his arms around Walker's neck. "I'm in."

Walker kissed him and threw him down on the bed. His shirt was getting damp but he didn't care. He ripped himself away. "We have reservations."

"We do."

"And you're still naked."

"No, I'm not!" Cameron glanced down at his body. His towel had fallen off. "Oh wait. I am."

Cameron went about getting himself dressed. Walker went by the window. The ocean kept doing its ocean thing. People bustled up and down Ocean Avenue. He called up Doug.

"Is he awake?"

"I was just about to put him to bed," Doug said.

"Can I say good night?"

"Yes, but don't stay on too long or else he'll have trouble falling asleep."

Walker wondered if Doug could tell he'd just had amazing sex. *Probably.* And he was probably jealous. That made Walker get a flash of Ron in his tight biking shorts. Yep, that image was stuck in his mind forever.

"Dad?" Hobie squeaked out.

"Hey, pal!" Walker didn't realize how much he could love someone's voice. "How's the other side of the rug?" Hobie asked.

"It's okay," Walker said, glancing at the waves and the row of palm trees. "But it's no Duncannon, P-A."

"That's what I thought."

"Hobie, I have someone here who wants to wish you a good night." Walker handed the phone to Cameron, who looked at it with a mix of love and trepidation.

"Hi, Hobie," Cameron said.

"Cameron!" Walker heard his son shout through the phone. "It's you!"

"It's me, buddy. I heard your Lego adventures are going swimmingly."

"There's no swimming."

Walker smiled. He hoped his son never realized how funny he was.

"I can't wait to play Legos with you," Cameron said.

"Are you coming to visit?" Hobie asked.

"No." Cameron held Walker's hand. "I'm coming home."

Walker stared at the beautiful guy in front of him, the guy who he was going to create a future with one day at a time. Cameron was right. There was no looking back.

THE END

Want to be the first to get details on the next Browerton University book? Become an Outsider. Outsiders always get the first scoop on my new titles, new covers, sneak peeks, members-only contests, and other cool goodies via my newsletter. Get in with the Out crowd today at www.ajtruman.com/outsiders.

Consider leaving an honest review at your favorite bookseller's website and on Goodreads. Reviews are crucial in helping other readers find new books.

Say "Hi" at www.ajtruman.com or on my Facebook page here: http://on.fb.me/1tejYE1

And then there's always plain old email. I love hearing from readers! Send me a note anytime at ajtruman.writer@gmail.com. I always respond.

Thanks for reading!

A.J. Truman remembers his college days like it was yesterday, even though it was definitely not yesterday. He writes books with humor, heart, and hot guys. What else does a story need? He loves spending time with his cats and his partner and writing on his sun porch. You can find him on Facebook or email him at ajtruman.writer@gmail.com